Y

D1639387

MAN TRACKS

MAN TRACKS

BENNETT FOSTER

SAGEBRUSH
Large Print Westerns

Copyright © 1943 by Bennett Foster
Copyright © renewed 1971 by E. Arlene Foster

First published in Great Britain by ISIS Publishing Ltd
First published in the United States by Doubleday, Doran

Published in Large Print 2009 by ISIS Publishing Ltd.,
7 Centremead, Osney Mead, Oxford OX2 0ES
United Kingdom
by arrangement with
Golden West Literary Agency

British Library Cataloguing in Publication Data
Foster, Bennett
    Man tracks. – Large print ed. –
    (Sagebrush western series)
    1. Western stories
    2. Large type books
    I. Title
    813.5'2 [FS]

ISBN 978–0–7531–8246–8 (hb)

Printed and bound in Great Britain by
T. J. International Ltd., Padstow, Cornwall

CAST OF CHARACTERS

LANE McLAIN . . . ran the Hatchet ranch, sometimes with his fists, sometimes with a gun.

MANVILLE SEAY . . . sold some cattle he didn't own and started a range war he couldn't finish.

NOSEY HARMON . . . had a brutal knife scar down his face and a nervous gun in his holster.

JUD WARREND . . . McLain's partner on the Hatchet ranch.

JUDITH WARREND . . . Jud's daughter, beautiful and spoiled.

GUY PRYOR . . . faro player and deputy sheriff.

CROSBY AGNEW . . . slickest sucker ever to come out of the east.

NEIL RODGERS . . . Lane's sidekick, hot tempered and reckless.

BETH VAN BRIMMER . . . sandy haired range girl, she loved Neil.

CHAPTER
ONE

Lane McLain halted beside the mesquite thicket which grew on top of the ridge and glanced at Neil Rodgers as he waited for the others to come up. Neil's hard young face wore a grin and his eyes sparkled. Somehow the younger man managed to swagger, although he was in his saddle and his horse stood still. Reluctantly Lane echoed his companion's grin. Neil, the blamed young fool, thought that he was riding into a fight and, as always when the going got tough, enjoyed the prospect.

"There she is," Neil drawled. "What do we do? Ride in?"

"Presently," Lane answered and turned to the others assembling about him. Cuff Doyle, the veteran, bulged a grizzled cheek with tobacco and stared with calm eyes down the slope. Saturnine Nebraska, tough and barbed as a mesquite bough, rested his forearm on his saddle horn as he leaned forward, and Ben Israel, his black face impassive, checked his restive horse and said, "Whoa, fool," almost gently. These were the Hatchet warriors.

Neil, with the impatience of youth, spoke again. "What are we waitin' for, Lane?"

1

Below the ridge the settlement of Handout squatted by the Rio Bosque, cottonwoods sprinkling it and making a pattern of light and shade on dusty street and adobe buildings. At the west end of town was a blacksmith shop and wagon yard, lifeless for all that the men on the ridge could see. East of the wagon yard was a store building, a single horse in front of it, and then, after a vacant space, a long and low adobe saloon. A hundred yards beyond this building were two more — an adobe and a mongrel structure composed of wood and tin and mud, and then no more, only the twisting road crawling through brush to the Rio Bosque's ford.

"This," said Lane McLain, "is a neighborly call. We ride in; I talk to Harmon, and we ride out again. That's Harmon's horse at Ryan's hitch rack."

"Neighborly!" Cuff scoffed and spat brownly in the dust.

"Neighborly!" Lane insisted and challenged Cuff with his eyes. "We lost the trail on those calves. We don't know who got 'em. If you've got doubts about it being neighborly, Cuff, you needn't come along."

Cuff subsided, and Lane, having stared hard at each of the others, spoke again. "I'm not looking for trouble, not this trip. Ben, you'll take the east end and Nebraska will take the west. Cuff, you'll stay in the middle while Neil and I go in. Got it?"

Heads nodded. Ben Israel turned his horse and loped away toward the east, the ridge crown shielding his progress. Nebraska held out his hand and took the plug that Cuff extended. Biting off a chew, he returned the tobacco; then he, also, loped away, following the ridge down toward the river. Cuff methodically slid his Sharps from its scabbard, opened the breach, and, having glanced critically at the brass of the exposed shell, closed the rifle and rested it across his saddle bows.

Neil laughed. "A nice, neighborly call," he derided.

Perforce Lane grinned. There was a fire in the younger man that called to Lane McLain, a devil-may-care recklessness tempered by unswerving courage and quick action. Of the four, Neil was closest to Lane, nearest in spirit.

"That's what it'll be — I hope," Lane stated. "Come on."

Topping the ridge, they rode down the slope, unhurrying, giving the others time to take position. In front of the store Cuff halted while Lane and Neil went on to the saloon's hitch rack. There, stopping, they dismounted and added their horses to the three that drowsed at the rail. The morning sun beat down with sledging strokes on street and adobes and, ducking under the rack, Neil pushed past Lane to reach the saloon door and open it first.

The interior was dusky after the brilliance outside, and Neil stepped in and quickly to the right, his shoulders against the wall. Lane, a pace behind, moved to the left, so that the door was flanked on either side. Fractionally their eyes adjusted to the light, and each surveyed the room.

It was long and low, ill lighted by two windows. Behind the bar a bald-headed man wearing a dirty apron stood motionless, his hand resting on a bar rag.

3

Against the wall a man, his hat tipped down so that his eyes were hidden, let his chair legs thump to the dirt floor, and at the bar two others turned slowly so that they faced the door. One of these was tall and hump-shouldered, while the other was squat and paunchy.

"How are you, Ryan?" Lane said.

The bald man relinquished the bar rag but kept his hand in sight. "Hello, McLain," he returned without enthusiasm.

Lane walked forward, and Neil stood, catlike, at the door. The man in the chair pushed his hat from his eyes and got up. "Hello, McLain," he said.

"How are you, Tybert?" Lane did not look at the speaker but kept his eyes on the two at the bar. At some time the tall, hump-shouldered man had suffered a catastrophe. A knife scar ran from forehead to lip, splitting his nose so that he seemed to have two widely separated nostrils. His eyes were small and angrily blue as he glared at Lane McLain.

"I wanted to see you, Harmon," Lane announced.

"You see me," Harmon growled.

"Up in the Cienega yesterday" — Lane's voice was deliberate — "we found some calves gone. We trailed them a ways and lost the tracks. We're on our way to Aspinwall, so we stopped by."

"I ain't got yore damned calves," Harmon growled. "Why hunt me up?"

"Because," Lane answered smoothly, "I don't figure to lose any more calves. Pass that around, Nosey. Tell

4

the boys that the Hatchet isn't losing any more stock this year."

"I ain't got yore damned calves," Harmon repeated.

"I didn't think you got 'em." Lane watched the man intently. "If I did I wouldn't be talking to you, Nosey."

The anger in Nosey Harmon flared suddenly. "You crowd yore luck," he snarled. "Someday, McLain, I'll meet you when you ain't got yore army with you. I'd like to have that happen. You wouldn't talk so big."

Blue eyes growing harder and more narrow, Lane surveyed the tall man. "Why, if it troubles you, Nosey," he drawled, "Neil could step outside. Or you and I could step out if that suited you. How about it?"

Harmon moved impetuously, and Garret, lifting muddy eyes, said: "Nosey!"

Harmon relaxed, and Neil, beside the door, laughed harshly. "Ain't the sign right?" he derided. "I wouldn't butt in, Nosey. I'd just as soon Lane killed you."

Harmon growled something in his throat, and Lane, turning, knowing that his challenge was unanswered, looked at Tybert beside his chair. "You too, Tybert," he drawled. "You buy a lot of cattle. Tell the boys that the Hatchet isn't losing any stock. None at all."

Tybert gulped, and Lane, pausing at the door, announced brusquely, "That's all. Come on, Neil." He went through the door and disappeared. Neil, grinning wickedly, backed through the opening, pausing just beyond it.

"Cuff's outside," he drawled, "in case you get ideas. So long, gents." He pulled the door shut. For a moment there was silence, and then leather squeaked and horses moved. This sound lessened, and after a time a single horse went by at a slow trot.

"They had that damned Ben at the west end of town," Ryan growled, picking up his bar rag again. "That was him went by."

"An' somebody at the other end," Tybert said. "Nebraska, likely. Rodgers said that Cuff Doyle was outside."

Harmon glared angrily at Garret. "What'd you stop me for?" he demanded. "I'd of gone outside with him."

"An' got killed." Garret's voice was cold. "You don't want no part of McLain, Nosey. He's too many for you."

"If he'd ever travel without that damned army of his," Harmon rasped. "I'd like to get him by himself."

"You'd better be glad he had his army," Ryan growled. "They saved yore bacon. Who got the calves; do you know?"

"You didn't get 'em, did you, Nosey?" Tybert asked quickly. "The last bunch of stuff I bought —"

"Came from the Secate, like they always do." Harmon's voice was contemptuous. "Some Mexican got them Hatchet calves. Take a drink, Tybert; yo're nervous."

"Yo're damned right I'm nervous." Tybert came to the bar. "I'm just nervous enough to pick up an' pull out. If McLain an' them Hatchet warriors are ridin' the country I don't want to stay. There's other places where a man can live longer an' do better."

"An' what would Seay think of that?" Harmon growled. "I'd ruther have McLain to buck than Seay."

6

"You've *got* McLain to buck." Tybert picked up the drink that Ryan had poured. "I ain't — not yet." He downed the drink and made a wry face. "I'm goin' out an' see if they've gone."

The door closed behind Bert Tybert, and Garret said, his voice as muddy as his eyes: "Birdsall got them Hatchet calves."

Harmon glanced toward his partner. "So what?" he growled. "Birdsall an' Tybert are *amigos*, ain't they? You'd think Tybert would of kept him off the Hatchet."

"Tybert don't know it." Garret did not lift his voice at all. "Birdsall sold them calves up north of Junction. Curly Bridgers bought 'em."

"What's on yore mind, Clay?" Harmon studied his partner's face. "You've got somethin' cooked up."

"Well," Garret said, "Birdsall wants in with us, don't he? He can't go back to Mexico right now, not after killin' that fellow. An' Birdsall took the Hatchet calves. McLain come in here askin' us to spread the news around. Why don't we spread it? Let Birdsall think McLain's lookin' for him, an' maybe we'll do some good."

Harmon scowled. Ryan said: "You don't want to let Tybert know. Tybert will keep Birdsall off McLain."

"Who said anythin' about Tybert knowin'?" Garret snapped. "Birdsall is in Aspinwall right now, an' McLain said that he was bound for town. Let's put 'em together."

"An' get Birdsall killed," Ryan stated. "That's smart. He's goin' to run you boys some competition, ain't he?"

"He won't get killed," Garret answered. "He downed that fellow at Piedras Negras from behind a shed. An' if he does get killed, it's no skin off of us."

Harmon made the decision. "We'll take another drink an' go to town," he announced. "After all, McLain asked us to spread this word around, didn't he?"

"If Birdsall gets killed Tybert won't like it," Ryan warned, placing a whisky bottle on the bar. "Tybert's sold on Birdsall; he got him in here."

"An' who's goin' to tell Tybert?" Harmon paused in the act of pouring his drink. "You, Ryan?"

Ryan shrugged. "Not me," he answered. "I make my money out of tendin' bar, not the other fellow's business. Only Birdsall don't stand much chance either way. If he kills McLain, McLain's friends will get him. But I don't think he'll kill McLain. It's been tried before without much luck."

"You worried about Birdsall, Ryan?" Harmon's face was bleak. "Because if you are —"

Ryan shrugged again. "What's one cow thief more or less to me?" he asked.

Lane McLain and Neil Rodgers, joined by Cuff outside of Ryan's Saloon, mounted and rode east to where Nebraska waited in the street. There, pausing, they looked back to watch Ben Israel come through the town. Israel rode at a slow trot, looking neither to right nor left.

"No excitement," Cuff reported. "Red Dowd stuck his head out of the store an' pulled it in again, like a turtle. What about Dowd, Lane?"

Lane shook his head. "One of the bunch, I guess," he answered. "Red used to be a good man too."

"Did Harmon do anythin'?"

"Heap brave," Neil stated and laughed. "He was goin' to step outside with Lane. Garret stopped him."

Nebraska scowled, and Cuff said slowly, "Nosey does the talkin' for that outfit, but Garret's the brains. Did you see anythin', Ben?"

Israel had arrived. He shook his head in answer to Cuff's question and looked at Lane, waiting for orders.

"You don't think Harmon got 'em?" Cuff divided his glance between Neil and Lane. Lane said, "I don't think so, Cuff," and Neil, grinning, answered: "Not Harmon. It was some new talent, if you ask me. Nosey an' Clay ain't the only rustlers around Aspinwall."

Lane touched his horse with spurs and applied the rein. "Let's go to town," he drawled.

He led the way, Neil beside him, Cuff and Nebraska following, and Israel, as always, bringing up the rear. They splashed into the Bosque's shallow ford and, slacking reins, let their horses water. "Too bad Pickles wasn't there," Cuff commented, easing himself in his saddle. "He's a good kid."

"Pickles is on the road to Aspinwall, cussin' every time the ambulance hits a bump." Nebraska held out his hand. "Give me a chew, Cuff. I'm goin' to buy some tobacco when I get to town."

"Well, I *hope* so," Cuff growled. "Here, Ben. Do you want a chew?"

CHAPTER
TWO

Fifteen miles stretched between Handout and the town of Aspinwall. Handout had been the original settlement, but when silver was struck in the foothills Aspinwall had been born and swiftly outgrew its older neighbor.

The horses kept a saddle gait, and Lane, dismissing what was past, fixed his mind on the next problem that confronted him. Neil hummed a song, gay as a girl going to a dance, and momentarily Lane envied the youngster his freedom from worry and his bold insouciance. It was fine for a man to be young and carefree and certain of himself.

Behind Lane and Neil, Cuff and Nebraska indulged in drawling conversation. Cuff said: "There's Harmon's place. Up on the hill. Now what do you think he wants a ranch for?"

Nebraska growled, "It's a good excuse, ain't it? Him an' Garret each got a brand, an' that makes things handy."

"I don't envy the Secate their neighbors," Cuff affirmed. "Harmon an' Garret an' Jack Buntlin — two rustlers an' the sheriff." He laughed contemptuously. "Maybe Seay likes 'em, though."

10

"Maybe he does," Nebraska agreed. "Say, Cuff. I've got —"

"Don't ask for my plug," Cuff warned. "Ben got the last of it."

"I wasn't goin' to ask for yore tobacco." Nebraska was indignant. "You think I sponge all the time?"

"Well, don't you?"

A faint grin hovered on Lane's lips. Nebraska and Cuff wrangling. They were always at it, no matter the place or circumstance. Why, in Mexico — the time he had gone after Manuelito — Cuff and Nebraska had quarrled over which was more poisonous, a tarantula or a scorpion, and right in the middle of the fight each had bet on his favorite. Dismissing Cuff and Nebraska from his thoughts, Lane turned his mind toward the town. Warrend had written to him. Right now Jud Warrend and his daughter were in Aspinwall, waiting. He wondered . . .

"What's on yore mind, Lane?" Neil asked, breaking off his humming.

"I was wondering," Lane said guiltily, "how Casa Alamos is going to stack up to the Warrends — after Boston."

"It'll stack up all right," Neil assured. "Casa Alamos is good enough for anybody. It's the best house in the country."

"But after Boston," Lane repeated, "it's going to look mighty small to them. Warrend's all right; he knows what he's coming to. But the girl —"

Neil grunted. "Casa Alamos has got wood floors, ain't it?" he demanded. "An' the beds are O.K. an'

11

Concha's a good cook. What more do you want? Quit worryin'."

Lane smiled in answer, and Neil resumed his humming.

A smoke plume from the stamp mill marked Aspinwall. The sun was sliding down, sending long slants of light into the eyes of the riders. They passed an adobe in a gulch, climbed swiftly, and suddenly were in town. Buildings lined a dusty, wheel-marked street. Heat, the rumble of the stamp mill, voices, horses at hitch racks, an ore wagon rattling by, Main Street, saloons and stores standing side by side under their tin awnings.

"There's Pryor, Lane," Neil said. "He wants you."

Lane glanced to the left and saw Guy Pryor, Aspinwall's city marshal, standing on the sidewalk.

Pryor was tall, with yellow hair too long for an ordinary man and a sweeping mustache. His amber eyes warmed as Lane bent in the saddle and held out his hand. "It's been a long time, McLain," Pryor greeted. "You haven't been to town."

"No." Lane released the marshal's hand. "We've been putting steers on summer pasture in the Chiricahuas. What's new in town, Pryor?"

"Not much. I want to talk to you when you have time. Your folks are at Mrs. Tindler's. They came on the morning stage."

"At Mrs. Tindler's, you say? I thought they'd go to Morton's."

Pryor nodded. "You'll see me before you pull out?" he drawled.

"I will," Lane promised.

"Then I'll not keep you." Pryor stepped back, and Lane rejoined the others in the center of the street.

"A good man," he said tersely to Neil. "The Warrends are at the hotel."

"An' sweatin', I'll bet," Neil commented. They rode along, presently to stop before a two-story building shaded by cottonwoods. Lane dismounted and handed up his reins to Neil.

"Pickles will be at the Star Wagon Yard," he stated briefly. "Put the horses there. And, Neil —"

"Yeah?"

"You boys keep together and watch Cuff." Lane's voice was low. "It's been a long time since he came to town. We've got to start early in the morning."

"Cuff will stay sober," Neil promised. "We'll see you, Lane." He joined his companions and, a compact cavalcade, they rode on down the street. Lane watched them go and then, turning to the hotel, glanced up, gave his belt a hitch, and crossing the porch, entered the little lobby.

In a room on the second floor of Mrs. Tindler's Hotel, Judith Warrend turned from the window and glanced at her father on the bed. Jud Warrend lay sprawled, coat discarded, collar open at his throat. His face was gray above his beard, and beads of perspiration lined his forehead. Although his eyes were closed he seemed to sense his daughter's glance.

"Tired, Judith?" Warrend asked.

"I'm tired of waiting in this — this —" Judith cast about her for a suitable expression. The room was small and dingily carpeted. The bed, too, was small, covered by clean rough sheets. There was a bureau and a washstand with white pitcher and bowl, and askew on the wall hung a sampler in a glassless frame: "HOME IS WHERE THE HEART IS." A border of faded blue forget-me-nots had been embroidered about the words.

"It's not so bad," Warrend said wearily. "Isn't it getting cooler?"

"Cooler!" Judith snapped. "The wind is like an oven. It just isn't as hot, Dad."

Warrend smiled faintly, and Judith continued. "Why doesn't this man McLain come?" she demanded. "You wrote to him? Why didn't he meet us in Junction? After all, he works for you. He might at least have —"

"McLain doesn't work for me." Warrend broke the angry speech. "He's not an employee, Judith. He's my partner. I own half of the Hatchet ranch and he owns half. I've explained that to you, Judith, and McLain isn't the kind of man to fail to meet us. I've no doubt that there's a reason why he isn't here."

The girl was unmollified. "Just the same, he should have met us," she announced. "There's no reason great enough to keep us stewing here."

Sound came from below. Judith looked out. The hotel was on a corner, and across the intersection was the White Palace Saloon. Across the street from the White Palace was the Orient Bar, its door gaping wide under the false front. Between these two came now a small procession, five riders who wheeled and, pausing

14

in the street, waited while one man dismounted. There was a brief colloquy, and then four of the men rode on. The other, pausing, glanced up, and Judith caught an impression of eyes, startlingly direct, gazing into her own. She turned hastily.

"I think Mr. McLain has come, Dad," she said.

Warrend sat up on the bed, looking toward the door. A pause, and then steps sounded in the hall and there came an even beat of knuckles. Judith, crossing hastily, opened the door, and Warrend said, "Come in, Lane. Come in."

Lane stepped into the room, a spur rowel jingling faintly as he advanced, hand outstretched. "I'm sorry to be late," he said. "Your letter reached me yesterday when I got back to Casa Alamos. How are you, Mr. Warrend?"

Warrend released Lane's hand and stepped back a pace. "Fine, fine," he said mechanically. "You haven't changed." His eyes caught Judith beside the door and he smiled. "Judith, may I present my partner?"

Turning, Lane saw the girl and for an instant moved no farther. Dark hair, piled high, graced her, and her eyes were dark, with lashes that drooped so that Lane could not determine their color. Her curved lips were firm but generous; her smooth cheeks were flushed with the heat, and her chin was rounded and determined.

"Judith, this is Lane McLain. My daughter Judith, Lane."

Judith caught an impression of strength. This man was tall and yet so broad that his height was lost;

15

broad-shouldered, narrow-hipped. His face furthered the impression of strength, not handsome, but pleasing, rather, with rugged jaw, wide blue eyes set under level brows, and a forehead white and fair compared with the tan of cheeks and chin. Muscles rippled under his shirt when he bowed.

"Your servant, Miss Warrend," Lane murmured. As he straightened he looked fully into the girl's eyes. They were gray.

"Sit down, Lane," Warrend urged, going to the bed and seating himself. "Tell me, how have you been? How is the Hatchet?"

Judith crossed to the chair beside the window, and Lane, not acting on Warrend's invitation, answered: "The ranch is fine. We've had a good year. Tomorrow you can see for yourself."

"We'd almost given up the idea," Judith said tartly. "Dad and I had nearly decided that you hadn't received his letter."

"I'm sorry that I kept you waiting." Lane looked steadily at the girl. "The letter reached me yesterday, else I'd have met you in Junction."

"No matter." Warrend brushed aside the explanation. "You're here now."

Judith glanced at the watch pinned to her dress. "Judge Morton and his wife are expecting us for dinner," she said. "I don't want to keep them waiting." She emphasized the last word.

"And you're expected too, Lane," Warrend announced.

Judith arose from her chair. "You men can talk," she said, "but if I'm to be presentable I must get ready. I'm

16

glad that you came finally, Mr. McLain." She smiled at her father as she crossed the room.

When the door closed Warrend looked at Lane. "Don't mind Judith," he apologized. "I've spoiled her, I'm afraid."

Lane smiled. "I made her pretty mad," he drawled. "You wrote me that you'd been sick, Mr. Warrend. How are you now?"

Warrend relaxed wearily. "Not too well," he admitted. "I played the game too hard, Lane. And too long. It seemed to be the only thing to do after my wife died. The doctors put me to bed this spring, and they've just let me up. I had to promise that I'd rest, and I knew of no better place than Casa Alamos. I wrote to you, and Judith insisted on coming with me. She had to look after me, she said." Warrend smiled faintly. "Do you think I can rest at Casa Alamos?"

"Rest and stretch out." The hard blue eyes of Lane McLain softened as he looked at the older man. "There's sun and quiet aplenty — and after a while a good horse to put under you."

"It sounds," Warrend said and hesitated, "it sounds like heaven to a tired man."

"Some claim it's hell." Lane's lips widened in a smile. "Either way, you'll find it hot enough and far enough off. Well —" He let the sentence die. Outside a bird fluttered in the cottonwood and a voice drifted up from the street below: "I'll buy a drink before supper."

"I suppose I'll have to get ready for Morton's," Warrend said. "You'll come?"

Lane nodded. "I keep a room and a change of clothes here in the hotel," he stated briskly. "I'd better clean up. I'll get a buggy to take us up to Morton's, Mr. Warrend."

CHAPTER
THREE

Candles shed a soft light over the Mortons' table, and Lane McLain watched the dinner party without himself taking part in the talk. Morton, at the head of the table, was a handsome, florid man, and Molly Morton, at the foot of the board, kept her guests in skillful play. Morton was the Federal judge for the district, an Eastern man who had lived long in the West.

Judith Warrend sat on Morton's right, and Mrs. Lawton, Colonel Lawton's wife, was at his left. The colonel sat between his wife and Lane, and across the table were Manville Seay, Crosby Agnew, and Jud Warrend. Seay, lean-faced and darkly handsome, was manager of the Secate Ranch, English-owned and bordering on the Hatchet on the north. Lane eyed him speculatively, then turned to Agnew.

Agnew, seated next to Judith, was a newcomer from the East. He was a handsome man, blond, with a wisp of blond mustache and brown eyes. Judith and Agnew, in conversation, had discovered mutual friends in Manhattan and in Boston. There was a constant interchange of quip and sally between the man and girl, and Judith sparkled. To Lane's right Lawton rasped a sentence, and Lane turned to the officer.

"What we need," Lawton stated in his parade-ground voice, "is to have Crook returned to the territory. He understands conditions and he can handle Indians."

Morton accepted Lawton's statement. "We do need Crook. But you'll catch the renegades, Colonel. You'll have them back on the reservation in a week."

"Perhaps." Lawton shook his head. "We're hampered, Judge. We make a three-day patrol and then return to our base for supplies and to recruit. While we're running back and forth the renegades go where they please. No telling how much damage they will do." He scowled gloomily. "It's Washington," he completed. "They don't understand Indians or how to fight them. Our orders limit us. What we need is Crook."

"Then you think the outlying ranches aren't safe?" Judith asked, looking at Lawton. "You wouldn't advise Father and me to leave Aspinwall?"

"The Hatchet is safe enough," Lawton rasped and glanced at Lane, who flushed.

"Why the Hatchet particularly?" Judith asked. "Have you an agreement with the Apaches, Mr. McLain?" All evening long, still piqued at her delay, Judith had baited Lane.

"An agreement on the Apaches' side only," Lawton amplified. "They've learned to leave the Hatchet alone."

Warrend, interested, turned from Molly Morton. "How is that?" he asked.

"McLain followed them into Mexico," Lawton explained. "How far did you go, McLain?"

20

"To Piedras Gordas." Lane cleared his throat and looked intently at his coffee cup.

"You wrote nothing about it," Warrend chided. "Tell me, Lane."

Color deepened on Lane's cheeks, and Morton, laughing, said, "You can't get Lane to talk, Warrend. I had the story from Cuff Doyle after they'd come back. I'll tell you."

Everyone turned to the judge, and he plunged into the tale, his voice deep with the importance many courtrooms had given it, making almost oratory of his words.

"Manuelito was out," the judge began. "This was two years ago, and he raided down the valley, bound for Mexico." The story went on, filled with rapine, savagery, and plunder.

"They made the mistake of stealing Hatchet horses," Morton said. "And they burned a camp and killed a man, so Lane took the Hatchet warriors and went after them. How many men did you have, Lane?"

"Cuff and Nebraska and Neil and Ben," Lane said. "We took some *vaqueros* along too. You're making too much of this, Judge."

"*I'll* tell the story. Lane and his men kept the trail right on into Mexico. They pushed the renegades so hard they had no time to rest. At Piedras Gordas Lane caught up. He burned Manuelito's rancheria and killed a few bucks and ran off the Apache's horses. Manuelito was afoot, and he had to come back to the reservation. Since then the Apaches have left the Hatchet alone." Morton completed the tale with unction.

21

"But why?" Judith asked. "Isn't it the Army's business to fight Indians, Mr. McLain?"

"We'd got a little tired of Apaches," Lane drawled, aware that every eye was on him. "The Army can't go into Mexico, but *we* weren't hampered." The attention made him uncomfortable, and he sought to change the subject. "I came through part of your country today, Seay. The grass is pretty good, considering how dry it's been."

"Fair," Seay agreed. "What part of the ranch did you cross?"

"I came to town by way of Handout."

"Handout?" Morton's eyes were sharp. "Did you stop?"

"For a minute." Again Lane felt attention center on him. "I wanted to see Harmon. We'd lost some calves."

"And you saw him." Morton scowled. "Was there trouble?"

"No trouble."

"I don't understand," Judith broke in. "What are you talking about, Judge?"

"A very serious situation," Morton answered heavily. "You haven't been in town for a long time, Lane. Have you heard the gossip?"

Lane shook his head. "I've been putting cattle on summer pasture," he replied, "and looking after the calves. What's new, Judge?"

"There's talk of running Pryor for sheriff. What do you think?"

Lane hesitated before answering, and Seay said quickly: "I don't like the idea, Judge. Pryor's not the man for sheriff."

"Then who is the man?" Morton demanded. "Pryor's cleaned up Aspinwall since we put him in. He could deal with the Handout bunch."

Lane said thoughtfully: "Pryor's a good man. Maybe a little quick, but I like him."

"You'd back him, then?" Morton asked.

"The Hatchet doesn't back anybody," Lane drawled.

Seay, who had been intent, leaned back in his chair, relaxing. Agnew said, "Of course I'm comparatively a newcomer and I don't know much concerning local politics. Or other conditions, for that matter. You say that you lost some cattle" — he looked at Lane — "and that you stopped to see Harmon. Do you think he stole your stock?"

"No," Lane answered bluntly. "I don't think Harmon got them himself. I had a talk with him some time ago and I think he knows better than to fool with the Hatchet."

"Then why did you go to him?"

"Because," Lane answered, "I wanted to spread word that the Hatchet wouldn't stand for rustling."

"But if you had a complaint you should have gone to the sheriff," Agnew insisted. "Certainly he's the man to handle such matters."

Lane laughed, and a reluctant smile spread on Morton's face. Agnew flushed, realizing that he had caused the mirth. "I don't think Buntlin would have done me much good," Lane drawled. "I don't know who got the calves and I wouldn't have sworn out a complaint if I did. I'd have gone after the calves."

"And taken the law into your own hands?" Agnew asked. "Is that customary?"

"It's the way things work," Lane replied.

Crosby Agnew locked the fingers of his hands and rested them on the table. He was still flushed, and he resented the laughter. "Then it's the wrong custom," he stated didactically. "Unless your officials are entrusted with the enforcement of the law you revert to chaos. Every man is a judge and jury, and you live simply by force. If that is true there is no need for Judge Morton or for a sheriff or any other officer."

Morton flushed uncomfortably. "I don't think you understand, Crosby," he said. "We have a difficult situation here in Aspinwall. There are two elements, two groups —"

"There *should* be two in our system of government," Agnew interrupted. "That makes for democracy. Now in Mr. McLain's place I should have gone to the sheriff, regardless of his political affiliations, and sworn out a complaint. The sheriff —"

"Would have laughed at me," Lane interrupted quietly. "In my place you'd have done just what I did, Agnew."

"Taken matters into my own hands? I think not."

"Then" — Lane's eyes narrowed — "you'd have been run over. In this country a man kills his own snakes and makes his own tracks. If he doesn't he's finished. Believe me, I know!"

Lawton's head was nodding agreement, and Morton also nodded. Lane's voice had grown rough with his

24

earnestness, and Judith, leaning forward, eyes sparkling, took up the argument.

"I agree with Mr. Agnew. It seems to me that you were wrong, Mr. McLain. You should have gone to the sheriff."

Molly Morton, catching the judge's eye, pushed back her chair and stood. "I think we had better all go in," she said. "There are some others coming, and Judith has promised to play for us." Turning to Lawton, she took his arm and the party left the dining room.

Later, in the long drawing room in which stood the only piano in southern Arizona, Lane McLain listened to Judith Warrend play. He was no musical critic, but he could watch the play of light and shadow on the girl at the piano and see her lips curve in a smile as she looked at Agnew, who stood by to turn the music. That was enough for Lane. He hardly noted the other guests and, had he heeded them, he would have seen nothing incongruous in the assembly: in Mrs. Tindler, plump and blowzy in her best, her cheeks bright with applied color; in Yelland, manager of the Mule Mine, stiff and out of place as a post oak in a formal garden; in Boss Darby, owner of the Orient Bar, or in Guy Pryor, his yellow hair long and smoothly brushed, his yellow eyes watchful as always. Lane would have seen nothing amiss in these or any of the others who listened to the music.

Judith, glancing up at Crosby Agnew from veiled eyes, was filled with questions and with banter. In Agnew she had found a familiar spirit, such a one as she had met in many places, at dances and cotillions, at receptions in stately Boston homes, or at theater parties in New York. They played a game, old and familiar to each, a game of quick smiles that meant nothing, of bright comment, of quip and bons mots and of questions.

"Who is the tall man by Mr. McLain?" Judith asked as she selected a composition. "The man with the blond hair?"

Agnew answered: "The city marshal of Aspinwall, Guy Pryor. He deals faro in the Orient Bar and dispenses justice with a gun. You can see it under his coat. Eight men killed; that's Pryor's record. A fitting subject for Molly Morton's musicale. Will you play this Brahms, Miss Warrend? It's a favorite of mine."

Late in the evening men and women bade good-by to the Judge and Molly Morton and, complimenting Judith on her music, took their leave. Lane and the Warrends were silent as they rode down the hill to Aspinwall, and not until Lane stopped the buggy in front of the hotel did Judith speak.

"What a strange party," she commented. "Why do you suppose Molly Morton invited all those people? That fat man — Boss, they called him — and that tall man with the long yellow hair. Why, Father?"

"The judge is in politics," Jud Warrend began. "He has to be friendly."

"And they are good people," Lane said tersely. "We'll leave early for the ranch, Mr. Warrend. I had the ambulance brought in for you. Can you be ready by five o'clock? It's a long trip."

"We'll be ready," Warrend agreed and, alighting, reached up to help Judith descend.

"Good night, then," Lane said. "I'll put up the buggy." He drove away, and Warrend, with Judith's hand tucked under his arm, went wearily up the steps of Mrs. Tindler's Hotel. At his door Judith kissed her father good night and sought her own room. A lamp was burning on the bureau, but the girl blew it out and, crossing to the window, sat down. Below her the street was lighted softly by the glow that came from the door and windows of the Orient and from the White Palace across the street. For a time Judith sat there, contemplating her experiences, the people she had met and seen, the things that she had heard.

So musing, she stared into the almost empty street, and as she looked she saw Guy Pryor, tall and blond, come to the door of the Orient and stand there, outlined by the light. Other movement attracted her. Lane McLain was striding purposefully along the street that stretched between the Orient and the White Palace, his hat pushed back and reflected light marking his uplifted face and the easy swing of his body as he looked up at the hotel. Again movement caught the girl's eyes. In the shadow of the White Palace a deeper shadow stirred, and a vagary of light glinted momentarily from metal. Something caught at Judith's throat, gripped like choking fingers. That glint, that soft, swift motion, so innocent and yet so sinister! Without knowing that she had moved, she was out of her chair, leaning from the window, and her scream pierced the night, ringing a tocsin of alarm.

Instantly below the scene dissolved. Lane McLain sprang forward, and in the shadow of the White Palace flame bloomed, a ring of fire that died instantly. A gun slugged the street's quiet, murdering it with thunder, and Judith saw Guy Pryor turn, his arm flung up. Again, shatteringly, a gun pounded in the street. Pryor's arm jumped with an impact, jumped again, and then from the shadow of the White Palace a man pitched out into the light, and Pryor and Lane were running and men came pouring from the two saloons, their voices clamoring.

Still Judith leaned across her window sill, terrified and yet unable to move. She saw Pryor stop and bend in the shadow. She saw Lane look up, saw his involuntary start as his eyes found her. Only then did she withdraw from the window and become aware of the pounding on her door and Jud Warrend's voice calling in the hall: "Judith! Judith!"

CHAPTER
FOUR

Aspinwall's main street was languid in the morning light, and the Hatchet ambulance, sturdy under brown canvas cover and with two mules hitched, stood in front of Mrs. Tindler's Hotel. Nebraska and a big-nosed youngster were loading a small trunk over the endgate, and across the intersection where last night the shadow of the White Palace had fallen, a languid swamper pushed a broom across the sidewalk, scattering cigar and cigarette butts over the boot-churned dust of the street. Lane McLain and Guy Pryor stood on the corner by the hotel. Lane's eyes were weary and sunken with lack of sleep, but Pryor appeared unruffled and fresh. Collar and shirt were immaculate, and his long coat was cleanly brushed.

"And why should he take a shot at you?" Pryor asked. "You hadn't jumped him."

Lane glanced toward the wall of the Orient, where in the adobe was a fresh pockmark. "I think," he answered, "that he got some ideas. I think I know where my calves went. Birdsall got 'em."

"And that was why he took a shot at you?" Pryor asked. "You didn't know he had 'em, did you?"

"No." Lane shook his head. "I didn't. But yesterday I stopped at Handout —"

"Cuff told me," Pryor interrupted. "So that was why?"

"Maybe."

"Harmon wasn't in town yesterday, as far as I know," Pryor said slowly. "He knows he's short here. Still, he might have taken a chance and seen Birdsall."

"He might have," Lane admitted.

"Well" — Pryor spoke with complete and callous indifference — "neither of us needs to worry about Birdsall now. There's talk of me running for sheriff this fall, McLain."

"Are you going to run?"

Pryor studied Lane's face. "I think I might do it," he drawled. "Buntlin and I don't get along too well anyhow. He doesn't help a lot."

"Didn't he give you a deputy's commission?" Lane asked.

"That?" Pryor spoke contemptuously. "Yeah. But Buntlin wants to come into town. He wants to run it as well as the county. I can't have that. I'm hired here to keep the peace."

Lane nodded, seeing Pryor's viewpoint. Pryor drawled, "I can't be sure, of course, but from the way Buntlin acts, he's in with 'em. He's greedy, McLain."

"I've thought of that," Lane admitted.

"So maybe I'll run for sheriff," Pryor said. "If I do, where will you stand, Lane?"

Lane considered the question. "The Hatchet has never backed anybody," he drawled. "I've tried to stay out of local politics. But if you run I'll back you."

"Because of last night?" Pryor's yellow eyes were hard. "You don't owe me for last night. In another minute you'd have had Birdsall yourself. Forget that end of it."

"Not because of last night. Because I think you're the best man for the job."

The yellow eyes warmed suddenly. "Thanks," Pryor said. "I appreciate that."

Neither man spoke for an instant. Then Pryor said: "How's Miss Warrend this morning?"

"I wish she hadn't seen that thing last night," Lane answered, scowling. "It upset her. She'd never seen a man killed before."

Pryor nodded his understanding. "Naturally, coming from the East," he drawled. "She did the right thing, though. If she hadn't yelled —" He let the thought trail off.

Lane nodded. "I've told her that," he said.

"I'd like to thank her." Pryor's voice was soft. "Not for her warning, but for playing the piano. It's been a long time since I heard a piano played in anything but a honky-tonk, and it's been longer since I've seen a girl like her."

"I wouldn't," Lane began awkwardly. "She —"

"Of course I won't see her," Pryor said quickly. "I would upset her all over again. No. I'll go along now. So long, McLain. Good luck."

With a quick, light pressure of his hand Guy Pryor turned and walked off down the street. Lane watched the marshal until he disappeared around the corner below the White Palace.

31

"Lane," Nebraska called, "we got that trunk loaded. Is there anythin' else to go?"

Lane turned. Judith and Jud Warrend were on the hotel porch, Mrs. Tindler beside them. Nebraska, Cuff, and Pickles gathered at the side of the ambulance, and Ben Israel, mounted, was behind it. Lane walked toward them, saying, "No, Nebraska. The freighter will bring out the rest."

Cuff, glancing at the ambulance springs, commented *sotto voce*, "An' a blame good thing."

"Now you come back," Mrs. Tindler said, "just any time at all. You come back, Miss Warrend. You too, Mr. Warrend. I'll have a room for you. I'm cer'nly glad to of met you all." She wiped her hands on her apron, shook hands with Judith and with Warrend, and followed them from the porch. Judith paused beside the ambulance.

"These are the boys," Lane said. "Cuff Doyle, Pickles, Nebraska, Neil Rodgers. Ben, come here." Israel appeared at the end of the ambulance. Each man had his hat in his hand. Cuff was sheepishly awkward, and Pickles was frankly fascinated, while Neil, a grin on his hard young face, gazed with worshipful eyes.

"Miss Warrend and Mr. Warrend," Lane completed.

Judith smiled. "I heard you named last night," she said. "I feel as though I know you all." Warrend gravely shook hands with each man, saying, "I've heard of you before. Lane's mentioned you in letters."

"And now," Lane said, "we'd better go. It's a long ways to Casa Alamos. Is the lunch in the wagon, Pickles?"

"Yes, suh," Pickles agreed. "I done put it in."

Lane nodded. "I'll drive," he stated. "Where do you want to ride, Mr. Warrend?"

"In the back," Warrend responded promptly. "Judith, you sit in front with Lane. Maybe he can tell you something about the country." Warrend hoisted himself up over the wheel and disappeared under the canvas. Judith, taking Lane's extended hand, mounted lightly to the ambulance seat, and Lane, seating himself beside her, assumed the lines as Judith settled her skirts about her.

In the doorway of the Orient, Boss Darby appeared. "Lane! Wait a minute," he called and crossed the street to the ambulance. Sun glinted from his well-oiled hair as he straightened from a stiff bow. "A little wine for the lady," Darby announced. "She might get faint on the trip."

"Thank you," Judith said as Lane took the proffered bottle and stowed it away.

"Good-by," Mrs. Tindler called. "Good-by, dearie!" She waved her plump red hand as the ambulance rolled, and Judith, leaning from the seat, waved back, her handkerchief fluttering. Lane turned his mule team at the corner, straightened them, and Aspinwall's dust puffed under their hoofs as they picked up a trot.

For a time there was no talk. Aspinwall's buildings rolled past, became scattering. The ambulance passed a long adobe, a salt-cedar hedge before it. "Last Chance," Lane said and laughed.

"Last Chance?" Judith inquired.

"That's what Mueller calls his place," Lane explained. "It's the last chance when you leave town and the first chance coming in. For a drink, I mean."

"Oh."

The mules jogged steadily. Now open country lay on either side, and ahead the road stretched, winding tortuously through brush and rocks, avoiding small steep-sided cuts. Far ahead were the Chiricahuas, the sun pouring down upon them, and when she looked back Judith could see Aspinwall dwindling and the high rugged walls of mountains making a backdrop. She sighed and relaxed upon the seat.

"Are you glad to be going, Judith?" Warrend asked, leaning forward.

"Awfully glad," Judith murmured. "I think — Aren't they queer people, Dad? Isn't Mrs. Tindler funny? She called me 'dearie', and almost cried because we were leaving."

"Mrs. Tindler," Lane said, staring straight ahead at the rumps of the trotting mules, "is the salt of the earth. She mothers the whole town."

"Of course she's fine," Judith defended, "but —"

"She calls everybody 'dearie'," Lane announced. "And she'll give you her shirt."

"You seem to be very fond of her."

"I am."

For the moment the conversation was closed. On the back seat Jud Warrend grinned. Lane's uncompromising directness would be good for Judith, he thought.

Through the brush, against a sloping ridge, a file of riders appeared. As distance closed Judith could see that these were troopers, each slouched in his saddle, each with a short-barreled carbine resting on his thigh. Lane kept the road, and as they passed Judith had a full view of the men. The young lieutenant in the lead, dust-covered and with his face burned red by sun, called a greeting, and Lane, lifting his whip in salute, answered it.

"Patrol," he said. "They're coming back. Lawton is right, Mr. Warrend. We need Crook back in this country."

Warrend answered in agreement and asked a question, and for a brief time there was talk between the front and back seats of the ambulance. Judith scarcely heeded. She was watching a rider spur out to the left of the road. Her fingers gripped Lane's elbow.

"Where is Mr. Doyle going? Isn't he going to the ranch with us?"

Lane cast a casual glance to the left. "Cuff's going to the ranch," he agreed. "Likely he's seen something that he thinks needs looking into."

"But — what could he see in this country?"

"There's lots of things to see," Lane answered noncommittally. "Cuff generally sees them. He's a good man."

"Last night," Judith offered, "Judge Morton spoke of the Hatchet warriors. What did he mean, Mr. McLain?"

"He was talking about Cuff and Nebraska and Neil and Ben," Lane said. "They call them that sometimes."

"But why? Tell me."

"Well" — Lane looked down and smiled at Judith — "I guess because they generally turn up when there's trouble. They've been with me a long time."

"The Negro too?"

"Ben?" Lane laughed. "I couldn't keep house without Ben. He came from Texas with me. He's the best cowman of the lot."

"That Negro?" — incredulously.

"Ben Israel."

"And what about Mr. Doyle and the man you call Nebraska? Hasn't he any other name?"

"Not that I've heard." Lane clucked to the mules and swished the whip threateningly. "Nebraska drifted in to the ranch five years ago. He'd been hurt pretty bad, and we looked after him. He's been there ever since, on the pay roll as Nebraska."

"How was he hurt?"

"Shot." The mules had slowed to a walk as they climbed a ridge. "There's a road runner," Lane continued, pointing with the whip. "The Mexicans call them *paisanos*. They can run as fast as a team. I've heard that they'll kill snakes, but I never saw one do it."

Judith paid no attention to the red herring flung into the conversation. "You don't know *anything* about Nebraska?" she demanded. "What if he was an outlaw? I should think you'd find out."

"He's all right," Lane answered. "I know all I need to know about Nebraska. I've never had to look back to find him. I've never had to do that with any of these boys."

The subject of Nebraska, Judith saw, was finished, but curiosity filled her, and she pursued her quest. "What about Mr. Doyle and Mr. Rodgers?"

"Cuff used to be a buffalo hunter," Lane said. "He had quite a stake one time, but he went broke on cards and whisky. He's been at the ranch longer than Nebraska."

"And Mr. Rodgers?"

"Neil?" Lane laughed. "I found him under a flat rock." Seeing Judith's face, he sobered. "Neil's kind of my boy," he continued. "His daddy was a missionary, and the Apaches killed him. Neil's mother too. Neil was raised in an Apache rancheria. He ran away from that and tied up with old Ramon de Griego. I saw him the first time I came into this country, before we started the Hatchet. We kind of joined up. He went back to Texas with me, and we've been together ever since."

"How old are you, Mr. McLain?" Judith asked.

"Thirty-two. Why?"

"Because you called Mr. Rodgers your boy. He must be nearly thirty himself."

"Neil's twenty-five," Lane drawled, "or thereabouts. He was just a kid when we came together. Maybe fifteen."

Judith sat quiet, pondering. Here was Lane McLain, seven years older than Neil Rodgers and referring to Rodgers as his boy. Lane could not have been more than twenty-two when, as he said, he and Neil "came together".

"Neil's my range boss," Lane said suddenly. "He's a cowman!"

"What is a range boss?"

"Neil covers the country I can't get to," Lane explained. "You see, the Hatchet is really three ranches.

There's Casa Alamos and Piedras Amarillas and the Benton Springs down south. I can't be every place at once, so Neil goes where I don't go."

"Oh," Judith said.

Cuff was returning to the road, and the mules topping the rise halted to breathe. The lines were lax in Lane's hands, and about the ambulance the country spread, immense and breathtaking.

"Big!" Lane said softly. "God's outdoors. Your father's asleep."

Judith, glancing back, saw that Warrend had disposed himself comfortably in the rear seat and that his eyes were closed. From him she looked again at the country about: wicked, yet soothing; fascinating, but dangerous; promising, yet diamond-hard. To the west clouds hung over the mountains, but above the sky was brilliant and clear as rock crystal. The girl breathed deeply, feeling air like wine fill her lungs. "God's outdoors," she echoed, her voice as soft as the man's. "I think Dad can rest here. I know he can."

"Geddup!" Lane ordered prosaically, and the mules moved again.

They nooned at a spring, Ojo Culebra, Lane called it and explained that the name meant Snake Springs. Mrs. Tindler had packed a basket, and while mules and horses grazed, the men and Judith ate and drank, seated in a circle on the ground. Judith marveled at them, their neatness, their ease. Ben Israel ate with the rest, accepted, one of them, indeed deferred to occasionally. He was older than any save Cuff Doyle,

38

and Neil, when he poured coffee from the pot, served Ben before he served himself or Nebraska.

After the meal there were cigarettes, and Cuff smoked a contemplative pipe. It had been a silent feast, relaxed and peaceful, and yet Judith noted that Cuff's big rifle leaned against a rock beside him and that each man was armed. She saw the guns upon their hips and noted their eyes, wary, always shifting, even as they stretched in the shade of rocks and paloverdes. Presently the nooning was done. Men rose and went to hitch the mules and tighten loosened cinches. Lane, on some mission of his own, strode off down the little stream that trickled from the spring and, stopping, gazed off toward the south. Judith, following, saw the man's footprints in the moistened sand, and because they were small and neat, the imprint of the high heel deep, she gathered her skirts in her hand and tested, with one small, kidshod foot, measuring her own against the imprint in the sand.

Beside her a chuckle sounded, and she looked up to see Ben Israel, mounted. The Negro's face was grave, but there was a twinkle in his eyes.

"You aim to follow them tracks, ma'am?" Israel asked. "They'd take you a long ways. Them's man tracks." He laughed again, deep in his throat, a fragment of sound, and, wheeling, rode away. Oddly Judith's cheeks were red as she left the rill and hastened to the ambulance.

It seemed, as they drove on, that the mountains had not neared appreciably. They lay ahead, bleak and unmoving; only now their peaks were lost in darkness.

The sun disappeared, shrouded by a cloud, and Lane frowned as he touched the backs of the trotting mules with the whip. "Rain," he said briefly. "We'll have to get along."

Presently the road led down a long slope, dropping into a valley. They crossed a dry stream bed, and as the team scrambled up the farther side Lane turned and spoke to Warrend. "We're on the Hatchet now."

"How much farther?" Warrend asked, and Lane answered, "Not far."

He let the mules blow when they were above the wash and the first big drops of rain spattered on the canvas top. The riders had dismounted. Judith saw Pickles struggling into a yellow slicker and, turning to the other side, watched Ben Israel, also in a slicker, approach and mount a protesting horse. Lane produced a gummed sheet and, fastening it to the dash, drew it up over their knees. "Maybe you'd better ride in back," he suggested. "You're apt to get wet here."

"I'd rather stay here," Judith answered.

Lane nodded and, gathering the lines, drove on, urging the mules to a faster pace. The first patter of rain became a rumbling drum roll, and Judith drew the gummed apron higher as wind whipped her hat and veil and fine drops stung her cheeks.

"It really rains in this country," Lane warned. "Sure you don't want in the back?"

"No! Don't stop."

Lightning, sharp as a sword thrust, flashed to the left, instantly followed by a peal of thunder. The mules

40

shied and broke into a run, and Lane pulled them down. Then with full force the storm struck.

It came like a wall, a deluge that roared down upon the ambulance. Judith had never seen its like for sheer ferocity. She could not see the slicker-clad riders on either side in that first attack, and in her fright she leaned close, her shoulder against Lane's arm. Lane grinned at her whitely as he controlled the running mules. Ben Israel pounded close to the ambulance and drew ahead, shouting something as he passed. Hail roared on the canvas cover, and water splashed on the apron that Judith held high for protection. There were hailstones on the apron.

"Fun!" Lane shouted above the roar of the hail. "This is a dandy!"

"Fun!" Judith cowered, utterly terror-stricken by the savagery of the storm, by the plunge and lurch of the ambulance that threatened, so it seemed to her, momentarily to overturn. Lightning made an almost continuous cannonade. Judith stared ahead and to the left, searching for Ben Israel, sure that he had been lost in the torrent. She caught a glimpse of yellow in the lightning's flash, saw Israel. The Negro's mouth was open as he yelled and, insanely, he was tearing at his slicker, ripping it open. Beyond Israel another rider was bearing down, a squat man, water streaming from naked shoulders and torso, a fillet of dirty, water-soaked cloth about his head turbanwise, his face wide, flat-nosed, with high cheekbones. A rifle was gripped in one upraised hand, and his legs were tight about the barrel of a rain-darkened horse.

Lane, jerking his head to the left, rasped out the words: "Apaches, by God!"

What happened then was too rapid for comprehension. The apron was snatched down, and wet leather was thrust into Judith's hands. She heard Lane shout, "Drive 'em!" and then a gun exploded, seemingly in her very ear, and she was struggling with the mules as they plunged against the lines she held. Lane's arm thrust past her face; she turned to avoid it, saw pale flame blossom from the pistol in his hand, and the ambulance lurched, seemed to drift upon its side for an instant, and then settled level again. The arm was withdrawn. The lines were taken from her hands. Judith could see Lane's profile, his strong, hard jaw. The pace of the ambulance began to slow. Only the rain was all about them now, and the mules were running up a long slope, going slower and slower, until they came to a toiling walk. There was a devastating flash and crash of thunder, and Judith, turning, hid her face against Lane's shoulder and clutched his arm with trembling fingers. She was hardly aware of her father's hands upon her own shoulders, or his voice. She heard Lane rumble, "Just scared. She'll be all right. Did you see the way she handled the team?" There was pride and praise in tone and words, and Judith, straightening, pushed herself away.

The rain was thinning. Jud Warrend, bent forward, repeated anxiously, "Are you all right, Judith? Are you all right, baby?"

Not for years had her father called her "baby". Judith managed a smile. "I'm all right," she answered, and

42

involuntarily her hands flew up to disordered hat and hair. Warrend sank back into his seat, and Lane said, "You bet she's all right. She'll do to take along, Mr. Warrend."

Ben Israel rode up beside the ambulance, slicker opened and streaming rain, rain running from his face. The Negro was grinning, and behind him came Pickles, also grinning, also with opened slicker and with a rifle across his saddle bow. The thunder muttered, low and ominous, and, turning, Judith saw Nebraska and Cuff on the other side. Both men wore wide grins.

"Is — was — ?" Judith quavered and then stopped, determined not to show her fright.

"They were Apaches all right," Lane said calmly. "The storm was driving them just like it was driving us, and they were just as surprised as we were. Nobody's hurt. How many were there, Ben?"

"Six of 'em, Mist' Lane," Israel answered. "Heah comes Neil."

Neil appeared behind Israel. Like the others, his face was alight with a smile. "Chee's bunch," he called through the thinning rain. "They came down a draw right onto us. We didn't stop any of them, Lane. Is Miss Warrend all right?"

"Fine," Lane assured. "She drove and gave me a shot at one buck. I don't know how I missed him."

"Too much rain for good shootin'," Neil said. "They didn't do any, did they?"

"I don't think so."

"Are they — ?" Judith began.

"Clear gone," Lane said cheerfully, interpreting the half-finished question. "They were headed south. If they don't run into one of Lawton's patrols they'll be in Mexico by morning. How heavy was the rain north of us, Ben?"

Surprisingly, Judith saw, the rain had stopped. Water dripped from the sodden canvas cover and ran down the apron. Her shoulders and blouse were wet, but watery sunlight was seeping down about them.

"Heavier in the nawth," Israel answered. "We better hurry if we want to cross the Santa Clara befo' she comes down."

Lane slapped the mules with the lines. "Lope ahead and take a look at the creek," he directed.

Neil and Israel stirred their horses, sweeping past the trotting mules.

"Is that all?" Judith demanded. "Isn't there anything for us to do? Is that really all?"

Lane's eyes were amused. "Unless you want to chase 'em," he drawled. "I wouldn't advise that. It's still kind of wet back there. No, that's all, I guess. We're nearly home."

"Home?" Judith echoed.

"Casa Alamos is just across the creek," Lane explained. "Maybe five miles yet to travel." The amusement spread from eyes to lips, and Lane McLain grinned. "You're all right," he praised. "You're fine, Miss Judith. Just keep it up and you'll be an Arizonan."

Judith gathered herself and straightened. For an instant she was angry. She didn't want to be an Arizonan; she didn't want the praise of Lane McLain.

Or did she? The tense shoulders relaxed, and Judith looked out over the backs of the now-docile mules to where the Chiricahuas jostled up into the light.

CHAPTER
FIVE

Casa Alamos was on the east bank of Santa Clara Creek, a collection of adobe buildings that had grown up about the main house and marked by the cottonwoods that gave the place its name. The Big House faced the creek, and south of it, fifty yards, was a small square adobe called La Casita, in which Lane had an office. Rain dripped on the cottonwoods, drizzled on the dirt roofs, and ran in rivulets toward the creek. Lane finished the letter he was writing, put his pen aside, and, stretching, stood up. The country needed rain, but Lane was ill pleased. This general storm removed his last excuse for staying at the ranch.

There had been other storms since the fierce downpour through which the Warrends had come. During the two weeks' interval small rains, swift-moving belts of wetness, had marched across the country, but this was the first big general wetting that the Hatchet had received for a month, and this rain would bring green grass. It was time to brand, and Lane must start the roundup wagons. The idea, for no reason at all, displeased him.

He walked to the door of the office and, looking out, saw a buggy on the Aspinwall road, a mile or more away. The vehicle was barely visible through the rain as it climbed out of one depression and dipped into another. Idly Lane wondered who might be coming. Molly and Judge Morton had visited the ranch, and Mrs. Lawton had spent a day with Judith. But the judge was now holding court at the west end of his district, his wife with him, and Lawton and his wife were back in Fort Clevenger, and the Army patrols had been recalled, the Apaches having returned to their reservation after a short raid. Guests would be welcome, for Judith enjoyed companionship.

Musingly Lane considered the Warrends. Having run for so long on nerve, Jud Warrend had collapsed when he reached Casa Alamos and had spent the first week at the ranch in bed. Only in these last few days had he felt well enough to sit in the patio and enjoy the sunshine. But Jud was getting well. Concha was plying him with hearty, well-cooked food, and the Easterner drank goat's milk, ate three meals, and pieced between times. His ragged nerve ends were padding, and the sagging hollows of his face were filling.

Judith was quite another matter. Automatically Lane's eyes searched the portal of the Big House for the girl. He had spent a great deal of time with Judith during the past two weeks. They rode together in the mornings, and often in the afternoons Judith came down to La Casita. She liked fine horses and was a good rider, albeit she used a sidesaddle. Lane grinned as he recalled Pickles fighting a horse in the corral, using the sidesaddle, and, with a gunny sack for a skirt, trying to accustom the pony to the new rigging.

Brightboy was gentle enough and wise, but it had taken considerable riding on Pickles' part to make the sorrel see the light. Like everyone on the place, Pickles thought that Judith Warrend was something special.

She *was* something special, Lane admitted. Not many girls could have taken the jolts as Judith had. Lane had expected hysterics and tears to follow that night in Aspinwall and the brush with the Apaches in the storm, but they hadn't come. Despite Judith's fright and shock, her principal concern had been for Jud. A mighty fine girl and a mighty game girl; all Lane's worry concerning her had been for nothing. She took the rough with the smooth and never murmured. And every man on the ranch, from Matias, the roustabout, right on to Cuff Doyle, was in love with her. It was funny to see old Cuff, gruff and surly as a grizzly bear, unbend and put on his company manners when Judith appeared. Lane grinned at the thought.

His thinking, abstract until now, became suddenly personal. Every man on the place was in love with Judith Warrend. How about Lane McLain? Was he in love with her? Reluctantly, because he was not given to introspection, Lane examined the evidence. He knew that he took pleasure in the girl's society. It was no real chore to stay at Casa Alamos, to delegate work to Neil or Cuff or to Carl van Brimmer, his foreman at the place. It was mighty nice to ride with Judith, to explain the workings of the ranch to her, to stroll with her, to answer her eager questions. But he wasn't in love with her, he decided. It wouldn't do. They were miles apart. Judith Warrend was accustomed to finer things than

Casa Alamos afforded: operas and parties and cities, trips on yachts, and fine homes. Some fellow like Agnew was the right man for Judith Warrend, not a cowman like Lane McLain.

The buggy crossed the Santa Clara ford and rolled along toward the Big House. Lane donned his slicker and, settling his hat, splashed out in the rain to greet the new arrival.

When Lane reached the Big House, Matias had already come to take the buggy team, and Judith Warrend was welcoming Crosby Agnew at the door. Lane was, for no reason at all, angry with the blond Easterner, but he forced the anger aside and made Agnew welcome.

"I suppose" — Agnew smiled as he divested himself of raincoat and hat in the entrance — "that any man would be foolish to undertake a trip in this kind of weather. But Judge Morton is gone and Molly with him, and I've worn out Aspinwall's resources. I was lonely, and so I came to visit."

"We've been wondering when you were going to visit us," Judith answered. "Welcome to Casa Alamos, Mr. Agnew."

Lane picked up Agnew's grip. "I'll show you a room, Agnew," he said, and if his voice showed a trace of surliness he did not realize it. "How far does the rain go? Clear to Aspinwall?"

"Beyond," Agnew answered and followed Lane.

When they returned to the living room Jud Warrend was there to welcome the guest, and for a time there was general conversation. Agnew had a budget of news, both from the East and from town, and he retailed it cleverly.

His news of Aspinwall was interesting. Guy Pryor had definitely announced for sheriff, backed by Morton, Yelland, and most of Aspinwall's businessmen. The Junction stage had been twice stopped and, so far at least, nothing had been done to apprehend the bandits. There was a fresh silver strike; the Mule Mine had hit a vein particularly rich in silver; a new minister had arrived to take the pulpit of the Methodist Church, and there were rumors of a new Indian agent on the reservation. In the midst of this report Neil Rodgers arrived, fresh come from Piedras Amarillas, and shortly thereafter supper was ready, and they all sat down at the table.

Talk continued during the meal. Neil reported that there had been three days of rain in the hills and that he had readied the roundup wagon. He had come in to learn Lane's pleasure. Agnew was politely inquisitive about the roundup plans, and Judith was eager.

"You'll take me with you, Lane?" she asked. "I've never seen a cow branded." Judith had long since discarded the formal "Mr. McLain."

Lane grinned. "You wouldn't like it," he replied. "And, anyhow, the wagons will start from Piedras Amarillas and from Benton Springs. We'll be branding for a month."

"But I want to see it done," Judith insisted.

"It wouldn't hurt her to learn where a beefsteak comes from," Warrend said.

50

"Well," Lane agreed, "when the wagons get to Santa Clara Creek they'll be close enough. You could come out then."

When the meal was finished Judith gave the men permission to smoke, and Agnew and Warrend lighted cigars while Lane and Neil rolled cigarettes. Agnew settled back in his chair, sipped coffee, and smiled contentedly.

"I've wondered ever since I came to this country how ranch coffee was made," he said. "It's good, but I've never had coffee like it before. How is it done, McLain?"

"Coffee," Lane drawled, "ought to be stout and hot. A cowpuncher generally tries his out with a horseshoe. If the shoe sinks he puts in more coffee. If the shoe floats it's just right."

Agnew laughed and took another sip. "Really," he said, "this is a business trip, McLain. Judge Morton advised me to talk with you."

"And I thought that you'd driven through the rain to see me," Judith flashed.

"I did, of course!" Agnew returned gallantly. "Judge Morton's insistence was simply an excuse. Still, to please the judge —" He laughed, Judith with him, and faced Lane again. "I'd like your advice, McLain."

"About what?"

"I am," Agnew said deliberately, "investigating the possibilities of this country for my father and myself. Some time ago Judge Morton wrote my father. Waite Agnew. Perhaps you've heard of him?"

Lane shook his head, but Warrend said briefly, "I've met Mr. Agnew. I know him."

51

"Then" — Crosby Agnew smiled at Warrend — "you know that he is always interested in new developments. There is a good deal of English and Scottish money going into Western ranches. Particularly in Texas. My father thought that Arizona might offer an equal opportunity, and when Judge Morton wrote, he sent me out."

"Arizona is as good a country as Texas," Warrend declared. "The Hatchet has made money."

"Exactly." Agnew nodded. "It seems that now would be a good time to invest. It happens that the Englishman who owned the Secate Ranch died last year, and his heirs are anxious to liquidate the estate. I'm here to examine that property."

"Do you like it?" Lane asked, wondering what an Easterner like Agnew could tell about a ranch.

"I do and I don't," Agnew answered. "Of course I don't know anything about the cattle business" — he smiled deprecatingly — "but it seems to me that there is money to be made in this country. I like the Secate Ranch, but it isn't big enough."

Lane waited without comment, and Agnew, having puffed on his cigar, continued: "The English people are anxious to sell. Father has been in correspondence with them and, I believe, has received a price. However" — he waved the cigar in a small gesture — "I've written Father that the Secate alone won't do. There are other adjacent properties that should go with it."

"Such as?" Lane suggested, his interest aroused.

"The Raoul Ranch, the Harbury Ranch, and the Porter Ranch."

52

A small glint of admiration came to Lane's eyes, and when he glanced at Neil he saw that youngster's approbation. "With those ranches and the Secate," Agnew continued, "a man would have natural boundaries. It seems to me that they complement and complete the Secate. What's your idea, McLain?"

"Really," Lane said slowly, thinking of the country, mapping it mentally, "they all go together. That would give you summer pasture in the Hermanitas and Santa Clara Creek for a boundary. You'd run down just below Handout and go clear to Rio Bosque on the west."

Agnew nodded, pleased, and Lane continued after a moment, "But you don't buy land in this country, Agnew. That is all open range. It's only usage that makes your boundaries."

"I know that," Agnew agreed, "but if I bought the cattle wouldn't I be entitled to the land? Wouldn't my claim to the range be respected?"

"Yes." Lane nodded. "That would be so if you bought the brands."

"And that," Agnew declared, "is what I intend to do. Manville Seay represents the English people, and he's negotiating with Raoul and Harbury and Porter for their places. If I can get them all together Father and I will buy."

"Then you'll be our neighbor," Judith said. "I hope that Mr. Seay can make the others agree."

Agnew smiled at the girl. "If you were to be here I'd consider it an added inducement," he said. "I'm not sure but that I'd urge the purchase whether we got the other ranches or not."

"That would make a big outfit," Lane drawled, reverting to the theme. "Who would run it, Agnew? You?"

"Hardly." Agnew laughed. "I know my limitations. No, I've promised Seay the management if he can make the deal."

Lane's face sobered, and Judith said: "Then you won't be our neighbor?"

"I intend to stay in the country and look after our interests, of course," Agnew replied. "But Mr. Seay will have the actual management. I've seen his reports to the present owners, and he's done well. I'm glad that you think it's all right, McLain. Judge Morton puts a great deal of confidence in your judgment."

"If," Lane commented, "you've gone this far with it I don't see why Morton sent you out."

"I want advice about the cattle," Agnew answered. "After all, that's what I'm really buying. There is very little deeded land on any of the places. I've checked at the courthouse. What about the cattle, McLain?"

"How do you mean?"

"I've examined the books of these ranches," Agnew explained. "They show that Raoul has a thousand head. Harbury two thousand, and Porter about fifteen hundred. Buntlin has some cattle north of Handout — about five hundred head — and the Secate shows fifteen thousand. We've set a tentative price of twenty dollars a head for all kinds of cattle. Do you think that's fair?"

Lane made a rapid mental estimate and then nodded. "That's fair," he agreed, "but you won't buy by a book count, will you?"

"A book count?"

"You won't take the numbers that show on the books and pay for them?" Lane amplified.

"Why not? Aren't these men honest?"

Lane deliberated before he answered. "They're honest, I think, but there's too much death loss and too much stealing for me ever to take range delivery on cattle in this country."

"Then what would you do?"

"Count 'em."

Warrend said, "Lane's right, Agnew. You should count these cattle."

"But that is twenty thousand head," Agnew expostulated. "That's impossible."

Neil grinned all across his hard, youthful face, and Lane's eyes held a twinkle. "That many cattle can be counted," he drawled. "You'd have to build a fence and put them through a gate, but it could be done. Your sellers would deliver at the gate. It would be up to them to get the cattle to you."

"I couldn't do it," Agnew declared.

"You could hire it done. Look here, Agnew: this deal runs into money. About four hundred thousand dollars. Five hundred head of cows at twenty dollars amounts to ten thousand dollars, and it would be easy to miss five hundred head out of twenty thousand."

"You're right, McLain." Agnew's face was sober. "I hadn't considered that. I hadn't thought that it would be possible to count so many cattle."

The corners of Lane's lips twitched, and Neil's grin broadened. Warrend said, "Lane could do it."

Agnew hesitated fractionally, then: "Would you count them, McLain?"

"I can't." Lane shook his head. "I'm busy with the Hatchet, and anyhow —"

"And anyhow?"

"The Hatchet has got enough enemies." Lane smiled. "The man who does this counting won't make friends, Agnew. I warn you of that."

"Then who would do it?" Agnew stared at Lane.

"If you don't do it yourself you ought to get some outsider," Lane said. "Someone not connected with the deal at all. He'll have to hire a crew and get a wagon and come in and count your cattle. You need a man with a good reputation and one that you're sure is honest."

Neil pushed back his chair and stood up awkwardly. "If you folks will excuse me," he said, "I got some things I ought to tend to."

"Of course, Neil." Judith nodded. "And I don't blame you for wanting to go. Business is boring."

"I'm sorry, Miss Warrend," Agnew said. "We'll talk of it no more."

"Good night, all." Neil bobbed his head to the others at the table. "I'll see you in the mornin', Lane."

"In the morning," Lane agreed. "Good night."

The others chorused, "Good night," and Neil went out.

When he left the Big House, with rain still drizzling, Neil crossed the yard to an adobe where a light burned. There was a second light in the bunkhouse, but Neil was not interested. He knocked on a door, waited, and when it opened stepped inside. "Hello, Beth," Neil said.

This was Van Brimmer's house, and Beth van Brimmer, a plump, sandy-haired girl with clear brown eyes, stood in the lamplight. She did not answer Neil's greeting, and Neil, removing coat and hat, dropped them beside the door.

"Where's Carl?" he asked. "Gone to bed?"

"He went to the north camp and hasn't come back." Beth crossed to a rocker and sat down, picking up her interrupted mending.

Neil grinned. "That suits me," he reported. "It's sure good to see you, Beth." He followed the girl and bent down, intending to kiss her. Beth pushed him away.

"I don't think you were very anxious to see me," she declared. "You came in at six, and it's after ten now."

"I couldn't get away from up there," Neil defended.

There was no lack of spirit and no lack of femininity in Beth van Brimmer. She had been in love with Neil for two years, but she would not let his neglect, as she considered it, go unpunished. Lately Beth had not been sure of Neil. When he came to Casa Alamos he spent his time with Lane or at the Big House, and Beth was resentful. Frankly, Beth van Brimmer was jealous of Judith Warrend, not that she would admit it even to herself.

When the Warrends first arrived Beth had tried to be friendly and — so she thought — Judith had answered with patronage. That had not set well, and tonight Beth was especially piqued. Carl was gone and Beth, left alone, had been omitted from the party at the Big

House. She had spent the evening in bitter recrimination, particularly since Neil's arrival, and, like all things feminine, she vented her spite on the person most dear to her.

"Say," Neil demanded, "what's the matter with you, Beth?"

"There's nothing the matter with me," Beth answered tartly, keeping her eyes on her mending. "I'm sure you were busy at the Big House. What did you talk about? Parties in Boston? I'll bet that you knew a lot about them!"

"Now look," Neil expostulated, utterly surprised by this attack and unable to defend against it. "I got down here as soon as I could. I couldn't just walk out an' leave 'em, could I? Lane said for me to stay for supper, an' I had to do it."

"Lane!" Beth sniffed. "You think the sun rises and sets in Lane McLain. He's as bad as all the rest of you. He follows her around like a puppy wagging his tail."

"Follows who around?"

"Judith Warrend. I suppose she told you to stay too. She wouldn't let you leave. Anything that walks and wears pants. She's not content with having Lane in love with her. She wants you too!"

Neil's eyes were narrow with anger. Lane was his idol, and to impugn him was to strike Neil in the face. And he had, in company with every other male at Casa Alamos, fallen under Judith's charm. "You lay off of Lane an' Miss Warrend," he warned. "They're all right."

"And I'm not, I suppose?" Beth snapped.

"I don't know what you're on the prod about an' I don't care," Neil announced. "I got down here as soon as I could, an' you snap my head off. I'm goin' to bed. When you can talk like a human let me know. Good night!"

He picked up his coat and slapped on his hat, jerked the door open, and stood in the opening.

"*Good* night!" Beth answered. "If you wait for me to come running after you, you'll wait a long time."

The door slammed behind Neil's angry back. Beth waited. She expected the door to reopen and a contrite Neil to appear. Instead she heard receding footsteps that were shortly deadened by the rain. For a while Beth sat, her unheeded mending in her hands. Then, dropping the mending, she turned to the table and pillowed her head on her arms, her shoulders shaking with her sobs.

Down in the bunkhouse Cuff Doyle stared at Neil Rodgers. "What's got into you, kid?" Cuff demanded. "You look like the back end of a cloudburst."

"None of your damned business," Neil flared. "An' I don't give a damn how I look! *¿Sabe?*"

CHAPTER
SIX

The hatchet ran two roundup wagons. One, with Neil as wagon boss, started from Piedras Amarillas and came west; the other crew, under Carl van Brimmer, began the work at Benton Springs and swung west, then north. They were to meet on Santa Clara Creek, pulling into headquarters at the end of the roundup.

Lane had complete confidence in Neil and Carl van Brimmer. Van Brimmer, a grizzled Texas cowman, had been with the Hatchet for years, and Lane had never seen a better man with cattle. Lacking that fiery spirit that drove Neil, that showed in Nebraska and Cuff, and that lay, latent, in Ben Israel, still Van Brimmer understood natives and handled them well. His crew was composed of vaqueros, with only sour Nebraska for leavening and company.

For two weeks the branding progressed without incident. Lane, riding between the wagons, managed to catch snatches of time at Casa Alamos. This was often out of his way, but he added miles to his rides in order to eat a meal with Jud and Judith Warrend and spend part of a night under the same roof.

Judith, without company, was frankly bored. "I never see you," she complained to Lane on the occasion of one visit. "You come in at night, eat dinner, go to bed, and are gone in the morning before I get up. Dad isn't any company. All he does is eat and sleep and get fat." She smiled fondly. "And of course that's what I want him to do, but it doesn't help matters for me."

"Well," Lane said, "you can ride. Matias will saddle Brightboy for you any time you want him, and he'll go with you. Only I don't think you'd better get very far from the ranch. And there's Beth. She'd ride with you."

Judith made a small and pretty grimace of distaste. "I've asked her," she said, "but I don't think Beth likes me. She won't ride with me and she's always busy. I've tried to be nice, but I'm afraid that I bore her. She'll hardly talk to me."

"What did you try to talk about?" Lane asked practically. "Boston? I don't expect that Beth's much up on Boston. Try her on something she knows."

"I don't know what that would be," Judith declared with asperity. "I've tried to talk to her about everything I could think of."

"Well," Lane said, "maybe you'll hit something if you keep trying. I'm sure glad your dad's coming along like he is. He'll be riding with you himself pretty soon."

Judith agreed, and the talk went to other matters. Before Lane left the next morning Beth waylaid him. The girl was wan, with deep circles under her eyes, and Lane, accustomed to her normal healthiness, was startled.

"When will you see Carl?" Beth asked and, when Lane said that he was going immediately to Van

Brimmer's wagon, handed him a note. "Will you give him that?"

"Sure," Lane agreed. He was tempted to make some comment on Beth's appearance but refrained, and Beth, her errand done, said, "Thank you, Lane," and returned to the house.

That day at noon Lane gave Van Brimmer his daughter's note. Van Brimmer read it through and then looked up, his eyes troubled. "Beth wants to go to town an' stay with Mrs. Tindler," he reported. "Mrs. Tindler's been after her a long time, an' Beth says she's lonesome at the ranch with me gone. What do you think, Lane?"

"I don't think it would hurt her to get away from Casa Alamos awhile," Lane answered. "She'd have a pretty good time in town."

"Then," Van Brimmer said, "I'll let her go. I've got to send in for some flour, Lane. We got a damn camp-robbin' horse in the remuda. He got into the wagon an' spilt the flour sack an' upset the sourdough crock. Cookie's figgerin' to kill him."

"Why don't you go in yourself," Lane asked, "and pack the flour back? You could talk with Beth, and I'll stay here and take over."

"Thanks." Van Brimmer nodded. "I'll do that if it's all right with you. We're goin' to work at Trampas Tanks tomorrow, anyhow, and there'll be short circles because we'll move the wagon."

The following morning Van Brimmer left for Casa Alamos, and Lane took over the work at the wagon. Van Brimmer returned that night with two sacks of flour and a small crock of sourdough on a pack horse. "Fellow named Agnew was at the ranch," he reported. "He's leavin' in the mornin' an' he said he'd take Beth in." Van Brimmer wondered why Lane scowled. Surely it was all right for Beth to go. Lane had suggested it himself.

Lane stayed with Van Brimmer's wagon another day and then, leaving, cut straight across country to where Neil's crew was branding calves. He reached the wagon at noon, just as the crew was saddling its afternoon horses, and just in time to see Neil hurt.

Neil liked bad horses. Time and again Lane had told him that, as range boss, he must ride a good string and leave the rough ones to Pickles and Epiminio Bautista. "They're hired for it," Lane argued. "Why don't you quit the broncs, Neil? It's not your place to ride 'em." Still Neil persisted. There was something in a bad horse that challenged Neil's combativeness. This day, as Lane rode in, Neil topped a black called Geronimo. Geronimo bucked, and Neil rode him, but when the horse stampeded blindly there were shouts of alarm. Geronimo went off a cut bank, fell when he struck, and when Lane and the others arrived Neil lay unconscious and white-faced, his leg twisted and blood running from a cut in the head. Hasty examination showed a broken collarbone, a bad cut in the scalp, and a leg that might be broken at the knee joint.

Taking Neil back to the wagon, they indulged in rough surgery. Cuff, veteran of many such occasions, used horse liniment and bandage on the cut, swore at the collarbone, and rigged a bandage that wound around Neil's body, forcing both shoulders back, and after some manipulation announced that the leg was not broken, but that it was "sprained aplenty". During these ministrations Neil sat and sweated freely and profanely.

"You and Ben unload the wagon and take him to the ranch," Lane directed Cuff. "You can send Matias into town for the doctor. I'll stay here."

"There's no use of that," Neil expostulated. "Who'll run the wagon if I'm gone? I'm all right. All I need is to lay around a day or so."

"I *might* manage to keep things going," Lane commented dryly. "And it will be more than a couple of days before you do any riding. That knee's already as big as a water bucket. Unload the wagon, Cuff, and haul him in."

Still protesting, Neil was taken to the ranch.

Cuff and Israel returned the next day, and Cuff grinned when he reported. "They done sent for the doctor, an' Miss Warrend's got Neil in bed. She's totin' him broth an' she's got Concha makin' plenty tracks in the kitchen. Neil's takin' to it like a sick kitten to a hot rock."

After five days with the crew Lane turned the job of wagon boss over to Cuff and departed for Van Brimmer's wagon. This time he went by way of Casa Alamos to see how Neil was progressing, he told himself.

He found Neil propped up by pillows in a chair, clean-shaven and primped within an inch of his young life, and his eyes followed Judith's every movement.

"I'll be all right," he told Lane. "Doc was out from town, an' he put a fancy bandage on my shoulder an' another on my knee. He says for me to stay off it for a while, but I could ride right now."

"You'll do what Doc says," Lane ordered sternly, and later, talking with Jud Warrend, made comment: "Judith's sure fixed Neil up all right."

Warrend grinned. "He was a godsend," he informed. "He's given Judith something to do besides nurse me. She nearly nursed me to death."

Lane joined Warrend's laugh. "I guess Neil can take a little pampering all right," Lane stated. "He's had little enough of it, and what he gets now won't spoil him."

The following morning Lane rode on to Van Brimmer's wagon, well satisfied with conditions at Casa Alamos.

The roundup wagons swung in their slow circles, moving from water to water. Calves were branded, entered in the tally books, and turned loose. Gradually the circle closed and the wagons drew together at a meeting point on Santa Clara Creek north of Casa Alamos. Lane was content with the calf crop, pleased with his crews, happy in a pleasant, peaceful world, looking forward to the time when he would be at headquarters again, the roundup over. And at Casa Alamos, Neil Rodgers fell in love with Judith Warrend.

At first it was simply that Judith was beautiful and kind to him. She read to him, made sure of his comfort, talked to him, and helped him pass the dragging hours. Inaction was hard for Neil, accustomed as he was to activity. Then the girl's presence began to mean more than these simple things. Neil's heart pounded when he heard her steps, his eyes burning deep in their sockets as he looked at her. Years spent in different environments separated the two, but Neil did not think of that. He knew simply that this woman was lovely and gentle and that he desired her.

And Judith? Gradually her new occupation palled and became a task. At first it was pleasant to be a ministering angel and to see Neil's eyes light up when she same. It was pleasant to read to him, to see that he was comfortable; pleasant to listen to the stories he drawled. But after a time Judith became uneasy under Neil's bright eyes, and the stories were old, and it was tiresome to sit and read. Like her patient, Judith was accustomed to activity, and more and more she found herself wearying of Neil. More and more she wished that Lane would come back to the ranch to stay, to ride with her again, to walk with her, to watch her with blue eyes that twinkled and that yet were kind. Judith, in short, missed Lane McLain more than she knew.

The roundup wagons met and began to work the country north of Casa Alamos. A little more time and the roundup would be done. Lane, leaving the camp, rode twenty miles to headquarters, counting the trip worthwhile when Judith welcomed him. At supper that night, when Lane mentioned that he would go back to camp in the morning, Judith announced that she was going along. Lane, watching the girl as she made her declaration, was pleased. He had seen her just once since Neil was hurt, and now he realized that he had starved himself.

"All right," he agreed. "You'll have to get up early, though. Sure that you're good for a forty-mile ride?"

"Of course I'm good for it. And I'm dying to get away from here."

"Hardly a compliment to us, Neil," Warrend observed dryly.

Judith flung her father a direct look. "You haven't bored me," she said, "but I do want to get away, and Lane promised that he'd take me. What time will we leave?"

"Sunup." Lane grinned.

Neil said, "I believe I'll go with you, Lane. I'm all right. No use of me stayin' here."

Lane was not to be so cheated. "No need of it," he declared. "There's just a little country left to work, and we'll be done by the end of the week. You'd better stay here and give that leg all the rest you can. There'll be plenty of riding left for you to do."

In the morning, dressing in the half-light, Judith put on a linen riding habit and a small hat with a jauntily cocked feather. When she joined Lane in the kitchen he grinned admiringly. "The boys," Lane drawled, "are going to be surprised. They sure are — and so are the cows. That's the fanciest roundup outfit I ever saw. Sit down and have some coffee, Judith."

The girl seated herself across the table, and Concha brought coffee, bacon, and corn cakes. Judith, whose customary breakfast was a cup of coffee and a thin piece of toast, made a gesture of distaste.

"Better eat," Lane warned. "That's got to do you until noon." He attacked his own breakfast, now and then glancing appreciatively at the girl. It was mighty nice, Lane thought, to have Judith sitting opposite him at the breakfast table.

They went to the corral when the meal was over, and Lane, having saddled Brightboy, put his own saddle on a bay gelding that he called Soldado. He helped Judith to her sidesaddle, mounted, and together they rode away, waving to Concha at the kitchen door as they passed. The horses were eager, active with the cool of morning and seeming to catch the high spirits of their riders. In time the edge wore off the horses and they settled into a saddle gait. Judith, happy as a child on a picnic, asked questions that Lane was pleased to answer.

"We take a scope of country and work it," he explained. "The foreman takes his crew out in kind of a semicircle and drops them off, two at a time. The riders gather cattle and push them onto the roundup grounds. Then the herd's worked and the calves are branded, and after that we mother 'em up and give them a shove back into the country that's been worked."

"Mother them up?"

"Make sure that the cows will claim their calves. We don't want to make any dogies."

"What are dogies, Lane?"

"Calves that haven't any mothers."

Judith's questions continued, and finally Lane laughed. "You'll just have to see it," he said. "I can't explain it to you. We're close enough now to help with the work. Suppose we take in a drive, Judith."

"I think that would be fun."

"Then you go on along this draw and I'll throw some cattle down to you." Before Judith could object Lane loped away, and presently a cow and a calf came lumbering down the hill. Brightboy, cow-trained and cow-wise, cocked his ears and sent the cattle along.

Judith, in the bottom of the draw, caught glimpses of Lane as he loped from place to place. The bunch of cattle ahead increased, cows stopping to bawl at their calves, calves trying to nurse, flies thick upon hairy backs, dust rising. This, Judith thought, was both tiresome and dirty. She turned Brightboy and loped up the slope.

Seeing her, Lane came back. "Here," he chided, "what kind of a cowboy are you? Never leave a drive like that."

"I'm not a cowboy and I don't want to be," Judith answered. "That's tiresome."

"Well" — Lane grinned — "Pickles and Israel are working this, anyhow. We might as well go on to the wagon."

They dropped down from the ridge and, leaving the cattle, rode on. The country was cut in a tortuous pattern, and Judith asked, "Where is the ranch, Lane?"

"Back there." Lane jerked his head. "The wagon's just ahead."

They came now to the edge of a series of small hills. A plain spread before them, and Judith caught sight of smoke from a fire and the naked bows of two wagons. Beyond these, horses grazed.

"Tired?" Lane asked.

"Not a bit."

Still, when they reached the wagons, Judith was glad enough to dismount. Twenty miles of steady saddling was different, she found, than a canter around the park, or even a ride out of Casa Alamos.

"Pancho's got coffee," Lane announced and gestured to the cook.

Pancho, resplendent in a clean flour-sack apron and wearing a yard-wide grin, had coffee ready. It was black and good, unsweetened, and in a tin cup that burned Judith's lips. She sipped the coffee while she surveyed the camp, her curiosity overflowing. The wagon, with its chuck box on the end, so compact and efficient, the keg lashed to its side, the miscellany of rope and branding irons and harness and many other things exposed by rolled-back canvas, intrigued the girl, and Lane needs must answer concerning them. Pancho's preparations for the meal, the sourdough crock, the Dutch ovens, and the big coffeepot, all these came in for inspection. Judith looked at the beds, some rolled, some open, that were close by the wagon; she saw this and that and everything, and, half a mile away, dark lines, drives of cattle, came streaming in to the roundup grounds.

Presently Pancho took the ovens from the fire and set them in a line. "We'll eat," Lane announced, "and then go out and relieve the men at the herd." Judith, armed with plate and cup, went down the line in approved fashion.

Now riders came in from the herd, grinning Ben Israel, worshipful Pickles, Nebraska, and the rest. Van Brimmer and Cuff arrived. Two men took the ends of long ropes attached to stakes that were joined by a rope, and into this improvised corral the wrangler drove the remuda. The rope holders closed their gap, and Israel and another roped out mounts as men called for their afternoon horses. Then saddles were changed, hasty toilets made, and the crew ate. By this time Judith was done with her meal, and Lane suggested that they relieve the guards at the cattle.

They rode out, Israel, Cuff, and Van Brimmer with them, and, taking the places of the watchers, sat around the herd. Lane stayed with Judith, occasionally leaving her to turn back some animal that sought to stray. Shortly the riders returned, and the business of the afternoon began. A trench was dug and a fire built in it where branding irons were put to heat. Van Brimmer sharpened a knife upon a whetrock, and a man placed a water bucket in the shade of a mesquite. Israel and Nebraska shortened their ropes and tightened cinches, and the others, save four who stood guard on the cattle, dismounted, hobbled their horses, and, hanging their chaps on their saddle horns, were ready.

"Irons are hot enough," Cuff announced, and Israel and Nebraska rode into the cattle.

Judith watched Ben Israel. The horse that the Negro rode fretted and tossed his head but minced along, stopping, then taking another step. Suddenly Israel bent forward; his rope shot out, and the horse, turning, came toward the fire, dragging a calf caught by both heels and bawling at every bump. An anxious cow followed the procession. Two flankers caught rope and tail, and the calf was turned upon its side, where one man knelt upon its neck, holding a foreleg doubled back. The other flanker, seated on the ground, braced a boot heel against a hock and held the calf's upper leg with both hands. Cuff came, carrying an iron, placed his foot on the calf's flank, and hair sizzled and the calf bawled. Van Brimmer bent down, was busy, and then straightened with a bloody knife.

"Steer!" he called.

"Steer," Lane answered and made a mark in the book he held.

"What are they doing?" Judith demanded. "They hurt that calf!"

"That's branding," Lane answered, watching Nebraska come out dragging a calf to another set of flankers. "Cuff brands and Van Brimmer earmarks and alters."

"Steer!" Van Brimmer called again.

"But it's cruel! Stop them, Lane!" Judith was excited.

"It's not cruel," Lane retorted as he made another notation in his tally book. "We have to brand calves. If we didn't every cow thief in the country would get rich. If we didn't brand no one would know who owned a calf or —"

"You won't stop them?" Judith faced the man angrily.

"No." Lane laughed. "They'd think I was crazy."

"Then I will!" Her quirt lashed down on Brightboy's flank.

Brightboy had been dozing, not interested at all in this familiar scene. Stung by the quirt, he woke up and jumped his full length. The flankers scrambled out of the way, letting a calf go. Cuff dropped a hot iron and dodged, and Brightboy, indignant and frightened, went straight into the cattle, Judith's pull on his light bit just enough to steady him and keep him running. Straight through the herd he went, and cattle ran on either side. At the edge a man yelled and another chorused the sound. Cattle were going every way at once, and the flankers ran for their horses, bending hastily to unhobble.

Lane went after Judith. Soldado struck his stride the second jump, and because Soldado was the best horse on the Hatchet, Lane overtook the girl like an express train overtakes a freight. Squarely in the middle of the herd Lane caught up, bent down, wrenched Brightboy to a stop, and confronted Judith, his eyes brilliant with anger. Cows were bellowing and calves bawling; on the edge of the herd men rode, twisting and turning to bunch the cattle again, and in the midst of that pandemonium Lane spoke his mind.

"Never do that! Never jump your horse at a herd, and don't interfere with things you don't understand. Now go to the wagon and wait for me! I'll take you home."

He released Brightboy's bits, and Judith gasped. Never, in all her life, had she been spoken to like that. Her face was white with wrath, and she lifted her horse, bringing him around. Once more Brightboy felt the quirt against his bright sorrel hide, and he lit, running. Coming out of the herd like water squirting from beneath a boot, the horse shot away. Brightboy headed toward the wagon, and Lane, thinking that his order had been obeyed, turned to help with the cattle.

There were fifteen minutes of close fast work before order was restored. Calves and cows were separated and bellowing each for the other. The herd spread out, loosely held, so that parents and offspring could get together again, and Lane, meeting Cuff at the edge, pushed back his hat and wiped his forehead.

"Whew!" he exclaimed.

"What got into her, anyhow?" Cuff demanded. "What put a fire under her?"

"She thought branding was cruel and wanted me to stop it." Lane rose in his stirrups and looked toward the wagon. Pancho was halfway between the herd and the camp and Pancho was running. In ten years Lane had never seen the fat cook get out of a walk. Simultaneously he and Cuff spurred their horses.

Pancho was out of breath, but he spluttered and gasped understandable Spanish. The señorita had gone past the wagon into the brush, and her horse was running away. Lane and Cuff looked at each other and then turned to Pancho.

"Certainly!" Pancho answered Lane's question, his dignity offended. "*Seguro.*" He had tried to stop the señorita. He had run out and waved his arms, but plainly the señorita's horse was stampeding. He, Pancho, had been a vaquero of note before he grew too fat for the saddle, and certainly he knew a stampeding horse when he saw one. The señorita had struck the brush and was gone. Where? *¡Dios solamente sabe!*

"Get the boys," Lane said quietly. "Leave enough to hold the cattle and bring the rest. We've got to find her." Soldado lengthened into a run toward the wagon, and Cuff spurred back to the herd. Pancho sat down and mopped his sweating head. Running in such heat! *¡Por Dios!*

Brightboy had scattered gravel when he passed the wagon, and his trail into the brush was plain. Lane rode in, following it, rising to look, and calling: "Judith . . . Judith . . . OOOOeeee . . . Judith!"

There was no answer. He went a short distance and then, as the trail mingled with other horse tracks, turned and came back. Cuff had arrived at the wagon with Van Brimmer, Nebraska, Pickles, and eight vaqueros.

"Miss Warrend," Lane addressed these, "came past the wagon about half an hour ago. Her horse was running, and you can see where she hit the brush. We've got to find her." He repeated the order in Spanish.

"An' hawse tracks all over the country!" Nebraska mourned.

"Cuff," Lane ordered, "you and Ben take the tracks. Keep on them. The rest of you spread out."

"Take a good look at the tracks, boys," practical Cuff commanded. "Make sure you know 'em."

To these veterans of the trail, horse tracks had identity. The men rode close, peered down, and, having marked the peculiarities of the hoofmarks, were ready. In a long thin line they entered the brush. Cuff said, "Come on, Ben. Le's cut sign."

As he rode Lane's heart was in his throat. He knew the dangers of the country and its potentialities. Suppose that Brightboy fell and threw Judith. Suppose that sidesaddle slipped. Suppose Judith was down, hurt, unable to move. Only trailing could find her, and even trailing might fail or be too slow. He glanced back. Cuff and Ben were riding in widening circles. As Lane had done, these two had lost the trail and were cutting for it. To Lane's left Pickles rode, and beyond him, Nebraska. Van Brimmer was almost out of sight, and beyond Van Brimmer were the vaqueros. For just an instant Lane was panic-stricken, and then he calmed. It wouldn't do to lose his head. He had to think. Brightboy was a home lover. Many a time Lane had sworn mildly at the horse for turning toward the corrals at Casa Alamos. After his fright was over and his stampeding done, Brightboy would try to head for home. Recollection filled Lane with gratitude and, lifting so that he could see above the brush, he called:

"Swing southeast, Pickles. Pass the word to swing southeast!"

He heard Pickles' voice rise, echoing the order. The boy could shame an Apache with his yell. Lane turned Soldado southeast and called again: "Judith . . . OOOOeeee . . . Judith!"

Three miles southeast of the men who searched for her, Judith stopped Brightboy and looked at the serenely marching mountains. A mile of running had been enough for the sorrel, but when he offered to slacken an angry quirt had kept him at a run. Brightboy was sweating, and now that he had stopped he blew hard. Judith scanned the hills. They were strange and unfamiliar, no peak appearing the same as from Casa

Alamos. She turned her head, saw more mountains, and was utterly confused.

Her mouth was hot and dry, and the sun burned her face and hands. The feather of her hat was no longer jaunty, and her once-crisp linen habit was limp and covered with dust. Judith was lost. A pulse fluttered in her throat, and her eyes grew wide with fright. Lost! She remembered Neil's stories of men lost in the desert, of finding skeletons not a hundred yards from water, skeletons of men who had died of thirst. She remembered the sudden swift appearance of the Apaches in the rain, how they had looked, their savagery. She shuddered. Brightboy, having blown, moved tentatively, turning so that he pointed to the southwest. He had had enough of this nonsense and was going home. Judith reined the horse, and obediently Brightboy changed his course, traveling southeast again. The reins fell slack. Brightboy laid back one sullen ear and again started home.

Now came a far-off sound, a weird and eerie call. Judith straightened convulsively, listened an instant, and jerked the reins tight. The sorrel stopped.

"Go on!" she commanded, her voice choking. "Go on, Brightboy." Brightboy stood his ground. Enough was enough, even for a well-trained sorrel horse.

To the right brush crashed. Judith, looking swiftly, saw a man appear on the ridge above her. He shouted — the words unintelligible — and came charging down. A sweating bay horse slid to a stop, and Lane was beside her. Lane! Lane, who reached up and lifted her from the saddle and crushed her against him. She could smell the sweat and leather and tobacco, the good, strong, *man* smell of him. Judith's arms closed about Lane's neck, and she did not turn her face from his kiss. His voice rasped, filled with anxiousness, the grandest thing the girl had ever heard.

"Judith! Judith sweetheart!"

"Lane —" Judith gasped. "Oh, Lane!"

Neither saw the Hatchet riders arrive: Cuff and Nebraska, Ben and Pickles, the swarthy vaqueros. The two stood, totally unaware of their surroundings, tight in each other's arms, engulfed in the wonder of the thing that gripped them both. Then Lane looked up and, seeing that they had an audience, stepped back, dull red suffusing the smooth tan of his cheeks. Judith, too, became aware that they were not alone. Her hands flew to her hair and hat, and her cheeks were rosy.

"I see you found her, boss," Cuff drawled and struggled with his grin. The grin won. It spread on Cuff's face and from there, like a contagion, reached around the circle. Everyone was grinning.

"Uh —" Lane said. "You boys can go back now. I'll take Miss Warrend home."

"Why, sure," Cuff agreed elaborately. "We'll go right back. I expect we still got time to brand them cattle if we hurry." Still he did not move.

"Well?" Lane rasped, recovering, challenging Cuff with his eyes.

"Yeah," Cuff said, and then with a start: "Come on, boys. We got a herd waitin' for us." He moved, turning his horse slowly, looking back over his shoulder. The others also moved, joining Cuff, riding back the way

78

they had come. They made a trailing cavalcade upon the slope, and as they reached the top Lane turned from watching them.

"I —" he began, not looking at the girl. "I'll take you home now, Judith."

"Lane!" Judith commanded.

The man raised his eyes. One long instant they stood and then, swift as summer lightning over the hills, Judith was in Lane's arms again.

CHAPTER
SEVEN

The ride back to Casa Alamos passed like a clock tick. Soldado and Brightboy traveled side by side, almost unguided, even making so bold, now and then, as to reach down and crop a mouthful of grass. At first Lane was tongue-tied in his wonderment, scarcely realizing what had happened and hardly daring to believe it. But there was a glory in Judith's eyes, and when he stretched out his hand the girl's hand, soft and warm, met it. There were no eavesdroppers on that ride, no one to note that, after a time, Lane found his voice and that Judith answered him, no eyes to see the horses stop and draw close together until they touched, to watch the riders merge until they blended into one. A hawk, circling lazily, dipped low, and beady-eyed lizards scurried in the shadows of the brush, but no one saw or heard.

Twilight came, and the two reached Casa Alamos, riding self-consciously and well separated. At the corral Matias took the horses, and Judith and Lane went to the house. Jud Warrend was in the living room alone. "Well" — he smiled, putting his book aside — "did you see the branding, Judith? Did Lane — ?" He stopped, for he had seen his daughter's eyes and Lane's face.

The girl ran to her father, dropping to her knees beside his chair, her arms reaching up to close about him. Absently Jud Warrend stroked her hair while he looked at Lane.

"I —" Lane stammered. "Judith and I —"

He could go no further, only stand and meet the older man's steady, questioning look. Then Warrend said: "She's all I have left, Lane."

"I know."

There was quiet again, and Warrend went on: "I've worried about the man for Judith." It seemed that he did not speak to these two but rather to himself. "I've seen the boys that came around. Some of them were good boys and some were spoiled. I'd hoped that she would find a man. Maybe this is why we came to Casa Alamos. I know you, Lane. I trust you."

"You can trust me." Lane's voice was steady and with a ring in it. "I love Judith, Mr. Warrend."

Warrend nodded. He sat awhile longer, his hand on Judith's hair, studying Lane. "You're a man, Lane," he said suddenly. "And Judith's grown into a woman. You haven't lived the same. You'll have to learn about each other from each other. I think you can. Be good to her, Lane."

"I will."

Judith sprang up, bent swiftly to kiss her father, then crossed to Lane. They stood, hand in hand, looking at the man in the chair, not yet dismissed.

"I think you will," Warrend said. "I know you will." He eyed the two almost wearily, his face tired and his shoulders slumped. The shoulders straightened and Warrend smiled.

"You'll want to keep this to yourselves awhile," he said, rising heavily. "This calls for a celebration of some kind. I think I'll see if I can't find the wine that Darby gave you, Judith." He crossed the room toward the hall.

Supper that night was a silent affair. Concha hurried back and forth from kitchen to dining room, smiling all across her face, eyes bright as she looked at Lane and Judith. Intuition informed Concha what had happened. Neil, engrossed in himself, feasted his eyes on Judith, all unaware. But when supper was finished and Neil would have attached himself to the girl Jud called him back, and the boy impatiently sat and answered questions, anxious to get away, but unable to leave, while outside Judith and Lane sat in the patio.

"I've got to finish roundup," Lane said regretfully. "I'll have to go back in the morning."

"And leave me?" Judith whispered.

"I've got to. But it won't be for long. And after roundup —"

"After roundup." There was a promise in Judith's voice.

In the morning Lane was gone, and Judith busied herself with Jud. She was especially attentive, as though she wished to make up something to her father. Jud let the girl fuss over him. Judith was kind to Neil, too, giving her companionship freely, a kind of sunlit happiness about her.

At the wagons Lane drove the men, making two circles a day, branding after supper, a flame consuming him. There were no complaints. The vaqueros smiled as though they understood, and Cuff and Nebraska, Pickles, Israel, and Van Brimmer grinned and put on added steam.

"He wants to get done," Cuff drawled to Pickles, "an' I don't blame him."

"Me neither," Pickles agreed.

Before the week was out the wagons pulled into Casa Alamos, the calves all branded and the work done. Men unloaded beds and belongings, and Pancho was boss in the cookhouse again. The bunkhouse temporarily overflowed. In a day or two riders would go back to Piedras Amarillas or to Benton Springs or to the camps strategically situated about the Hatchet, but for one night at least, all the crew was at headquarters.

Neil, limping slightly, came down to the bunkhouse and found Cuff Doyle putting his bed on a bunk. Israel was washing clothes, and Nebraska dourly took spare clothing from between his blankets and placed them in a battered bureau.

"You didn't take long to wind things up," Neil offered, seating himself.

"The boss was in a hurry to get done." Cuff sat down on his bed. "I don't blame him, neither, but he like to wore the hide off us these last few days."

"Gals," Nebraska said sourly. "They sure raise hell with a man. Two circles an' brand after supper. I'm goin' to sleep a week."

"You didn't kick," Cuff snapped.

"Naw. I didn't kick." A slow grin spread across Nebraska's face. "I'd done the same if I was the boss."

"You been here, Neil." Cuff turned to Rodgers. "When's the weddin' goin' to be?"

"Weddin'?" Neil demanded. "What weddin'?"

"You mean to say you don't know? They ain't told you?"

Neil shook his head, his eyes narrowing as he looked at Cuff.

"Tryin' to keep it a secret!" Nebraska laughed. "An' every man on the outfit knowin' about it."

"What weddin'?" Neil insisted.

"The boss an' Miss Warrend," Cuff said. "Hell, as soon as I seen 'em together I knew there was goin' to be a weddin'."

"When did all this happen?" Neil drawled. "What was it, anyhow?"

"At camp. The time the gal come out to see us brand." Cuff went on, telling the story with relish, concluding with a simple statement: "They meant business, I tell you. They never even seen us when we rode up; they was too busy kissin' each other. Any time a man kisses a gal like that there's goin' to be a weddin'."

Israel took his bucket of dirty water out the door, and Cuff got up from his bed and resumed its making. Nebraska had done with the distribution of his clothing. Neil said: "Well, that's news to me," keeping his voice level, but not looking at Cuff or Nebraska. "Guess I'll go congratulate Lane." He limped out of the bunkhouse and as he cleared the door saw Judith standing beside a clump of hollyhocks that grew against the wall of the Big House.

Judith smiled as Neil arrived and then, seeing the strange intentness on the man's face, asked, "What is the matter, Neil?"

"I just heard," Neil blurted.

84

"Heard what?"

"About you an' Lane."

"About Lane and me?" Judith flushed slightly. "I'm glad, Neil. I know how much you think of Lane and I know that you're my friend. I'm very happy that you know."

"You didn't tell me!" Neil accused.

"We haven't told anyone except Dad." Judith's flush deepened. "Are you going to wish me happiness, Neil?"

The boy was awkward and confused. His face reddened and he turned away his eyes. "Sure," he rasped. "Yeah. I hope you'll have a lot of luck!" He wheeled swiftly and limped away, and Judith stared after him. Down at the cookshack Pancho beat upon his triangle, calling all hands to come and eat.

The meal was half done before Cuff looked up suddenly and asked, "Where's Neil? Still eatin' at the Big House?"

At the dining-room table in the Big House, Judith asked the same question: "Where is Neil?"

"Eating with the boys, I guess," Lane answered.

"I told him today, Lane," Judith said. "About us, I mean."

"I meant to tell him myself," Lane responded. "I haven't had a chance. Anyhow, I didn't know —"

"It's no secret." Judith laughed. "You will fall in love publicly, Mr. McLain. Remember, we had an audience!"

Behind the corral Neil Rodgers sat and rolled another cigarette. Stubs littered the ground beside him, and he lighted his fresh smoke from the coal of his last. His eyes were moody as he looked out toward the hills, growing dim as the light failed, and his young face was not hard, but softened with hurt.

In the morning, while Lane sat at his desk in La Casita, adding figures from the tally books, Neil came limping in. The younger man hesitated at the door, and Lane, looking up, smiled his welcome. "How's the leg, Neil?" he asked. "Hurt you any now?"

"No." Neil came on to the desk. "I reckon I'll congratulate you, Lane. Judith told me about you two. I'd heard it from the boys before she told me."

"I meant to tell you myself," Lane said kindly, "but I've been with the wagons."

"She's gettin' a good man." Neil's voice was almost grudging. "When's the weddin'?"

"We haven't talked much about that. I don't know."

Neil limped to the window, looked out, and spoke over his shoulder. "I guess I'll pull out."

"There's no need for you to go to Piedras Amarillas." Lane misunderstood Neil's meaning. "I thought I'd send Cuff up there for a while. You can stay here."

"I don't mean that." Still Neil did not turn. "I reckon I'll take my time."

"You mean you want to quit?"

"Yeah."

Hardness began to creep over Lane's face. "What's wrong, Neil?" he drawled. "Have you had a jangle with somebody?"

"No. I'd just like to move around awhile."

"I've counted on you," Lane said slowly. "I figured that you'd take most of the riding for a while. If it's money I expect the Hatchet could stand a boost."

"It ain't money." Neil turned, and Lane was almost shocked by the look on the boy's face. "I'm just tired of bein' a home guard. I want to get out."

The hardness settled on Lane's face. "You're grown," he said. "It's your privilege."

"Then," Neil drawled, "what are you waitin' for? Write out my check."

"I'll figure up your time," Lane assured crisply. "You've got quite a little coming."

"Yeah." Neil limped to the door. "Leave the check with Van Brimmer, will you? I'm goin' to run in my privates an' get ready."

Lane, hurt, not understanding Neil at all, said, "I'll leave it with Van Brimmer."

Neil paused by the door, half turned as though to speak, turned back, and, his voice harsh, flung words over his shoulder: "So long. I hope you have a lot of luck."

He stepped on out, and Lane, opening a drawer of the desk, pulled out a ledger and, turning pages, came to that headed "Neil Rodgers". He scowled as he scrawled figures on the bottom of the page.

At noon Lane casually reported, "Neil quit today. I gave Van Brimmer a check for him."

Judith looked up, startled. "Neil? But why?"

"No reason. He just quit." Disappointment and a little bitterness tinged Lane's voice. "All he said was that he was tired of being a home guard and that he wanted his time."

"But — I thought you could depend on Neil."

"So did I. I was mistaken."

Judith searched Lane's face. "He's hurt you," she said. "I could hate him for that. What will you do, Lane?"

"Put Cuff on the job. He can handle it if he stays sober, and I'll keep him sober."

"Then it won't make any difference?"

"Not to you and me." Lane smiled fondly at the girl. "The Hatchet would be a poor outfit if it couldn't get along when a man quit. Still — I'd depended a lot on Neil."

That afternoon Neil, on a good bay horse and driving another that carried his bed, rode away from the Hatchet. His fellows in the bunkhouse watched him go, and when he was out of sight Cuff commented: "Somethin' in Neil's craw, I reckon. Somethin' happened to that boy."

"Somethin' stuck there, all right," Nebraska concurred. "Wonder what it was?"

"I talked to him some," Pickles ventured. "I was aimin' to ask him why he was pullin' out, but I never got round to it."

"Yo're young!" Cuff drawled contemptuously. "Neil's business ain't none of ourn."

"Likely" — Nebraska squinted toward the spot where Neil had disappeared — "it's a gal. Neil was sweet on Beth, an' they had some sort of jangle before brandin'. Remember, Cuff?"

"Yeah." Cuff nodded. "Well, Beth's in Aspinwall an' Neil's headed for town. If that's what's achin' him it ain't nothin' that Beth can't fix. Neil'll be back."

"No," Ben Israel drawled, "he won't be back."

88

"What makes you say that, Ben?" Nebraska turned to the colored man.

"Nobody," Israel stated, "quits Mist' Lane but one time. Nobody!"

Neil's departure made a hole in the Hatchet crew and necessitated some taking up of slack. Cuff went to Piedras Amarillas, and in addition Lane sent Nebraska to Benton Springs. This left Israel, Pickles, and four vaqueros at headquarters, where Van Brimmer found plenty of work for them to do. Pickles was starting some new horses with Israel's help, and Van Brimmer and the vaqueros did the outside riding. Lane spent some time making sure that the new setup functioned smoothly and then devoted himself to Judith. Man and girl were far too engrossed in each other to be influenced by anyone or anything else, and Jud Warrend, feeling more and more his former self, daily grew better content and happy in his daughter's happiness.

Judith never tired of talking to or about Lane, exploring his life before her advent. She learned of his childhood spent in a Texas laboring under "Reconstruction"; of his father, killed in the last year of the War between the States, and of the mother who had inspired him.

"She said I had to amount to something," Lane stated simply. "We were mighty poor, but she made me study. I didn't go to school, but I read everything I could lay hands on, and when she died I kept it up. I knew I had to get ahead because she'd expected me to."

Judith tucked her hand under Lane's arm, and the two were silent for a time. "I'd like to have known your mother," Judith said then.

"I wish she could have seen you," Lane answered wistfully.

On another occasion Lane spoke of the founding of the Hatchet. It was an epic, sketched, rather than drawn, and there were great gaps in the story. Lane told of how he had worked for Colonel Grayson in Texas, of how he had delivered a herd of the colonel's cattle in Arizona Territory and seen the new land. "I liked it," he drawled. "I had a little money and I speculated in cattle. Ben was with me, and I brought a herd of my own out of Texas and sold it at a profit. They were stocking this country then, and I wanted in on the ground floor, but I didn't have enough capital. The colonel knew your father and he got us together."

"I remember Colonel Grayson," Judith said. "He visited us in Boston. I was just a little girl."

"You aren't much more than that now," Lane said fondly.

"And then?" Judith reverted to the story. "After you met Father?"

"Why," Lane said, "your father was game. He was willing to bet with me. He came down to Texas to Grayson's place, and we made a deal. I got a herd together and hired some men, and Ben and I brought it across. We settled here in the valley and we've stayed."

"But," Judith persisted, "is that all? Isn't there any more to tell?"

90

Lane shook his head and smiled. "Nothing worth telling," he drawled. "We had some ups and downs, but your father stayed with me. He came out a time or two, you know. After a while the ranch got on its feet and we began to make a little money, and these last few years we've showed a profit. I guess that's all, Judith. Until you came."

The conclusion was satisfactory enough, and Judith rewarded Lane properly, but she was still vaguely dissatisfied. She was certain that there was a great deal more to the story than Lane had told. She questioned Jud, but he could supply few details.

"Lane had a pretty tough time of it when he came in here," Jud said. "All I did was put up a little money. I never questioned his judgment after I met him at Grayson's. I came down a time or two and visited the ranch. That was before your mother died. Why don't you ask Ben Israel, Judith? He was with Lane and he can tell you."

Accordingly, on the first occasion that presented itself, Judith sought the Negro. Ben Israel was squatted in the semishade of the corral fence, mending a hackamore, when Judith found him, and the girl seated herself on an old feed trough and began her questioning. Israel surveyed her with mild brown eyes and put his work aside.

Yes, Israel admitted, he had been with Mist' Lane when he first came from Texas. Yes, he had helped bring the cattle. At first all that the Negro would do was answer Judith's questions and then, warming gradually, he talked. No great gift of words had black Ben Israel.

He could neither read nor write, and his speech was sparse and lean as a greyhound's body, but he told Judith those things she wanted to know, and when he was done the girl's eyes were shining.

"Mist' Lane," Israel concluded, "doan' nevah look back, Mizz Judith. Nevah!"

"What do you mean, Ben?" Judith bent forward on the trough.

"Mist' Lane," Ben Israel said, "is *with* yo'. He stahts with yo' an' he ends with yo'. Yo' nevah look ovah yo' shouldah to fin' him, an' he doan' look ovah his. No mattah what, he nevah looks back!"

A freight wagon and trailer came creaking into the yard and stopped. The teamster dismounted, and his helper dropped down from the trailer, and they walked to the cookhouse. Lane appeared at the corner of La Casita, a bundle in his hands, and, spying Judith, walked toward her.

"The mail's in, Judith," he called cheerily. "There's a big bundle for you."

"Thank you, Ben." Judith arose hastily. "Thank you for telling me."

Ben Israel's eyes were dull as he picked up the hackamore. "Doan' thank me," he said. "Yo' had to know, Mizz Judith."

Judith's mail contained a note from Molly Morton. She read it to her father and Lane while they sat in the living room, going through their letters. Molly wrote that she and the judge had returned to Aspinwall and that they would welcome a visit from the Warrends and from Lane. Molly named a date: the following Thursday.

"Can we go?" Judith asked. "I'd like to visit Molly."

"I've got to go to town, anyhow," Lane said. "I have some business at the bank at Aspinwall."

"No reason why we can't go," Warrend announced. "It would do us all good to visit the Mortons."

On Thursday the Warrends and Lane McLain left the Hatchet in a buckboard drawn by two mules. The buckboard went past the north camp, for Lane wanted to inspect a new stud that the Hatchet had recently purchased.

"It's not much farther by the camp," he said, "not more than ten miles or so. You'll get to see some new country, and I can size up the mares that Cuff's put with the horse." Judith and Jud were both agreeable.

They reached the camp at noon, finding two men in the little house. The stud and his *manada* were five miles out, the riders said. Judith, Jud, and Lane ate dinner with the riders, and after the meal Judith stayed with her father while Lane went out with a rider to see the horses. It was midafternoon when Lane returned, worried because he had delayed their trip.

"We had to hunt the horses," he apologized, "and after we found them I had to cut the bunch. There were some mares in it that didn't belong there. I'm sorry that I've kept you waiting."

"No matter," Warrend said. "I've had a sleep, and Judith rested, too, didn't you, Judith?"

"For a while," Judith admitted. "But we'll have to hurry. Molly's note said that we were expected to dinner."

Lane cast an apprehensive glance at the sun. "We won't make Aspinwall before dark," he prophesied.

The mules were harnessed again and the trip resumed. From the north camp a dim road led westward, and the mules trotted swiftly while Lane and Judith talked, Warrend adding an occasional word. The sun sloped down and, when the buckboard approached the Rio Bosque, hid itself behind the peaks of the western hills.

"Twelve miles to go," Lane commented when they had crossed the ford.

With the sun gone, twilight lingered. The shadow of the mountains reached out across the valley, and the mules jogged through the growing dusk. As the dusk deepened the buckboard passengers relaxed in a quiet broken only by wheels purring over sand. Judith turned to Lane, a question forming in her mind, and as she turned she saw two riders on the road, bearing down upon the buckboard. Men and horses blended in the dusk, and Judith felt Lane move.

The riders neared, and in the evening light Judith saw them more clearly. One was short and sat his horse ungracefully. The other was tall, hump-shouldered, with a scowling face, his nose slit as though by a knife. Judith caught a glimpse of metal in the tall man's hand.

"Lane!" she gasped. "That man has a gun in his hand!"

The lines lay lax on the dash of the buckboard. Above the purring of the wheels Lane's voice came evenly, hard as a blow:

"So have I!"

CHAPTER
EIGHT

"And when I looked at him Lane had his pistol in his hand!" Judith paused dramatically. They were in the Mortons' drawing room, Judith and her father, Lane and Crosby Agnew, the judge and Molly Morton. This was the second telling of the story, and repetition enlarged and enhanced it.

"And then what happened?" Molly asked, although she already knew.

"They simply disappeared. They went into the bushes by the road, and when I looked again Lane's pistol was gone."

"Look, Judith," Lane said uncomfortably. "After all, nothing happened. Couldn't you just let it go?"

"Of course I won't let it go!" Judith flared. "I don't see how you can be so casual, Lane! Those men might have shot you! They might have killed us all. Something ought to be done about them!"

"I expect something will be," Lane drawled, "but we can let it go for now. I don't think these folks are interested in Nosey Harmon and Clay Garret."

"I can mention something that will interest them," Warrend announced, his eyes twinkling. "Shall I?" He glanced at his daughter.

"Dad!" Judith protested.

"I think I will," Warrend said. "Judge, Molly, Mr. Agnew, it gives me pleasure to announce the engagement of my daughter Judith to Mr. Lane McLain!"

"Dad!" Judith exclaimed again. "We weren't going to —"

She had no opportunity to complete her protest. Molly was beside her. "I'm so happy for you, Judith!" Molly cried and kissed the girl. Morton, pumping his hand, clapped Lane on the back.

"Fine! Fine, my boy!" he rumbled. "This is the best news I've heard for months. So you beat the Easterners, did you?"

Lane's cheeks were flushed under his clear tan and his smile embarrassed. Warrend was enjoying the commotion his announcement had caused, and Agnew came to Judith, smiling.

"I wish you every happiness, Miss Warrend," he said. "And you, McLain" — he turned — "I congratulate you."

"When did this happen?" Morton demanded. "Judith, I'll give you credit for good judgment. You're getting a fine man."

"You should congratulate Lane, Judge," Molly reproved. "When will you be married, Judith? Are you going to Boston for the wedding?"

Judith, flushed, her eyes bright and her lips smiling, shook her head. "We haven't decided," she answered. "Of course I'd like to be married at home, but —"

"We'll have the wedding right here!" Morton boomed. "An Arizonan should be married in Arizona, and you're both Arizonans now. I insist on it; Lane, you'll be married in my house."

Lane was momentarily growing redder. "If Judith wants —" he began.

A knock at the door interrupted. The judge, frowning, said, "Now who can that be?" and left the room. For a moment no one spoke, and Morton's voice came clearly. "McLain? Yes, he's here, but he's busy."

Again a pause, and then Morton said reluctantly, "I'll call him. Lane!"

Lane went into the hall, and the judge returned. Voices murmured, then Lane came back. "I'll have to leave you for a while," he said apologetically. "I've got to go into town. You'll excuse me?"

"What is it, Lane?" Judith asked anxiously. "Can't it wait until morning?"

"I'm afraid not. I'll get back as soon as I can." He bowed to Molly, smiled at Judith, and stepped into the hall. The outer door closed, and Judith said, "Who was it, Judge? What did they want of Lane?"

"A man from town. Pryor sent him for Lane. Let's sit down. I don't think Lane will be gone long."

"Pryor?" Judith said. "Isn't he — ? Why, he's the marshal. You don't think it's any trouble, do you, Judge?"

Morton, seating himself, shook his head. "I don't think so," he answered comfortably. "Sit down. Sit down. Now, Judith, you must tell us your plans. I insist on the wedding's being here at my house. Warrend, I don't think you're well enough to give away the bride. I'll take that matter off your hands." The judge's laugh rumbled.

The others seated themselves. They had dined well; they were content, and the momentary rift of Lane's departure caused none but Judith uneasiness. Judith said: "You don't think Lane was called because of what happened this evening, Judge? It isn't about those two men?"

"No." Morton shook his head. "I don't think so."

Warrend eyed his daughter. "If I were you, Judith," he commented, "I wouldn't talk so much about that occurrence. Particularly to Lane."

"Why not?"

"Because if you make so much of it Lane is very apt to take it up. You heard what he said?"

"What was that?"

"You said," Warrend reminded, "that something should be done about Harmon and Garret. Lane told you that something would be done."

"But surely —" Judith began. "He didn't mean —"

"You're in love with Lane," her father interrupted, "but you don't know him very well. Lane isn't the man to let a thing like that pass. He'll take it up himself."

"He can't!" Judith exclaimed. "I won't let him. Those men are dangerous, Dad."

"They're no more dangerous than Lane," Warrend drawled. "You've fallen in love with a very simple man, my dear, a man who takes a direct course. If I were you I wouldn't mention the occurrence again."

Judith's eyes flashed from face to face. Both Molly and the judge were serious, and Agnew nodded. "Your father is right, Miss Warrend. The first time I met Mr. McLain we argued the matter. You were there. You remember what he said."

"But —" Judith began, and then, regaining her assurance, "Lane won't do anything. I'll ask him not to."

"Perhaps that would be a good idea," Morton stated deliberately. "I'm certain that Lane will do anything you ask him."

"Of course."

"And this all goes to prove my thesis." Agnew leaned back in his chair. "The logical method to pursue in matters such as this is to turn them over to the regular officers. No individual should try to deal with lawlessness. The thing to do is to have Harmon and Garret arrested, brought in before a justice, and put under bond to keep the peace."

"Could I do that?" Judith asked. "How would I do it?"

"Judith," Warrend began, "I wouldn't —" He stopped short, knowing that what he was about to say would only alarm his daughter and make her more determined.

"Certainly," Agnew answered. "You could do it, Miss Warrend. You would have to draw a complaint and swear to it, and then a warrant would be issued."

"Why not forget it?" Warrend asked. "How have you progressed with your business, Agnew?"

"Very well." Agnew turned to the older man. "Mr. Seay has persuaded the other three to sell their cattle. We're having a meeting at the bank tomorrow. I — Could you and McLain attend, Mr. Warrend? I'd like to have you there."

"I've put business away for six months." Jud Warrend smiled as he shook his head. "Doctor's orders."

"Would you play for us, Judith?" Molly asked. "The piano hasn't been touched since you were here."

Agnew sprang up and went to the instrument. "Please," he seconded.

"My fingers are so stiff, I'm not sure that I can play." Judith laughed. "But if you'll forgive my mistakes —" She went to the piano.

The others listened while Judith played. The piano was across the room, and they leaned back in their chairs, enjoying the music. Agnew, standing by the instrument, bent down, and man and girl and piano made a picture in the lamplight. Judith, the music unnecessary, looked up at the man and her lips moved, but the sounds of the instrument drowned her voice, and Warrend and the Mortons could not hear what she said.

"Would you help me, Mr. Agnew?" she asked. "You're a lawyer."

"Help you with what?" Agnew bent closer. "Of course if I can be of any assistance I'll be glad to help."

"To do what you said I should: make a complaint against those men."

"You're going to do that?"

"Of course. Isn't that what you advised?"

For an instant Agnew did not answer as the keys rippled under Judith's fingers. Then: "I suggested it, but I don't think it would be wise for you to take action, Miss Warrend. You should leave it to your father or McLain."

"Dad won't do anything. And Lane — I can't have him meet those men! Please, Mr. Agnew."

"Of course," Agnew agreed. "I'll help you. You want me to draw a complaint?"

Judith nodded. "Tomorrow."

Agnew thought rapidly, and a smile touched his lips. Judith Warrend was a beautiful girl, a very desirable woman. "I've moved to Mrs. Tindler's Hotel," Agnew informed. "You can find me there in the morning, Judith." Daringly he used her first name instead of the formal Miss Warrend. "If you'll come I'll be glad to help you."

"Play the Schubert, Judith," Jud Warrend called. "It's a favorite of mine."

The music stopped. Judith murmured, "Then I'll come in the morning, Mr. Agnew." She turned from the instrument. "The 'Serenade', Dad?" she asked. "Do you have it, Molly?"

"It's on the piano," Molly Morton answered. "Isn't it time for Lane to come back, Judge?"

"He should be here," Morton rumbled. "I wonder what's keeping him?"

Trouble was keeping Lane. When he left Morton's he walked down the hill beside Pryor's messenger. The judge had built his house on a rise above Aspinwall, and below the lights blinked at Lane. He asked one question: "Where's Pryor?" and when his companion answered, "In the Orient," they wordlessly followed a steep path that leveled behind Mrs. Tindler's Hotel and, walking along the side of the building, entered Aspinwall's main street. Crossing to the Orient Bar, Lane found Guy Pryor standing impassively beside a faro layout, watching the game.

"Hello, McLain," Pryor greeted, and then with a nod to his messenger, "Thanks, Tony. Tell Boss to give you a drink and put it on my bill."

Grinning, Tony sought the bar, and with a nod Pryor left the faro layout, Lane following. In the small back room of the Orient the two paused.

"Where is Neil?" Lane asked quietly. "What's he doing, Pryor?"

"He's in the White Palace," Pryor answered. "He's drunk and making a nuisance of himself. He's your man, McLain. I didn't want to run him in."

"Neil," Lane announced slowly, "quit the Hatchet a week or so ago. He asked for his time and I gave it to him."

"Then" — Pryor shrugged, watching Lane narrowly — "you're not interested?"

"I didn't say that" — quickly. "I said that he'd quit the Hatchet."

"He has," Pryor drawled, "been raising hell since he hit town. Drunk about half the time and mean the rest. He's been hanging out with the wrong crowd too. Over at the White Palace. Red Dowd's been with him. I've had my eye on Dowd."

"You think that Dowd — ?" Lane questioned.

"Dowd's pretty fast company for Neil," Pryor interrupted. "I'm about ready to tell Dowd to stay out of Aspinwall. Do you want to talk to Neil or don't you?"

"I'll talk to him," Lane decided. "Maybe I can do something."

"Then" — Pryor settled his coat with a shrug of his shoulders — "let's go. Are you heeled?"

"No."

The marshal frowned. "That's a bad habit to get into in this country," he observed. "That bunch at the White Palace — Well, never mind. Let's go."

Leaving the Orient, the two crossed the street, stepping up under the awning of the White Palace. Pryor moved swiftly ahead of Lane, glanced through the door of the saloon, and, saying, "He's at the bar," went in. Lane followed, pausing briefly at the door.

There was no crowd in the White Palace. Two poker tables were quietly occupied, and there was a little play at the faro bank. Half a dozen men were at the bar. It was a typical weeknight crowd. Only at the bar Neil Rodgers stood with Dowd, and Neil's hat was pushed back, and his face wore an ugly scowl as he snarled at a bartender. Pryor waited, and Lane, walking on, pushed up between Neil and the man closest to him: Red Dowd.

Dowd, freckles splotching his face and his spatulate, hairy hands, was a little drunk but cheerful. Everybody liked Red Dowd, and no one quite trusted him. Dowd had worked on the Hatchet; he had been a miner; he had done a dozen different things, from keeping bar to prospecting, and made a fair success at them all. Right at present no one knew for sure what Red Dowd did, but there were ideas circulating, rumors.

Dowd grinned and said, "Hello, McLain. Off yore regular beat, ain't you? I thought the Hatchet always went to the Orient when it came to town."

Lane nodded and said, "Hello, Dowd," making no other comment. Neil turned very slowly, setting down his whisky glass.

"Hello, Neil," Lane said.

Neil was disheveled, and his eyes were small and bloodshot. This was not the neat, self-respecting boy who had been the Hatchet range boss; this was a drunk, a mean drunk.

"I seen you when you come in," Neil rasped. "I'd of spoke to you if I wanted to."

A dull color began to creep into Lane's cheeks, but his voice was even when he spoke. "I'd like to talk to you if you've got a minute," he drawled and jerked his head toward the back of the room, inviting Neil to step away with him.

"If you got anythin' to say to me say it out loud," Neil answered. "I ain't got time to listen, anyhow."

"I think," Lane stated, low, hard-voiced, "you'll have time to listen to this. You're making a fool of yourself, Neil."

"Ha!" Neil tossed back his head and laughed, one short bark of sound. "*Me* make a fool of myself. Hell, I done *been* made a fool of. You ought to know that, McLain."

It was going to be difficult, Lane saw. Neil was drunk. He had always been reckless; in a way, that quality had endeared the younger man to Lane. There was nothing that he could do; Lane saw that he could not reason with Neil. "That's all, then," Lane said and began to turn.

"No, it ain't all!" Neil rasped. "Not by a jugful. Look here, McLain."

Lane waited. Neil surveyed him with glittering eyes. "How come the warriors ain't with you?" he demanded. "Where's Cuff an' Ben an' Nebraska? Ain't you afraid you'll be caught without 'em?"

Now Lane did turn and stepped away from the bar. Neil wheeled, took a lurching step, and was between Lane and the door. Neil was not so drunk that he could not move. Neil's gun jutted at his hip, and his eyes were narrow.

"Don't run out on me!" he snarled. "You wanted to talk. Well, listen. *I* ain't the fool, McLain. *Yo're* the fool."

"Get out of the way, Neil," Lane ordered tightly. "You're drunk."

"I ain't so drunk I don't know what I'm sayin'! *Yo're* the fool, McLain. I *was* a fool, but I got over it. *Yo're* the sucker now. That Warrend girl's playin' you just like she played me. She honeyed aroun' me till she saw she could get you. I didn't have money enough. I wasn't the big auger. But —"

"Shut up!" Lane rapped the two words like blows.

"Shut up, hell! I'm goin' to tell you about what yo're marryin'. I'm goin' —"

Lane's hand flashed up in a short, hooking blow, swift and vicious as the swing of a long-horned steer as he strikes at a wolf. Neil's arms flew wide, and his eyes glazed as Lane's fist caught the angle of his jaw. Instinct made his hand fly to his gun, and it was half drawn by reflex action as Neil pitched back and down. Lane stood, legs spread, glaring at the man sprawled on the floor; then, lifting his eyes, he stared around the silent room.

"You're his friends," Lane said thinly. "He's been drinking with you. Does anybody want to take this up?"

There was no answer, and Lane stalked toward the door. Pryor, moving swiftly, joined him and they passed out.

"We'll go to the Orient and take one drink," Pryor drawled when they were outside the White Palace. "I'm sorry that I got you into this, McLain. But I thought —"

"The young fool!" Lane choked on the words. "By God, Pryor, I could have killed him back there."

"Yeah," Pryor drawled, "I reckon. Come in here now."

They stepped into the Orient. The men in the place, seeing Lane's face, ceased their talk suddenly. Pryor said, "We'd like a drink, Boss. My private bottle."

Watching Lane, Darby fumbled under the bar, found the bottle, and set it out. Liquor was poured, and Lane drank automatically. Pryor said, "Better stick here awhile, McLain. I'll be right back." He caught Darby's eyes, and the owner of the Orient followed along back of the bar as Pryor moved toward the door. At the bar end the marshal bent and spoke to Darby. "Keep him here till I get back. Give him another drink, but don't ask him what happened and don't let anybody else get to him."

"O.K., Guy," Boss Darby agreed stolidly.

Pryor went on out, and Darby, returning to Lane, drawled: "Long time no see, McLain. How are things at the Hatchet?"

Guy Pryor crossed the street again and entered the White Palace. Neil was on his feet, at the bar, in the act of taking a drink. He put down his glass as Pryor came up.

"You," Pryor said, his face expressionless, his yellow eyes thin, "are done in Aspinwall, Rodgers. You too, Dowd. Pull out."

Lane's blow had sobered Neil, but his head still rang with it. Red Dowd's eyes were wide. "Why, what have we done?" he demanded. "I ain't crowded you, Pryor."

"And won't," Pryor assured. "You're short in this town, Dowd. Get out, both of you!"

"You can't do this," Neil blustered. "I've got a right in Aspinwall. I got a right to —"

"I've told you," Pryor snapped. "That's enough." He paused, his eyes watchful, his voice almost thoughtful as he spoke again. "I ought to kill you, Rodgers, after what you've done. Get out before I change my mind!"

Red Dowd took a lurching step. "Come on, kid," he said thickly. "Who in hell wants to hang around this dump, anyhow?"

Neil hesitated and then unsteadily followed the redheaded man. They went through the door, and

107

Pryor, having watched them out, looked at the room. No one moved; no man had anything to say. The marshal made a long inspection, searching each face. Then abruptly he turned and walked out of the place, crossed the intersection, and, pausing at the entrance of the Orient, looked up and down the street, composing himself, making up his mind. Some things Guy Pryor could do; some he could not, and he still had to deal with Lane McLain.

CHAPTER
NINE

The Sheriff's office in Aspinwall occupied a corner of the courthouse, and the streaming sun made the room as hot as the street outside. Buntlin, occupying a swivel chair behind his desk, mopped at the sweat that was trickling from his partially bald head and teetered back and forth, the chair squeaking.

"No sir!" he said. "Not me. I don't stick out *my* neck!"

Opposite the sheriff, sitting out of the sun, Manville Seay creased his forehead in a frown. "You're going along with me," he stated definitely. "That's what you're going to do, Jack."

The tempo of the chair's squeak increased, and Buntlin's voice was plaintive. "First you come along an' tell me that Agnew is goin' to buy on range delivery," he accused. "You got me to say I'd deliver five hundred head when I ain't got two hundred. An' now you come in here an tell me that Agnew's goin' to count 'em. I ain't goin' to that meetin', Manville."

"You're going" — Seay glanced at his watch — "in about fifteen minutes. You're going down to the bank and sign that contract; that's what you're going to do." There was a threat in Seay's voice, unspoken but very definite. Buntlin mopped his streaming forehead again.

"Do you think," Seay continued, the hardness still in his tone, "that I'm going to pass up this chance? Not much. You're yelling about signing up for five hundred head when you haven't got two hundred. I'm going to mark the Secate down for fifteen thousand, and there aren't ten thousand on the place. I've *got* to go through with this. It's the only out I've got."

"But —" Buntlin protested.

"Look here, Jack," Seay rapped. "You know what's been going on. You know that Nosey and Clay and their boys have been taking Secate cattle and that Tybert's been selling them. We've been doing that ever since you took office. You've given us protection and you've been paid to keep still. You've laid off of Nosey and Clay and the rest, and that's fine. But we know some things too. I could do some talking about Red Dowd, for instance, and about why the taxes haven't been collected from the west end of the county, and some more things. Are you going along with me?"

Now it was not the sun's heat that made Buntlin sweat. He mopped his forehead again and tried one more plea. "But what good can *I* do? There's no need for me to sign that contract."

"I'll tell you what good you can do," Seay rapped. "Nichols' heirs in England are hell-bent to sell. They're going to do it whether I want to or not, and I've got to account for fifteen thousand head of stock. I'm going to do it. Then when this is over we'll keep going for a year. I'm going to run the Secate for Agnew and I'm going to clean up. At the end of the year I won't give a damn. I'll have mine and I'll pull out for Mexico some night, and Nosey and Clay will go along with me. After that you can turn your dogs loose or you can come with us. I don't care. But right now you're going down to the bank and sign Agnew's little contract. You're going to agree to everything he says, except one thing. When it comes to counting these cattle you and I are going to insist that Agnew does the job himself. *¿Sabe?*"

"But —" Buntlin made ready to expostulate.

"It would be a damned shame," Seay interrupted, "if we couldn't get him twenty thousand head to count. We'll show him cattle until hell looks level. Nosey and Clay will move the stock around and around, and he'll count the same ones two or three times. And when we get done he'll have twenty thousand head and we'll have the money."

Buntlin was a fleshy man with pursy bags of flesh under his small eyes. Now his eyes widened. "What about Porter an' Harbury an' Raoul?" he demanded. "They'll get wise."

"I can handle Raoul and Harbury," Seay assured. "You know I can. Besides, they'll not give a damn. They'll be getting theirs. And if old man Porter gets out of line" — he paused ominously — "I guess Porter could be handled too. Nosey don't like him, anyhow."

Silence filled the office. Buntlin broke it. "Where did Agnew get this idea?" he demanded. "Who got him into the notion of counting?"

"McLain, damn him!" Seay grated. "He had to stick his nose into my business. He's got an idea that he knows what's going on at the Secate."

111

Again the sheriff began to teeter in his chair. "McLain," he said. "If he's goin' to help Agnew —"

"He won't!" Seay rapped. "That's why you're going with me! That's why we're going to make Agnew do his own counting. We're going to run McLain out and keep him out. Now get your hat and let's pull out for the bank. It's time."

Buntlin picked up his hat. "McLain's in town," he informed. "He came in last night." He pulled the hat on. "Him an' Rodgers had a jangle."

Seay, already at the door, stopped short. "McLain and Rodgers?" he demanded.

"I'll tell you." Buntlin reached the doorway. "Wait till we're outside." They walked along the hall, gained the entrance, and emerged into the sun.

"Now tell me," Seay commanded.

"It was down at the White Palace," Buntlin complied. "Rodgers has been in town about two weeks. Him an' Red have been teamin' around together, an' Rodgers has been drinkin' an' mean as hell. Last night Pryor an' McLain found Rodgers in the White Palace, an' McLain tried to talk to him. Rodgers was ugly. He jumped McLain about that Warrend girl McLain's goin' to marry —"

"McLain's going to marry *her?*" Seay interrupted.

"That's what they say. Rodgers got to givin' up head about McLain an' her, an' McLain knocked him stiff as a poker. I didn't see it, but they say it pretty near come to gunplay."

"McLain's going to marry Judith Warrend," Seay said slowly. "Warrend's his partner. That'll give McLain

112

all the Hatchet, the lucky bastard! Then what happened?"

"Why, McLain an' Pryor went out. After a while Pryor come back an' told Rodgers an' Dowd to pull out of town."

"Did they go?"

"Uh-huh. They went to Handout."

Seay's eyes narrowed. "It looks like the Hatchet is breaking up," he commented. "Rodgers, huh? I've been wanting to cut that little rooster down to size for quite a while. So has Nosey. Maybe we'll do it now."

"You lay off of Red," Buntlin warned. "Don't mix him up in it."

"We'll lay off Red," Seay agreed.

They had approached the First Territorial Bank of Aspinwall as they talked, and now as he reached for the knob of the back door Seay reverted to the business at hand. "Don't forget," he warned. "Nobody but Agnew does the counting. Back me up." He opened the door.

The back room of the bank was small and contained a long table. On the side of the table opposite the door Francis Raoul, with Jimmer Harbury and Able Porter, occupied chairs. Oscar Lundell, a lawyer, sat at one end of the table, and at the other end were Crosby Agnew and Judge Morton. Lane McLain stood beside the room's only window.

"Sorry to be late," Seay said, nodding to the assembly. "Jack had a little business in the sheriff's office." He took a chair opposite Porter, and Buntlin seated himself.

113

"We haven't waited long," Agnew announced. "Here is a copy of the contract, Manville." He slid two documents across the table to Seay and the sheriff.

Harbury, Raoul, and Lundell returned to their reading as Seay picked up the paper, and for a time there was quiet in the room. Then Seay put down the contract. "It looks all right to me," he stated. Harbury nodded, and Raoul lifted his eyes from the agreement.

"Are there any questions?" Agnew asked. "Do you see anything you would wish changed, Mr. Lundell? You're representing these others."

Lundell said grudgingly, "It seems to be all right."

"Good!" Agnew glanced around the table. "There is one more thing to discuss. You'll note the contract reads that the cattle are to be delivered at a place or places designated by me, but within Aspinwall County, and that a date is to be set for the delivery. I've been talking to Mr. McLain, and he suggests that you deliver at Blocker Gap. I can put a fence across the gap and count the cattle through a gate."

"Wait a minute!" Raoul put down the contract. "I thought that this was to be range delivery. That's what you said when you talked to me, Seay."

"That's what I thought," Seay agreed smoothly. "But Mr. Agnew came to the ranch a few days ago and told me that he intended to count the cattle."

Harbury and Raoul were both frowning, but Able Porter remained impassive, a stub of a cigarette protruding through his grizzled beard.

"Naturally I intend to count the cattle," Agnew stated. "Mr. McLain has advised me that death loss,

114

and so on, make an accurate inventory impossible and that they should be counted."

The men at the table turned to Lane. Raoul said, "Are you going to receive for Agnew, McLain?"

"I tried to employ Mr. McLain," Agnew forestalled Lane's reply. "He tells me that he can't accommodate me and I'll have to get someone else."

Seay had been leaning forward, but at Agnew's statement he relaxed. McLain had eliminated himself, and their apprehension died. Buntlin sighed gustily.

Porter growled, "I thought there was a catch to this someplace when you told me range delivery, Seay. I didn't think anybody would be that big a fool."

"Do you object, Mr. Porter?" Agnew asked.

"No," Porter growled. "I said I'd sell out an' I'll sell out. Who are you goin' to have count for you, Agnew?"

"I haven't decided yet." Agnew looked around the table. "There are several possibilities. I'd hoped that McLain would reconsider."

"You won't do the countin', Lane?" Porter glanced at the man beside the window. "It'ud suit me if you did. We'd get a straight count."

"I've got the Hatchet to look after," Lane said. "That keeps me busy."

"Who did you think you'd get, Agnew?" Seay questioned. "I think we all ought to agree on who receives the cattle. We're as interested as you are."

"I don't see any objection to that, Crosby," Morton said. "Mr. Seay's right."

"What about this fence?" Raoul demanded. "I'm not goin' to pay for puttin' up any fence; are you, Jimmer?"

"No," Harbury growled. "An' I wouldn't have agreed to sell at twenty dollars if I'd known I had to round up an' deliver."

"I'm paying market price," Agnew reminded. "You would round up and deliver your cattle if you were shipping them."

"I still want to know about the fence," Raoul growled.

"I intend to pay for the fencing." Agnew turned to the little man. "McLain, I wish you'd explain your ideas to these gentlemen. You know more about it than I do."

Reluctantly Lane stepped forward. He had no business here at all, he felt. He had come to the meeting only because of Morton. Agnew had asked him to receive the cattle and, having refused, Lane did not feel that he could reject the request of both Agnew and Morton to come to the bank.

"I thought," Lane said diffidently, "that a fence could be put up across Blocker Gap. Most of your cattle are north and east of the gap, anyhow. You could work the country below and throw the cattle back. Then you'd bring them down and they could be counted through a gate."

"That makes the Secate the only outfit to work cattle below the fence," Seay objected. "I don't like your idea, McLain. I don't see what business it is of yours, anyhow. You're not going to receive them and you aren't selling any."

For an instant Lane almost liked Seay. The man had given him an out, a way to escape from the meeting.

116

Then he began to anger. Seay's words were intended as a slap in the face, and Lane's eyes narrowed.

"I asked McLain to come," Agnew defended, frowning at Seay. "I want him here and I appreciate his advice."

Lane stepped back from the table. "Seay's right," he drawled. "I've got no business here." He wheeled abruptly toward the door. Morton sprang up, and Agnew called, "Wait, McLain," and followed the judge. On the sidewalk Lane halted.

"I wish you'd stay, McLain," Agnew pleaded. "Won't you?"

"Come back, Lane." Judge Morton added his request to Agnew's. "There's no sense in your leaving. Seay —"

"If I come back I'll tangle with Seay," Lane stated quietly. "You'll do better without me."

In the back room of the bank Harbury, Raoul, and Porter had turned toward the door. Seay bent swiftly to Buntlin. "As easy as that," he murmured triumphantly. "McLain's out. Stay with me and we'll make Agnew receive these cattle himself." Buntlin nodded, and Morton and Agnew returned, their disappointed faces showing that they had failed.

Lane, having shaken free of Agnew and the judge, walked on toward the Orient, his frown darkening his face. He was angry with himself for being out of place; with Seay for his rudeness. A black mood had possessed Lane all day, a carry-over from the night before, and this fresh anger increased the blackness.

117

Lane had, after leaving the White Palace, waited for Pryor at the Orient. He nursed his one drink, paying no attention to Boss Darby's attempts at conversation, immersed in anger and in the hurt of Neil's outburst. Pryor came in, quick and quiet as always, touched Lane's arm, and jerked his head toward the back room. Lane, carrying his drink, followed the marshal. In the Orient's poker room Pryor closed the door.

"I have told Dowd and Rodgers to get out of town," he said without preamble. "I don't want them here. I can't have trouble in Aspinwall. You see how that is, McLain?"

Lane nodded.

"Rodgers was drunk," Pryor continued. "He's not responsible for what he said. This is my fault, McLain. I'm sorry that I got you into it, but I thought that you could handle him."

"Nobody can handle him," Lane said bitterly. "He's gone bronc."

"Yes," Pryor agreed. "He's off the reservation. It will be different when he sobers up. He'll come around."

Lane shook his head. "I hit him," he reminded. "You don't know Neil, Pryor. He'll not forget that."

The marshal was silent an instant. "You can't stop talk," he stated abruptly. "This will get around, McLain."

"Yeah."

"And what will you do?" Pryor's eyes were keen.

"Nobody" — Lane's voice was thick with anger — "will talk to me and get away with it."

"I don't think," Pryor drawled, "anybody will try to talk to you. McLain, I don't ask you to lay off this, but I'll take it as a personal favor if you keep the trouble out of Aspinwall. Rodgers will stay out of town, and you won't meet him here. I'll see to that."

Lane finished his drink and put the glass on the poker table. "If I don't run into Rodgers," he drawled, "I won't have any trouble with him."

"No," Pryor agreed. "Where are you headed now?"

"To Morton's," Lane answered.

"I'll walk a piece with you," Pryor stated.

At the judge's house, having left Pryor at the foot of the path, Lane found that Agnew was gone, but the others were waiting for him. They sensed that something was wrong, and Morton and Warrend were tactful enough to ask no questions. But Judith was insistent. She believed, apparently, that Lane's absence had been connected with Nosey Harmon and Clay Garret, and she played upon the theme. Lane, immersed in this more immediate trouble, had almost forgotten the two, and finally, to reassure Judith and to escape her importunities, he made a promise.

"I'll not look for Harmon. Garret either. I'll leave them alone if they'll leave me alone. Does that satisfy you?"

Perforce Judith was content, although far from satisfied. Molly Morton tactfully took command, sensing that Lane would be better by himself. She and the judge showed their guests to their quarters, refusing to hear Lane's suggestion that he occupy the room he kept at the hotel. Good nights were said and, one by one, the lamps in Judge Morton's home were extinguished. For a long time Lane lay awake, thoughts revolving in his mind, hurt and anger, the vain wish that he had not come to Aspinwall but had stayed at the Hatchet. Finally he drifted off to sleep.

Morning brought fresh difficulty. Lane had planned to spend the day with Judith, to get his mother's old square-cut amethyst ring from his strongbox in the bank and give it to the girl, but his plans were changed. First Judith announced at the breakfast table that she and Molly were going shopping in the town, and, to cap that, Morton insisted that Lane and Warrend accompany him to a ranch south of town to inspect a buggy team that he contemplated buying. The trip took all morning, and Lane fumed.

At noon, returning to Aspinwall, Lane found Crosby Agnew at the judge's house. They all lunched together, Judith bright-eyed and very gay, hiding something under her gaiety. After lunch the men went to Morton's study, and there politeness forced Lane to listen to Agnew as he talked of his impending business; to answer questions, and even to help plan the details of the transaction. Somehow Lane managed to retain his equanimity, although he could cheerfully have choked Agnew for keeping him from Judith. Lane was even courteous when the Easterner again broached the idea of Lane's acting for him and receiving the cattle.

"It will be a long job," Lane said, "and I can't spare the time from the Hatchet."

"I'll give you two thousand dollars and all expenses," Agnew insisted. "I want you for the job, McLain."

120

"I'm sorry." Lane shook his head.

"Three thousand?"

Here Warrend intervened. "You'll have to get somebody else, Agnew," he said. "Lane can't spare the time from the ranch and, besides, there's Judith to consider."

That had stopped Agnew's importunities, and yet, having refused the task, Lane felt that he could not reject Agnew's request, seconded by Morton, that he accompany them to the bank. So now, as Lane strode along the street, he reviewed all this. Of all the things he had planned for the day he had accomplished only one: His mother's ring was in his pocket.

The bank was a block from the Orient, and as Lane passed the White Palace he saw Beth van Brimmer on the porch of Mrs. Tindler's Hotel. Lane crossed the street to speak to the girl. "How are you, Beth?" he greeted. "How do you like living in town?"

Beth's face was pale, her freckles plainly marked. "I miss the ranch, Lane," she answered, and then quickly, "How is Dad?"

"Just fine. He misses you. When are you coming home, Beth?"

"I don't know," Beth answered. "I —" She frowned. "How long is Mr. Warrend going to stay?"

"Till fall, I hope."

The girl studied the toe of her shoe, moving it back and forth, making small, invisible marks on the porch. She looked up suddenly. "I heard about what happened last night," she said. "I — Why did you hit Neil? He was drunk, and you know how he is when he's had a drink!"

For a moment Lane was at a loss, then: "Neil had it coming," he snapped.

"Because of what he said?" Beth demanded. "I don't blame him for what he said. That woman —"

"Now wait a minute, Beth," Lane warned. "Neil was out of line. He was drunk, but that's no excuse."

"It is too!" Beth's eyes were angry. "Neil worshiped the ground you walked on, and you know it. You couldn't do anything wrong. It was Lane this and Lane that, until sometimes I hated you. And then Judith Warrend came and made all this trouble. It's her fault! Neil quit and came to town and got to drinking and — and —" Tears choked the girl's voice. Turning, she fled blindly into the hotel, leaving Lane standing on the porch, staring after her. In a moment or two he crossed the street to enter the Orient.

"I want a drink," he snapped to Boss Darby. "Whisky."

Darby set out the bottle. "Go kind of easy, Lane," he drawled, watching the drink that Lane poured. "You ain't used to it, you know."

"Maybe I'll *get* used to it," Lane growled.

Lane was still at the bar, and Boss Darby was worried when Morton and Agnew entered the saloon. They came straight to Lane, and Morton, smiling at Darby, ordered a drink for them both. "We had quite a time after you left," he told Lane. "There was a good deal to settle."

Lane had his fourth drink in his hand. The whisky had not helped. "But you got it settled?" he drawled.

"We did," Agnew agreed. "At first I didn't think we would. Raoul objected to my counting the cattle at all. He said that he understood I was to receive the cattle on the range, and that was the way he wanted it, but we brought him around. Then I suggested that Mr. Easlip count the cattle for me, but that didn't suit Buntlin. I mentioned every man you spoke of, and none of them suited. Finally Seay asked why I didn't count the cattle myself. It seemed to be the only thing to do, and I said that I would."

Lane's lips drew down in a small grimace. Seay, he thought, was smart; mighty smart.

"I don't know how I'll come out." Agnew laughed nervously. "But we had to reach some agreement. I'm counting on your help, McLain."

Before Lane could reply Porter came in with Raoul and Harbury, Seay and Buntlin only a step behind them. Seay's face wore a triumphant smirk. Seay could afford to grin, Lane thought, and cold anger seized him again.

"I'm going to buy a drink," Porter announced. "What'll you all have? Well, we got done with it, McLain."

"Agnew was telling me," Lane agreed dryly.

"We're goin' to count through a fence at Blocker Gap like you said," Porter continued. "Name it, boys. This is on me, Boss." Darby placed a row of small glasses on the bar.

"Whisky?" he queried.

"That's good for me," Porter stated. Raoul nodded. Porter's voice boomed on. "You'd ought to have taken the job, McLain. There's goin' to be a lot of cattle come through Blocker Gap."

Down the bar Seay was filling his glass, the smirk still evident on his face.

"Twenty thousand head of cattle — maybe," Lane drawled, the pause between his words significant. "You'll learn to count cattle by the time you're done, Agnew."

"I don't see why you wouldn't count them." Porter poised his glass. "Well, here's to the new Secate." He tossed down the liquor.

"I offered McLain three thousand dollars to take the job," Agnew informed. "He turned me down."

"Three thousand?" Raoul looked at Lane. "That's a lot of money."

At the end of the bar Seay put down his glass. He had done what he wanted to do; he had forced McLain out, and Agnew was to do his own counting. Seay could not resist the jibe that rose to his tongue.

"More money than most of us can turn down," he drawled. "But then it makes a lot of difference when a man's going to marry the boss's daughter. When he's done that, he doesn't have to get out and rustle for a living any more."

Morton felt Lane move and put his hand on the younger man's arm. Lane's face was livid. Gradually the color drained away. Buntlin growled, low-voiced, "Shut up, Seay! Keep still, can't you?"

124

Between Lane and Seay, Porter, Raoul, and Harbury stepped back hastily, so that the way was clear. Lane shook off Morton's restraining hand. Seay's sallow face became sallower, but he held his ground. He had, he knew, said too much.

"I was going to keep out of this," Lane murmured, as though to himself. "I wasn't going to mix in it at all." He looked at Agnew. "You're going to count through a fence at Blocker Gap, you say?"

Relief showed on Raoul's face. Porter looked at Lane, frankly disbelieving. Agnew nodded.

"Then," Lane said deliberately, "you'll need a crew to help you receive your cattle. I'll be glad to work on that crew, Agnew, and I think I know where you can get some more men."

Agnew's eyes widened. "You'll work on the crew?" he said. "You — Do you mean you'll count for me, McLain?"

"Why," Lane drawled, "I'll work wherever you put me, of course. Just anyplace. It's going to be quite a thing to see twenty thousand head of cattle come through that gate. I wouldn't want to miss it."

Morton regained his hold on Lane's arm. "Let's go home," he said. "Judith's waiting, Lane. Come on, Crosby." He pulled Lane toward the door. For an instant Lane resisted; then, smiling thinly at Seay, he let Morton propel him along. Agnew, puzzled but pleased at this sudden turn, followed. The three went out, and at the bar end Jack Buntlin growled, low-voiced: "You damned fool, Seay! Now look what you done!"

CHAPTER
TEN

THE TERRITORY OF ARIZONA
TO THE SHERIFF OF ASPINWALL COUNTY,
GREETINGS:

You are hereby commanded to arrest
and take the body of
Z. O. HARMON, ALIAS "NOSEY" HARMON
and keep him safely so that you have his body
before the Circuit Court of the United States,
within and for the County of Aspinwall at the next
term thereof, either regular or special, then and
there to answer unto an indictment for ASSAULT
WITH DEADLY WEAPONS and this you do under
the penalty of law.

WITNESS: The Hon. Henry Morton, Judge of the
_____ Judicial District of the Territory
of Arizona, and the seal of the
Circuit Court this _____ day
of August A.D. 188—.

CLERK: *Wm. Jinns*
_____

Jack Buntlin shuffled the warrants as his horse trotted. The second was identical with the first save that the name Clay Garret filled the blank. The time was noon, and east of the officer a spiral of smoke rising in a windless sky marked a camped wagon. Buntlin returned the warrants to his pocket as his horse waded into Rio Bosque and, lowering his head, drank thirstily. When the horse had watered, Buntlin splashed on across the shallows, pulled up the eastern bank and, emerging from the timber, sighted a roundup wagon a quarter of a mile away.

As Buntlin arrived Manville Seay, a coffee cup in his hand, strolled out from the canvas fly the cook had spread for shade. "Get down, Jack," Seay invited. "You're just in time. What brings you out from town on this hot day?"

Buntlin dismounted, loosened his cinch, and hobbled his horse. He pulled off the bridle deliberately, and as he hung it on the saddle horn he answered Seay. "I wanted to see you."

"Eat and then we'll talk," Seay suggested as he led the way to the fire. Buntlin took a plate, filled it, and squatted by a wagon wheel. There were ten men and a cook with the outfit, all Secate hands and all but two natives. Seay, lighting a cigar, sat beside Buntlin, well apart from his men.

"We're coming along pretty well," he stated. "Three or four more days and I'll start in above Agnew's fence. McLain's got it about built."

The wrangler had brought the remuda in to the rope pen, and a roper was catching horses. Buntlin gulped his coffee, and Seay, rising, called, "Get that Leon horse for me, Tony, and put my saddle on him."

"*Seguro, señor,*" the roper answered, and Seay sat down again.

"Well" — he stared at Buntlin — "what's on your mind?"

"A lot of things," Buntlin growled. "Are you goin' to try yore stunt on McLain?"

"On McLain or anybody else," Seay answered levelly.

"I wish you hadn't talked out of turn." The sheriff mopped his plate and stuffed the half biscuit in his mouth. "If you'd kept yore mouth shut in the Orient we'd of had easy sleddin'."

"We'll *still* have easy sledding," Seay drawled. "I'm kind of glad McLain's going to be with Agnew. I'd just a little rather put this over on him than anybody else. He thinks he's so damned smart!"

"He is smart," Buntlin assured. "You know he is, an' you won't put it over on him."

"Maybe not" — Seay's face was thoughtful — "but I think we will. I've got Nosey and Clay lined up. We'll just be careful, that's all. We won't run any markers past him twice and we'll shift stock around the fence at night. We'll be careful."

"An' it *still* won't work!"

"All right!" Seay glared at the sheriff. "Suppose it don't work. Suppose McLain gets wise. Then what?"

"Then —"

"McLain's bluffed everybody in this county," Seay declared angrily. "He don't bluff me! Where did he get his reputation, anyhow? He had a tangle with the Apaches. He's run it over a few two-bit would-be toughs. He's up against something different this time. He's up against me. McLain gets tough and I'll kill him!"

"That has been tried," Buntlin pointed out. "Frank Birdsall tried it, and look what happened to him."

"Birdsall ran into Pryor, not McLain," Seay snapped. "Nosey and Clay ribbed that up. But if I start after McLain I'll get him and there won't be any slips. Do you think I'm going to get stuck now when I've got this whole thing staked? Not much! Not by Lane McLain."

The riders were ready to go. Seay stood up and called to his foreman, giving directions and adding that he would join them presently. He remained standing as the men rode off and Buntlin carried his dishes to the wreck pan. When he returned Seay proffered a cigar, and the men reseated themselves.

"I tell you," Seay continued, "that we're all set, Jack. Nosey and Clay have got four or five men, enough to move cattle. I think this thing is going to work as slick as a greased gut, but if it doesn't I won't care. I made up my mind quite a while ago that I was going to have a showdown with McLain, and now is just as good a time as any."

For all Seay's bravado Buntlin knew that the man was uneasy. He had seen Seay and McLain in the Orient Bar, and while the sheriff knew that Seay was dangerous, he believed that the Hatchet man was more dangerous. But Buntlin's fortune lay with Seay and he had to go along. Now he drew the warrants from his pocket.

"I got these this mornin'," the sheriff stated. "What do you think of that?"

Seay took the papers and scanned them. "Who swore these out?" he rapped, looking sharply at Buntlin.

"Judith Warrend signed the complaint," Buntlin answered. "Let me tell you. This mornin' Morton brought these down an' dumped 'em on my desk. He was mad. Yelland was with him, an' Morton said that he wanted returns on these an' wanted 'em quick."

"He's wanted returns on warrants before," Seay drawled. "You could file these in yore wastepaper, Jack."

"No, I can't." Buntlin's reply was quick. "They've got me over a barrel this time."

"Why?"

"Because Pryor's runnin' against me for sheriff. If I don't make a stab at servin' these he'll beat me too. Do you think Nosey an' Clay would let me take 'em in?"

"You are kind of up against it, aren't you?" Seay pursed his lips and stared at the cigar in his fingers.

"I'm plenty up against it. I want a favor, Seay. I want you to get Clay an' Nosey to let me take 'em in. It won't be bad. They won't be held. Morton would put 'em under a peace bond an' they'd have to appear, but we can fix that up. You fellers can't afford to let Pryor beat me. You need me too bad."

Seay shook his head. "I need Nosey an' Clay too," he affirmed. "You can't take 'em in now."

130

"You ain't goin' to throw me to the wolves!" Buntlin began hotly. "Look here. I ain't goin' to be beat in this election. You want to remember —"

"Wait a minute!" Seay commanded. "I'm beginning to get an idea, Jack."

"It had better be good."

"This *is* a good idea!" Seay laughed and slapped the warrants in his hand. "Morton and Yelland and Pryor think they've got you in a pinch, don't they? We'll show them!"

"Show 'em what?" Buntlin was suspicious.

"A couple of things they never thought of. They want to make political capital out of these warrants. We'll make some ourselves!"

"How?"

"This" — there was relish in Seay's voice — "will be easy. Pryor holds a deputy sheriff's commission, doesn't he?"

"Yeah. But I don't see —"

"You will. Pryor wants to be sheriff. All right, you'll give him a chance to show that he can do the job. You'll hand him these warrants and tell him to serve them."

"Are you crazy?" Buntlin's eyes were wide.

"Not a bit. See here, Jack. You'll give Pryor these warrants and let everybody know that he has them. Either Pryor will have to serve them or he'll have to back down. If he doesn't serve the warrants he'll be a fourflusher, and everybody will know it. Wouldn't that elect you?"

"But he'll serve the warrants."

131

"No, he won't." Seay's smile broadened. "He'll never even see Clay and Nosey. They'll know he's got the papers for them and they'll lay low. I'll be using them, anyhow, and Pryor won't find them in a month. Then when Pryor falls down you'll take these warrants back and come out and serve them yourself. You'll have done what Pryor couldn't do, don't you see? These papers will beat Pryor and elect you!"

Buntlin's eyes had brightened as Seay talked. "That's smart!" he praised. "By gosh, that's a real scheme. Do you think Nosey an' Clay will let me take 'em in?"

"They will if I tell them to. We'll get this lined up beforehand, have a bond made and everything ready. You take these and go on back to town, Jack."

Buntlin took the warrants. "I'll give 'em to Pryor tomorrow," he promised. "By gosh —"

"No, not tomorrow. You'll have to wait awhile. I need those boys now. I want them to move cattle and not have to spend their time dodging Pryor."

The spark died in the sheriff's eyes. "What'll I do then?" he complained. "I'll be rode from here to hell an' back if I don't serve these warrants. It'll be all over the county that I've got 'em and that I'm afraid to serve 'em."

"You'll be ridden some, I guess," Seay admitted. "But you'll just have to stand it. I've got to have those boys right now, and, anyhow, the nearer it is to election when you do this, the better off you'll be. That's right, isn't it?"

"I guess so." Buntlin was sullenly doubtful.

"Sure it's right," Seay assured. "I'll tell you, Jack. You get out of town. Go over west and act like you were collecting taxes. Dig out some old stuff and say that you're working on that. Stall awhile. I've got to have Clay and Nosey, but as soon as I can spare them I'll let you know. Then you can hand these to Pryor and go to bat."

Seay stood up, Buntlin rising with him, and the Secate man put his hand on the sheriff's shoulder. "You go back to town," he urged, "and sit tight. Don't let them stampede you. We'll pull this off. You're going to make some money on this cow deal. That's worth a little riding, isn't it?"

"I guess so," Buntlin said doubtfully. "Well — all right, Seay, I'll do it."

"That's the way to talk!" Seay pushed gently against Buntlin's shoulder, urging him toward his horse.

"It all rains at once," the sheriff complained, moving reluctantly. "First McLain gets mixed up in receivin' for Agnew, an' now this warrant business. Damn it! I'll be worried until it's all over."

"We've figured how to use the warrants," Seay reminded. "Don't worry about that, and don't let them get you down by riding you. Sit pat. And don't worry about McLain. I'll take care of him. You'll be O.K., Jack."

"I hope so," Buntlin growled. "Things had better be O.K.!" Voice and attitude were threatening. Seay's eyes narrowed speculatively as he looked at the officer.

"They will be," he assured. "Go on back to town and leave the worrying to me. I'm a good hand at it. I'll let you know when I can turn Nosey and Clay loose, and then you can start with Pryor. So long, Jack."

Buntlin unhobbled his horse, tightened his cinch, and mounted. "So long," he answered and then, as a final thought, "Don't keep me waitin' too long, Seay. I can take just so much off that bunch in Aspinwall."

He rode away, Seay watching him. When Buntlin reached the trees at the river and disappeared Seay turned back to the wagon. Buntlin was a weak sister, a poor man upon whom to depend. Seay's face was dark with his scowl as he walked to the wagon.

It was nearly five o'clock before the sheriff reached Aspinwall. He had stopped at Handout en route and spent half an hour with Ryan. Leaving his horse at the livery barn, Buntlin walked toward the courthouse, and as he reached the door he encountered Morton. The judge, just departing, stopped and spoke. "Good evening, Sheriff."

"Evenin'," Buntlin growled.

"You've been out, I see." Morton eyed the dust on Buntlin's clothing and boots. "Have you served those warrants?"

"Not yet, I ain't." The sheriff raised defiant eyes. "You just gave 'em to me this mornin'."

"I'm particularly anxious to have a quick return on those warrants," Morton stated. "That's why I asked."

"You'll get a return on 'em," Buntlin growled and went on into the building.

Morton stood a moment, frowning thoughtfully, and then left the courthouse door. He spoke to several men

134

as he walked along and, stopping in the Orient, had one drink with Boss Darby. Darby seemed unusually jovial.

"I seen Buntlin come to town," the owner of the Orient informed. "He wasn't lookin' very happy, Judge."

"No?"

"Not a bit happy." Darby chuckled. "I reckon he don't like them warrants you handed him this mornin'."

"You know about the warrants, then?"

"Everybody knows about 'em," Darby informed. "Yelland was tellin' me. You've got Buntlin acrost a stump, Judge. If he don't serve them warrants Pryor will beat him this fall, an' if he tries to serve 'em Nosey an' Clay will be sore. So will the whole west side of the county. Either way, Buntlin's over a stump. Yo're smart, Judge."

"Do you think so?" Morton put down his glass.

"I know so. We all kind of wondered where you stood in the election, but we know now. Yelland an' me an' everybody else is tickled, now that you've come out for Pryor."

"I —" Morton began.

"You are for Pryor, ain't you?" Darby's face became anxious. "Ain't that right?"

Judge Morton did not answer, and Darby's grin returned. "I forgot," he apologized. "Of course you can't come right out an' say, bein' a Federal judge like you are. That's all right, Judge. You gave Buntlin them warrants. We all know where you stand. That drink's on the house, Judge."

"Thank you," Morton said gravely and left the Orient.

When Morton reached the top of the path he heard laughter coming from his house. As he entered Molly and Judith met him, each taking an arm. Molly kissed her husband, and Judith squeezed the arm she held.

"We missed you at luncheon, Judge," she said. "Molly's cook made the best tamales!"

"Have you had a hard day, dear?" Molly asked.

"Fairly." The judge freed one arm and removed his hat. "I'd like to speak with you a moment, Molly. You'll excuse us, Judith?"

"Of course." Judith flashed a smile. "I'll wait here for Crosby."

"Crosby?" Morton looked at his wife.

"He's coming for dinner," Molly explained, moving with her husband toward the hall. "You don't mind, do you?"

"No," Morton answered. "Of course I don't mind. Crosby's always welcome."

In their room the judge seated himself on the bed while Molly, having closed the door, remained beside it. Morton stared steadily at his wife, and Molly shifted uneasily. "What is it, Henry?" she asked.

"This morning" — the judge's voice was deliberate — "Jinns brought in two complaints for me to issue warrants. Judith had signed them. What do you know about them, Molly?"

"Why" — Molly crossed the room and sat down by her husband — "Judith got Crosby to draw the complaints, Judge."

"Why wasn't I told?"

"Because I didn't want to trouble you." Molly leaned against the judge, "I wasn't going to have anything bother you during your vacation."

Morton patted his wife's hand. "When did Judith have the complaints drawn?" he asked.

"The day after Lane and Mr. Warrend left." Molly turned her hand uppermost and gripped the judge's fingers. "I went with her. I didn't want her to do it, Henry, but she insisted, and I couldn't let her go to Crosby's room alone. Are you angry, Henry?"

"I don't like it," Morton admitted. "I wish that Judith could let things alone."

"She was worried about Lane," Molly said. "She'd treated Lane abominably, you know, and I think she was sorry. And then Crosby had said that the thing to do was to have those men arrested. Remember?"

Morton nodded. "Judith pays a good deal of attention to what Crosby says," he observed dryly. "And he has plenty of opportunity to say it. He's been here constantly since Lane left."

"They're young and they know a good many of the same people," Molly defended. "Judith's pretty, and naturally Crosby likes her and spends his time with her. You can't blame him, Henry."

"I don't blame Crosby particularly," Morton agreed. "But for an engaged girl Judith seems to enjoy his company."

"That doesn't mean anything. Judith likes to talk with him. Any woman would like Crosby. He has charming manners."

"And not too much good taste," Morton added. "He's poaching on another man's preserves. I wish that Judith had gone back to the Hatchet with her father."

"Don't you enjoy having her here?" Molly looked up quickly. "I couldn't help inviting her."

"No." Morton smiled reluctantly. "I know you couldn't help it. She made it impossible. Of course I enjoy having her. Judith is very lovely. She is also a nuisance and she needs to be controlled. I had to issue warrants on those complaints."

Molly waited, knowing that her husband would continue.

"I couldn't do anything else. Yelland was in my chambers when Jinns brought in the complaints. He saw them and he saw that I was not pleased. I had Jinns draw the warrants and I signed them and took them down to Buntlin myself."

"And why does that worry you, Henry?" Molly asked softly.

"Because," Morton said, "the word of them has gone all over town. Men are identifying me with this fight for the sheriff's office. They think, because I issued those warrants, I did so to embarrass Buntlin and that I'm backing Pryor in the election."

"Don't you want Mr. Pryor to be elected?"

"Of course. But I can't appear to take sides. And there is another thing, Molly. I hope that Lane doesn't learn about those warrants, but I'm afraid he will."

"Why do you hope that, Henry?"

Judge Morton looked steadily at his wife. "Judith signed the complaints," he said. "Harmon and Garret are dangerous men."

138

"But surely you don't think they'd harm Judith!" In her alarm Molly stood up.

"I don't think they'd harm Judith," Morton answered. "I don't think they would have an opportunity to harm Judith. But Lane —"

"What about Lane?"

"Lane might have another idea," Morton said heavily. "And if he did he'd look for those two men — and kill them."

CHAPTER
ELEVEN

Blocker gap, forty miles from Aspinwall and twenty-five from Handout, lay athwart the country opening to the southeast. The Pinnacles marked its western end, and Popes Nose rose at the east, while behind the gap lay a basin bordered by mountains. Twenty miles north the Hermanitas marched, and on the east were the upper Chiricahuas. These, with the Pinnacles, comprised the basin's rim. Here was a natural funnel, with the gap forming the narrow end, and across the opening Tio Abran Feliz and a crew had strung a two-wire fence for Lane McLain.

A Hatchet wagon was camped near the center of the gap, where a gate opened the fence, and above the fence another camp had been made. Here in a tepee lived Manville Seay, attended by a cook and wrangler, while in the hills and flats to north and east and west Raoul, Harbury, Porter, and Seay's two foremen, Juan Madrid and Alejandro Paiz, swung their crews in long circles and, gathering cattle, brought them down.

Lane McLain received those cattle. To be sure, Crosby Agnew was at the gate when the herds came through, sitting his horse, deafened by bellowing, choked by dust, but it was Lane who counted. Before the first hour had passed Agnew had lost count and become confused. He realized now how hopeless it would have been for him to attempt this task alone. But Lane was always there, a knotted rope sliding through his fingers, his eyes alert. At the day's end it was Lane who quietly told Agnew the figures to enter in the tally book.

Opposite Agnew and Lane, Manville Seay counted for the deliverers, sometimes with Raoul or Harbury or Porter beside him, sometimes alone. When the last cattle for the day had been pushed through the men would meet to compare and balance their figures, reaching an agreement as to the count.

Lane was not happy. The work was familiar and engrossing enough; the weather was good, with steadfast sun and little wind, and for companionship he had not only Agnew, but Cuff, Nebraska, and Ben Israel, and still he was not pleased. There was a continuous, ever-present friction between himself and Seay, a thing not so much of words but of spirit, and Lane was constantly alert and apprehensive, looking for something that was not there, some trick, some attempt to beat him. Too, Lane begrudged the time, knowing that he was stealing it from his own work at the Hatchet and, more than that, from Judith.

When Lane thought of Judith he was half hurt, half angry. The girl had not made it easy for him to leave, and she had refused to understand that, having given his word, he must keep it. They were sitting at twilight in the patio of Morton's house when Lane told Judith that he had agreed to help Agnew receive cattle. The girl had seemed pleased at first, but when she understood that he would be gone perhaps a month she changed.

"I don't see why you did it," Judith chided. "You knew it would take you away from me. Why did you, Lane?"

Lane could not answer honestly, could not tell the girl that he had been angry and that four drinks of whisky had helped his sudden decision; so he did not answer at all.

"You'll be gone a month," Judith continued. "Can't you tell Agnew that you won't help him? That you've changed your mind?"

"I can't do that," Lane answered.

"I don't see why. I'll tell him I won't let you go!"

Lane straightened. "No," he said firmly, "you'll not tell him that. I promised that I'd help receive these cattle and I'll keep my word."

Tone and bluntness angered Judith. "You'd rather keep your promise than be with me," she accused.

"I've got to keep my promise," Lane corrected. "You know I'd rather be with you. It won't be so bad, Judith. I'll come down to the ranch from the gap. I'll not be gone all the time."

"I'm not going to the ranch," Judith said coolly. "I'm going to stay here. Molly will invite me. I'm not going to stay at Casa Alamos with Dad and Concha for company."

"But I can't come to town," Lane expostulated. "I'll have to ride down to the Hatchet and keep things going, but I won't be able to come to Aspinwall. I'll not get to see you if you stay in town."

"You should" — Judith's voice held no warmth — "have thought of that before you promised Mr. Agnew. I'm sorry, Lane, but I'll not stay at Casa Alamos and spend my time waiting for you. I'm going to stay in town with Molly." She walked toward the house, Lane remaining on the bench beneath the salt-cedar tree, a dead cigarette between his fingers.

Judith was as good as her word. Later in the evening, by laughing innuendo and gentle hints, she extracted an invitation from Molly and the judge. Molly recognized the girl's machinations, but the judge had no thought of her design when he said, "You'd better stay here with us while Lane's busy. You and Molly will be company for each other." Perforce Molly seconded her husband, and Judith gratefully accepted. That done, she turned to Agnew.

"And you'll be gone too?" she asked.

Agnew glanced at Lane. "I'm not sure," he answered. "Is there any need for me to go to the gap, McLain?"

Lane shook his head. "Not while we're building fence," he said. "Of course when we receive cattle you'll be there."

"Of course," Agnew agreed. "But it will take some time to build the fence. I believe I'll stay in Aspinwall until we're ready."

Judith seized the opportunity. "You're robbing me of Lane," she said, smiling. "You'll have to make amends for that, you know."

"Gladly," Agnew agreed. "I'll do my best to make you forgive me, and I'll see that you're not lonely while McLain's away."

In that instant Lane hated Crosby Agnew, his smile, his blond mustache, his polished urbanity. Lane was being punished, although he did not realize it, and Judith, seeing Lane's face, used her whip again. "I'm sure you will," she said brightly, and then, turning to Molly: "It's so kind of you to ask me. I'd much rather stay here than to languish at Casa Alamos."

Lane spent the next day in town buying wire, hiring Tío Abran Feliz to build the fence, attending to various details. When Lane saw Judith she was aloof and distant and, having a temper of his own, Lane lost it. He made no other attempt to reconcile the girl, and that was a mistake, for Judith knew that she had been wrong and was ready to repent. She had no opportunity. As she had been aloof, so now was Lane, and when Lane and Jud Warrend left for the Hatchet the parting was strained. Lane took little consolation from Jud's drawled "She'll get over it, Lane. I've spoiled her." And Judith, roundly scolded by Molly, grew angry again and was more than cordial when Agnew called.

Lane stayed at Casa Alamos while the fence was being built. He made arrangements for the conduct of the Hatchet during his absence, stocked a wagon, and selected his crew. He rode to Benton Springs and to Piedras Amarillas, then on north to note the progress of the fence. All the while he was morose and moody, and Jud Warrend, fond of Lane and knowing the cause of his unhappiness, was angry with Judith. He should,

Warrend thought, have used a paddle on his daughter long ago. Then the fence was completed, and Lane sent word to Agnew in town and, with a wagon and his crew, pulled out for the north.

"I'll come back every chance I get," Lane told Warrend as he shook hands. "You and Van can hold it down all right."

"Good-by," Warrend said. "And, Lane —"

"Yes?"

"Never mind. Get done as soon as you can. Good luck."

"*Adiós*," Lane answered and rode after the wagon.

That afternoon, when the wagon was camped, Agnew came to the gap, piloted by Israel, whom Lane had sent to Aspinwall. The Easterner was jovial, in excellent spirits, although tired by his ride. He brought Lane messages from Judge and Molly Morton, but there was no personal word from Judith, and in a way Lane was pleased by that. Agnew, speaking of happenings in town, told of taking Judith to various functions and parties, of visiting at Morton's, and Lane's pleasure died. It was apparent that Agnew had been good as his word and spared Judith from loneliness.

The day after arriving at the fence Lane established camps at either end of the wire, placing Cuff and Emilio Pacheco in one, Pickles and young Telesfor Feliz in the other. That done, they waited, and early on the following day Seay's foreman, Madrid, brought a herd down to the gap and the counting began.

For the first few days the work mounted. Harbury's hands were working near the gate, and these were augmented by Seay's crews with the stuff that had been thrown back from the south. Daily there was a stream of cattle through the gate, and Agnew had visions of a task soon completed. Lane disabused him of the thought.

"It will slow down," Lane stated. "There are a lot of cattle close to the fence now, and they're easy gathered. After a while they'll be working back in the hills, and the drives will be longer. There'll be times when we won't get any cattle for a day or two."

The last of the day's herd had passed through the gate, and Lane and Agnew were waiting for Harbury and Seay. Harbury, riding across, was in time to hear Lane's statement.

"You've been getting plenty of cattle right now, though," he said, entering the conversation. "I make it twelve hundred an' ten today. What did you get?"

"Twelve hundred and twelve," Lane answered, glancing at his tally book.

"I check with McLain." Seay stopped beside the men.

"Twelve-twelve, then." Harbury laughed. "I won't quarrel over two head when it's in my favor. That makes" — he consulted his own tally — "five thousand eight hundred an' ninety head for the week. That what you got, McLain?"

"That's what I've got," Lane answered and turned his horse to ride toward the camp. Agnew paused a moment to speak further with Seay and Harbury, then, loping his horse, caught up with Lane.

"That's a lot of cattle," he said, reining in.

"There's about fourteen thousand head still to come," Lane reminded shortly.

"But aren't you pleased?"

"Pleased enough."

They reached the wagon and, dismounting, began to unsaddle. As Lane turned his horse loose Pickles came up, and Lane raised his eyebrows inquiringly. Pickles, camped at the west end of the fence, had no business to be at camp. His job, with Telesfor, was to ride the fence and a line east of it, throwing back to the south any stock that drifted up from below. On the other end of the fence Cuff and his partner performed a like service, and both Pickles and Cuff had been at the wagon at noon.

"I come back along the fence this evenin'," Pickles reported, answering Lane's unspoken question. "These cows are awful sticky, Mr. McLain, an' I thought I'd make another push at 'em. There's a lot of wet cows hung up against the fence, bawlin'."

"Wet cows?" Lane asked. "They weren't there this morning?"

"No suh. They turned up after dinner."

"They're trying to get back to where they came from," Agnew announced, airing a bit of newly acquired knowledge. "Cows will do that, you know."

Pickles grinned broadly and looked at Lane.

"How about east of the fence?" Lane asked.

"Telesfor says there's a lot of cattle there."

"Any horse tracks?" Lane's eyes narrowed.

"None but ourn," Pickles replied.

"Save Soldado for me," Lane called to the wrangler at the rope corral. "All right, Pickles. Better eat before you go back."

"I done et," Pickles announced.

Taking his bridle, Lane went to the pen, where the wrangler had roped out Soldado. He had finished saddling and was washing, preparatory to eating supper, when Nebraska joined him. Nebraska and Ben Israel, in company with two vaqueros, were pushing the cattle toward water south of the fence. "The kid tell you about them wet cows?" Nebraska drawled.

"Yes," Lane said. "Have you seen anything below the fence, Nebraska? Horse tracks that don't belong, cattle moved, anything like that?"

Nebraska shook his head. "We ain't," he answered. "But then we ain't been all over the country. We went to the Rio Bosque today. There's cows spread pretty well along the river."

"I'm going up to talk to Cuff right after supper," Lane announced, putting his towel aside. "Tomorrow Ben and I are going to make a swing south. You'll count with Agnew. Hold everything below the fence after you count it."

Nebraska nodded his understanding. "Goin' to call Seay's hand?" he drawled.

"I'm going to raise him a blue chip," Lane snapped and, having rolled down his sleeves and thrown the water out of the basin, he went to the tail gate.

148

As soon as supper was eaten Lane mounted Soldado and, in the twilight, rode west along the fence. A mile from camp he came upon his first wet cows, three of them, their heads thrust across the wire, bawling to the calves that had been left behind. Lane left these and went on. He encountered others and when he reached Cuff's camp had counted twenty-one. Cuff came out as Lane approached and walked beside Soldado back to the little tent and fire.

"Get down an' have a cup of coffee," he invited. "Somethin' wrong?"

"Wet cows and no calves," Lane stated, dismounting. "You didn't ride the fence this afternoon?"

"Emilio rode it. He said he'd seen some wet cows an' pushed 'em back."

"There's twenty-one head against the fence now," Lane informed, "and Pickles says there's a bunch down his way. They just turned up this afternoon."

Cuff poured coffee into two cups and handed one to Lane. Emilio, hair tousled from sleep, appeared at the tent door and grinned.

"That's too many," Cuff drawled. "They might miss a few calves, but not that many. Not if they were tryin'. Who brought 'em down?"

"Madrid. We counted his bunch yesterday, and Nebraska and Ben took them on south. They've just about had time to get back from the river."

Cuff thoughtfully sipped coffee. "I thought they'd try to go around the fence," he complained. "I didn't figure on this wet-cow stunt. It'll be hard to stop, Lane. Them wet ones will go back."

149

"It won't be hard to stop," Lane answered curtly, emptying the last of his coffee. "I'm going back and stop it now. I still think there'll be a play to drive cattle around the fence or through it. Tomorrow Ben and I are going to make a circle south."

"You'll go to Handout?" Cuff asked.

"Not that far, I think."

Cuff scowled speculatively. "That's where yore trouble comes from," he growled. "Handout! There ain't an honest man in that town. They're all bad! From Ryan right on to Cotton in the store an' that jasper runnin' the wagon yard. They live off the rustlers an' throw in with 'em. I tell you, Lane, them little jackals on Rio Bosque need lookin' into, an' Handout needs cleanin' out. It's too bad adobe won't burn!"

Lane's eyes were amused. "Maybe we'll get around to cleaning Handout someday," he suggested. "Well, I'd better get back."

Cuff nodded. "Do you want me to go back with you?" he asked.

"No. I'll handle it. I want you to keep riding the fence and a line west of it."

"Day an' night, too, I reckon," Cuff drawled. "We could use more men, Lane."

"We could, but we haven't got 'em."

Cuff scowled. "Damn it!" he swore. "I wish Neil hadn't gone haywire! This would be just his kind of business. We could sure use him." Cuff stopped, noting Lane's face. "Mebbe," he completed lamely, "we could get Van an' some of the boys from Benton Springs."

150

"They're needed on the Hatchet." Lane tossed his cup into the dishpan. "You and Emilio stay with it, Cuff. I'll see you tomorrow."

"Oh, we'll stay with it," Cuff assured, and Lane, mounting, rode back toward the east.

As he rode he could hear the bawling of the cows against the wire, and his frown deepened. It was a smart idea, this bringing down cows without their calves, smart and hard to detect as the cattle came through the gate. Cows and calves rarely stayed together when they were driven, particularly this late in the summer. Those cows on the fence would try to go back to where they had left the calves, and a two-wire fence was not enough to stop them. Beyond the ends of the fence there was nothing at all to stop them except the line riders. Here was a situation that Lane had not foreseen, but he was prepared to deal with it. He passed the gate and rode on to the wagon where firelight sparkled in the dark.

Reaching the wagon, Lane dismounted and, pulling off the bridle, staked Soldado. As he approached the fire his name was called, and Able Porter stood up in the firelight.

"How are you?" Porter greeted as Lane arrived. "Countin' lots of cattle, Lane?"

"Some." Lane shook hands with Porter and sat down. Harbury had accompanied Porter and with Agnew and Nebraska occupied the firelight.

"Five thousand eight hundred an' ninety head." Harbury rolled the figures from his tongue. "I claim that's gatherin' 'em in a country as rough as this."

"Is Seay at camp?" Lane asked abruptly.

"We left him there," Harbury answered.

Lane got up. Porter's eyes were sharp as he, too, arose. "Somethin' wrong?" he asked.

"I want to talk to Seay."

"Let's go talk to him, then. Come on, Jimmer."

Harbury got up, and Agnew said, "Do you need me, McLain?"

"I'd like to have you along."

Agnew grunted as he stood up. "I'm stiff as a board," he complained. "I've been on a horse all day and I'm going to walk."

Lane said, "We'll see you at your camp, Porter. I'll walk with you, Agnew."

"Sure," Porter agreed, and Lane, with Agnew, moved toward the fence. When they reached it Lane held down the wire, and Agnew stepped across. "What do you want of Seay?" the Easterner asked as the wire twanged back in place. "Is there something wrong?"

"I think," Lane said deliberately, "that Seay's trying to put one over."

"But I thought everything was going so well," Agnew protested. "What is it? What's Seay done?"

"There are too many wet cows coming down," Lane answered.

"Wet cows? I don't understand."

"You will," Lane promised. The Secate camp was close, and Harbury and Porter were dismounting beside the fire. As Lane and Agnew arrived Seay came out of the tent. "Hello, Crosby," he greeted. "How are you?"

"Stiff," Agnew replied.

"McLain's got somethin' on his mind," Porter growled. "Get on with it, McLain!"

"I've got wet cows on my mind," Lane stated, looking at Seay.

"Wet cows?" Seay drawled.

"Pickles came in this evening," Lane informed, "and reported that there were wet cows hanging on the fence, bawling for their calves. After supper I rode to the west end and I counted twenty-one."

"Well?"

"You're leaving too many calves in the hills," Lane snapped. "These cows were bought with calves at side."

"I've got every damned calf!" Porter growled and threw away his cigarette. "How about you, Jimmer?"

"I haven't left any!" Harbury's voice showed his anger.

"Of course," Seay said smoothly, "you don't expect us to get every calf, McLain. We're bound to miss a few. Maybe you should have waited until fall to receive these cattle, Agnew. We can't help making a few dogies at this time of year."

"This isn't up to Agnew," Lane said bluntly. "Talk to me, Seay. Agnew's hired me to receive these cattle, and I'm going to do it. You'll make no more dogies. From now on we'll hold below the fence and mother up the calves. Any wet cow that doesn't have a calf sucking her goes back through the gate and won't be counted."

Seay's sallow cheeks showed a crimson flush in the firelight, and Harbury and Porter were angry. "You won't get away with that!" Seay snapped. "Once a cow

153

goes through that gate she's yours! You'll not cut her back!"

"If she's wet and not sucking a calf I will," Lane promised uncompromisingly. "Beginning tomorrow."

"Mebbe you think we ain't got the cattle!" Harbury blustered. "Mebbe you think we can't deliver twenty thousand head. You been actin' like it, puttin' riders on the wings an' all that!"

"That's exactly what I think," Lane agreed succinctly. "You contracted to deliver twenty thousand head and you'll deliver them without us counting any twice."

"Agnew," Seay said slowly, "McLain's accusing us of deliberately leaving calves north of the fence so that their mothers will go back to them. Do you believe we'd do that? I made this contract in good faith, and so did Mr. Porter and Raoul and Harbury. I've agreed to manage the Secate for you after you've received these cattle. Do you think I'd cheat you?"

"I don't know what to think," Agnew stammered. "Mr. McLain didn't tell me about this. I —"

"You'd take McLain's word before you took mine?" Seay fixed the Easterner with his eyes. Agnew glanced helplessly toward Lane.

"I've employed McLain —" he began.

Porter's growl interrupted. "Them are my cattle you'll count tomorrow, McLain. Do you think I'm crooked?"

"No," Lane said candidly, "I don't. All these wet cows are branded Bar S."

Silence followed that statement, broken only by the popping of a juniper log in the fire. Finally Seay said, "Meaning that *I'm* crooked, McLain?"

"Meaning anything you want that to mean," Lane said and waited.

The juniper popped again, and Agnew jumped. Porter took a step, so that he stood between Lane and Seay. "We're goin' to think about this," he growled. "You'd better do some too, McLain."

"I've done my thinking," Lane said quietly. "Good night. Coming, Agnew?" He wheeled abruptly and walked into the darkness.

Agnew hesitated an instant and then followed and went on toward the fence in silence. As they neared it Agnew said, "I wish you'd told me what to expect, McLain. There was no use in doing what you did. This could all have been handled without friction."

Lane stopped and pushed down on the wire. "You don't know Seay yet," he said quietly. "There's just one way to handle a man like Seay."

"I don't agree with you." Agnew came on toward the fence. "I think —" He was paying more attention to his thoughts than to his footing, and now, striking loose rock, he stumbled, falling forward and flinging out his arms. The wire sang, and an exclamation was torn from the Easterner.

"What is it?" Lane demanded. "Did you hurt yourself?"

"I've cut my hand on the wire." Pain colored Agnew's voice.

"Bad?" Lane's hand was on the man's arm. "Here, let me help you." The fence creaked as Lane placed a boot on the top strand.

In the darkness a man appeared out of the north, silent as a shadow. "Ah'll hold the wiah, Mist' Lane," Ben Israel said. "Yo' take him to camp."

The light of Pancho's lantern revealed a raw and bleeding cut. The wire had ripped across the palm of Agnew's hand, laying it open. Agnew's face went pale at the sight of blood, and he retched with nausea. Lane, after a quick glance, made the Easterner lie down. He washed the cut and stanched the bleeding with firm pressure. Then turpentine was applied and a clean rag bound tight.

"That's a bad cut," Lane said as he finished. "That's what I don't like about wire."

Agnew, his face pale and perspiration beading his forehead, was too ill to answer.

"Get me the whisky, Pancho," Lane directed.

Agnew rested for a time after he was in bed. The shock wore off gradually, and the whisky warmed and comforted him, so that he dozed. He wakened once to hear Porter's gruff bass and Harbury's thinner tones and Lane's smooth voice in reply; then he dozed again. At midnight he awakened fully. The hand ached and burned, and he could not ease it. Striking a match, he noted the time; then by loosening the bandage he checked the throbbing somewhat. For a while he lay cradling the hand and dozed off again, waking only when full day had come. Forgetfully Agnew pushed

156

against the ground as he sat up, and searing pain shot up his arm.

Nebraska, seeing that Agnew was awake, came to the bed. "How you makin' it this mornin'?" Nebraska drawled.

"My hand is pretty sore," Agnew replied, glancing down at the injured member. "Where's McLain?"

"Him an' Ben pulled out at daylight," Nebraska reported. "I'm goin' to count with you today, an' we'd better get goin'. Porter's bringin' his cattle down."

Agnew got up. His whole arm seemed afire and was swelling at the wrist, but he made no mention of it. Lane was gone. Crosby Agnew was as tough as the next man, and, a little ashamed that he should feel so ill and upset, he dressed.

Later Agnew sat beside Nebraska at the gate. Cattle streamed past in an endless line, but he scarcely noted their progress. His hand throbbed dully; his cheeks were flushed, and when he closed his eyes the saddle seemed to rock beneath him. No one noticed his plight, for all were intent on the work at hand.

At ten o'clock Pickles arrived from his camp with a report for Lane. "Where's Mr. McLain?" he demanded, and then, noting Agnew's paleness, the glassy fever in his eyes, and the faint flush on his cheeks: "Say, Mr. Agnew's sick!"

Nebraska took one hasty look and rode out to check the flow of cattle. "Hold on a minute," he commanded. "Agnew's sick. Shut the gate, Pickles."

The riders thronged around the Easterner: Nebraska, Pickles, Porter, and Seay.

"What's wrong?" Porter demanded.

"My hand," Agnew said dully, and Nebraska added: "He cut it on the wire last night."

"Let's look at it!" Porter's voice was gruff, but his fingers were gentle as he took Agnew's hand. "Say, this is swollen pretty bad."

Not only was the hand swollen, but it was inflamed. When the bandage was unwrapped the wound showed red and angry with small fiery streaks running toward the wrist and arm. Again Agnew was faint and nauseated, and they took him to the wagon where, leaning against a wheel, he soaked the hand in cold water while the others consulted.

"If it was me," Porter growled, "I'd have a doctor look at that hand an' I wouldn't waste no time."

"Think you can make it to town, Mr. Agnew?" Nebraska asked. "I'll send Pickles with you. Dang it" — he turned to Porter — "I wish Lane was here."

"You can't wait for McLain," Porter rumbled. "That hand's bad. He could mebbe lose it."

"Do you think you can ride?" Nebraska bent above Agnew. "Here, take a drink of this."

The whisky helped. Under its stimulus Agnew said that he could ride to Aspinwall, and preparations began immediately. Fresh horses were caught and saddled, and Nebraska drew Pickles aside.

"You get him to town," Nebraska directed. "Take him right to the doctor an' tell Judge Morton what's happened. You think you can make it?"

"Sure I can make it. Why not?"

Agnew felt better after the drink and the cold water on his hand, but he was frightened and anxious to get to Aspinwall. They helped him mount, and Nebraska, standing beside Pickles' horse, cautioned: "Now you get back. Lane'll want to know he got to town all right, an' we need you here. Better take this with you." Nebraska held up the pint of whisky that Lane kept in the wagon.

"I'll get back." Pickles stuffed the bottle in his chaps pocket.

It was a five-hour ride from camp to Aspinwall. Pickles and Crosby Agnew made it in six hours. At first Agnew was easy, reassured because he was going to town; his hand, cooled by its soaking, not so painful. Then the jolting got in its work, and the wound, despite a sling Porter had fashioned, ached and throbbed again. The red streaks spread from wrist to forearm, and the whole arm began to swell. Agnew was forced to stop.

This development frightened Pickles. He dosed Agnew liberally from the bottle and kept going, determined to get to Aspinwall and help. The whisky aided in spreading the infection. Agnew's eyes grew bright with fever; his cheeks flushed unnaturally. Whenever Agnew would have stopped, Pickles resorted to the bottle, and two hours out of Aspinwall Agnew grew delirious. The ride from there on gave Pickles a taste of undiluted hell. He was more than thankful when he sighted the smoke from the stamp mill, and he could have danced a jig when, as he led Agnew's horse into Aspinwall's main thoroughfare, he sighted Judge

Morton. By this time Agnew was sodden with liquor and fever, and Pickles had tied the man to his saddle.

Morton took charge, and at his direction Pickles took Agnew straight through town and up the hill to the judge's house. There the man was carried in to bed, and Judith and Molly Morton, greatly alarmed, did what they could to make him comfortable until the judge came with Dr. Folling. Pickles waited, trying to make himself as unobtrusive as possible. After a time the doctor came out of Agnew's room.

"Are you the man that brought him in?" he demanded, glaring over his glasses.

"Yes suh," Pickles agreed.

"Then you're a fool!" The medico was blunt. "Don't you know that whisky is the worst thing you can give for fever? You gave him enough to make him drunk. You might have killed him."

"He ain't goin' to die, is he?"

The doctor disdained to answer but snorted and returned to his patient. When Morton appeared Pickles repeated his question.

"No," the judge said, "he isn't going to die, Pickles. But he's a sick man. His arm's infected, and he has a high temperature."

"I got to tell Lane," Pickles said. "He'll want to know."

"You tell Lane that we'll look after Mr. Agnew," Morton instructed. "He'll be all right now that he's where the doctor can look after him."

"Judge!" Judith called, and Morton hastened away.

160

Pickles debated. He wanted to wait and find out more about Agnew, but Judge Morton had said that Agnew would be all right. Nebraska's caution was recalled, and Pickles knew that he was needed back at camp. If Judge Morton said that Agnew would be all right, then he would be. That was enough for Pickles. He slipped out of the house and rode toward town.

Twilight had come, and lights began to appear on Aspinwall's street. Knots of men stood on the sidewalk, and there was movement back and forth. Pickles, dismounting in front of the Boston Store, was hailed by an acquaintance.

"Hi, Pickles. What you doin' in town?"

Pickles said, "I just come. What's all the excitement?"

"Ain't you heard?" The townsman paused beside the boy while Pickles tied his horses. "The stage was held up this mornin'. Red Dowd an' another fellow. Old Asa Goodin an' Bill Camm was on the stage, an' they cut loose. Dowd was killed."

"The hell!" Pickles stared at his friend. "Who was the other fellow?"

"They think Rodgers. He's been runnin' around with Dowd. Buntlin's got a posse out now lookin' for him."

"The hell," Pickles said again and crossed the sidewalk to the store, the townsman following. While Pickles bought a sack of candy he learned more details, and when he left the store his friend asked, "Ain't you goin' to stay in town? Mebbe they'll catch Rodgers an' bring him in."

Pickles shook his head. "Got to get back to camp," he answered and untied his horses.

A mile north of Aspinwall on the Junction road Pickles turned right. Here was the road to Handout, and Handout lay almost in line with Blocker Gap. In the growing dark it would be easier to follow a road than to strike across country, and Pickles juned along, the lead horse following. By changing horses, Pickles thought, he could make time and not hurt either animal. Both were tired, but he would split his riding, and when he got to camp both horses could have a good long rest. He munched a piece of candy, staving his appetite, and reached into the sack for another piece. The lead horse's reins snapped tight, and under him Pickles' mount shied violently. Pickles swayed, balancing with the sudden movement, and pulled the horse down. "Now what's got into you?" he complained. "Ain't you tired enough to behave?"

The horse stood trembling, ears cocked and nose thrust out toward a mesquite beside the road. Pickles' eyes grew wide and he dropped the candy sack. A boot protruded from the mesquite, and above the boot a blue-jeaned leg. Pickles tied the lead horse firmly to his saddle horn and dismounted. Holding the reins, he advanced cautiously toward the mesquite.

"Hey!" he challenged. "Hey there!"

Neither boot nor leg moved. Bending, Pickles reached into the shadow of the brush and dragged a body into the road. He knelt and stared at the pallid, bloodstained face.

"My Lord!" There was awe in Pickles' voice. "It's Neil! My good gosh!"

162

CHAPTER
TWELVE

False dawn streaked the top of the Chiricahuas when Lane, with Ben Israel and Jimmer Harbury, rode off toward the east. Harbury's company had not been requested, but after the brief and fiery visit Lane and Agnew had made to Seay's camp north of the fence the night before, Porter and Harbury had come to the Hatchet wagon.

"We been talkin'," Porter announced, "an' we figure we want to see them wet cows. I'm goin' to count tomorrow with Seay, an' we decided that Jimmer could ride the fence in the mornin'. Have you got any objections, McLain?"

"I'd be glad to have him ride the fence," Lane answered. "Ben and I are going to pull out early and make a circle south. We'll take Harbury along if he wants to go."

"You won't be on deck to count, then," Porter said and, after a moment, "Maybe that's a good thing. You rode us pretty hard up there, McLain. You got on Seay worse than you got on Jimmer an' me, but I'll tell you straight, we didn't like what you had to say to us."

"I laid my hand out for you to look at," Lane stated. "I can't help it if you don't like the looks of the cards."

163

"You didn't have to be so all-fired tough about it," Harbury snapped. "As far as I'm concerned you can go to hell, McLain, but Able thinks I ought to go 'long tomorrow an' see if there are cows bawlin' on the fence an' how many there are of 'em."

"We'll leave by daybreak," Lane said. "You're welcome to come if you want to."

"I'll be here, then," Harbury agreed.

True to his word, while Lane and Ben Israel drank a final cup of coffee in the weird light a fire makes just at dawn, Harbury came trotting up to the Hatchet wagon. He refused the coffee and waited in hostile silence until Lane and Ben were done. Mounting their waiting horses, the three struck out along the fence toward Pickles' camp.

The fence ended at the foot of Popes Nose, seven miles from the gate. A mile out from the wagon Lane and his companions found their first wet cows, four of them in a bunch, where the fence crossed a small draw. Lane made no comment, and Harbury's scowl deepened.

"That ain't many," he stated. "Anybody could miss four calves. I ain't seen no wet cows yet, not any number of 'em."

Still Lane was silent, and they rode on. For a quarter of a mile they found no cattle on the fence, and then in another draw they came upon six head, all with swollen bags, all close to the wire, all bawling.

"Could anybody miss ten head?" Lane drawled, and Israel, farther down the fence, called: "Theah's two gone through down heah."

Harbury and Lane joined Israel. The sign was plain. Strands of hair were caught in the wire's barbs, and there was blood where a cow, crawling the fence, had cut herself.

"Twelve head," Lane said. "You can go on to Pickles' camp, Harbury. You'll find some more. Ben and I branch off here."

"Where are you goin'?" Harbury demanded.

"To Dog Draw." Lane waited while Harbury made up his mind.

"What do you think you'll find at Dog Draw?" the man asked.

"I don't know. We're going west from Dog Draw and hit the Rio Bosque. We'll come back north on it."

"An' what's the idea of all that ridin'?"

"I think," Lane drawled, "that I'll find horse tracks. I think that I'll find some cattle gone from where they were located. I might find something else. We'll push along now, Harbury." He turned his horse and started toward the south, Israel following. They had gone almost a hundred yards when Harbury loped up.

"I'm goin' with you," he announced.

"If you want to," Lane replied without enthusiasm.

The sun topped the Chiricahuas as Lane and his companions rode on south. They reached Dog Draw and rode part of its length. There were cattle along the draw, and Lane and Israel took their time, inspecting the animals, working out on either side of the draw, covering country. When the three riders drew together again Israel reported. "There's been none moved from heah, Mist' Lane."

Harbury snorted triumphantly. "Ready to go back now?" he demanded.

"I told you the ride we were going to make," Lane answered.

From Dog Draw they went on south, swinging slightly toward the west. By noon they had reached a water hole below Concha Tank. There were no cattle here but plenty of horse tracks. Lane and Israel had no comment, but Harbury said: "Lots of horses waterin' here."

"And some of them smoke," Lane drawled, stooping to pick up a fresh cigarette butt.

They nooned at the water hole, the horses grazing, Lane smoking a contemplative cigarette and Harbury his pipe. Ben Israel sprawled in the shade of a rock, relaxed, and when an hour had passed they tightened cinches, remounted, and went on.

Now they rode straight west toward the Rio Bosque, and as the sun crawled above them toward the west, gaining on them, they topped a rise and saw the river, its green wooded banks and water glinting.

"Heah's wheah we put the most of the cattle, Mist' Lane," Israel announced and led the way down the slope.

The river disappeared behind long swells of brush-grown land. The horses' hoofs crunched in the sand, and chaps rattled brush as the men skirted it. Silence had held them all day, and now it grew more tense, as though each man expected something. Israel's horse tossed its head and pointed its ears. Israel held up his hand, reining in. The others halted.

"What is it, Ben?" Lane asked, low-voiced, and Israel cautioned silence.

"I don't hear a blame thing!" Harbury's voice was loud and petulant. "I don't —"

"Hush!" Israel snapped, and then, barely audible: "Theah, movin' through the brush ahead."

Harbury flashed the Negro an angry glance. "Don't tell me to hush!" he rapped. "What's movin'? Where?"

Lane rode ahead cautiously, and Israel moved. They were in a depression, and as the horses climbed Harbury came past, riding ahead to reach the crown of the rise first. He paused there, silhouetted boldly, and looked back.

"There ain't a damned thing —" Harbury began.

A rifle bit into the sentence, breaking it short. Harbury's horse reared, pawing air with futile forefeet, and continued to rise until, overbalanced, it fell back, crashing into the brush. With the shot Lane had slid a rifle from beneath his fender and spurred. Israel, too, was forging ahead. They crowned the rise, their horses running, and Israel slid his mount to a halt. His rifle jumped to his shoulder and chanted two quick notes. Three hundred yards away running cattle appeared in an opening. A horse, its rider bent low, showed beyond the cattle, and then another rider passed the first. Lane fired, fought his bucking horse, and fired again. Sand spurted at his horse's feet, and a puff of smoke between the running cattle and the rise was whipped away in the breeze. Israel had gone on down the slope, and now he fired again as Lane fought with his horse. There was a staccato rasp of gunfire; then the opening where the

167

cattle had been was vacant. Dismounting, Lane let his horse go and ran to a vantage point. When he reached it cattle, horses, and men had disappeared. The brush moved in the wind, and farther west Lane caught a flash of color in the trees along the river. He scanned the country, searching every foot, and then, turning, walked back along the ridge top.

Lane's horse had trapped a rein between two rocks. He fought his tether as Lane came up and continued to fight, despite soothing voice and restraining hands. Not until Lane put his rifle down did the horse stop and stand, trembling. Quieting his mount, Lane held him securely and, reaching the rifle, placed it in the boot. He had mounted when Israel appeared farther north along the ridge. Brush rattled and, facing the south, Lane saw Harbury on foot and carrying his rifle. A bloody welt stood out on Harbury's red cheek. He reached Lane almost as Ben Israel arrived. The man was out of breath, and for an instant no one spoke. Then: "Damn 'em!" Harbury rasped. "They killed my horse. He come close to gettin' me when he fell. Who were they, Lane?"

"Too far to see," Lane answered. "Did you get close, Ben?"

"No suh. Ah thought they'd hit yo' an' Ah come back."

"Well," Lane drawled, "that's that, I guess. They were moving stock north to the fence. Are you satisfied, Harbury?"

"I'm a damned fool," Harbury growled by way of apology and acknowledgment.

168

"No." Lane smiled suddenly. "You're not a damned fool, Jimmer. You're honest and you expect everyone else to be."

"Do we follow 'em?" Israel asked. "They went to the rivah."

Lane looked at Harbury and then at the Negro. "We go to camp," he decided. "We'd not get far following them. There's two horses for the three of us."

The sun was down when the three men reached the gap. Nebraska, the two hands, Pancho, and the wrangler spied their approach and ran out to meet them, and for a time the air was filled with questions. Lane answered briefly and then, missing Agnew, made inquiry.

"I had to send him to town," Nebraska reported. "His hand got bad, an' he pretty near passed out on us. Pickles took him in."

"How bad was that hand?" Lane questioned sharply.

"Bad enough that Porter thought he was goin' to lose it."

Lane turned to the wrangler. "Get in the horses," he directed, "and get me Pronto."

"You ain't goin' to town?" Nebraska demanded.

"Ain't you goin' to talk to Porter?" Harbury asked. "An' to Seay?"

"They'll have to wait." Lane's voice was crisp. "I've got to find out how bad Agnew is. You can talk to Porter, Jimmer."

"Yo're damned right I can!" Harbury agreed. "But I'd like to have you do it. I'll back you up."

"Not now. I've got to go to town."

"You'll eat first," Nebraska stated, "if I have to hawg-tie you an' feed you. Pancho, rustle the boss some supper. You got time, Lane. The horses ain't in yet."

Lane grinned at Nebraska. "All right," he agreed. "I'll eat." Pancho brought a laden plate, and Lane sat down.

"We counted Porter's cattle an' held 'em below the fence like you said," Nebraska reported as Lane ate. "Seven hundred an' fifty-six head. I rode through 'em just before you come, an' there wasn't a wet cow in the bunch that didn't have a calf suckin' her. I put the figgers in the tally book."

"Good." Lane spoke around a mouthful of steak.

"An' Cuff come down —" Nebraska continued with his report, and Lane listened.

"Tomorrow," he said when Nebraska was done, "take those cows down to Dog Draw and spread them out. Go quite a ways south with them."

"You think that's safe?" Nebraska asked.

"It's safe," Lane said grimly. "They won't try again so soon. I'll be back here tomorrow or the next day. When I get back we'll ride the country south. I'll stop with Cuff when I go in, and I'll try to hire another man or two in Aspinwall." He put his plate aside and stood up. The wrangler, leading the saddled Pronto, had arrived at the wagon.

"Hold it down, Nebraska," Lane directed. "Harbury, you tell Porter what happened. I'll be back as soon as I can get back."

170

Harbury nodded. "Loan me a horse an' I'll go home," he said to Nebraska. "Good luck, Lane."

Pronto was a *grulla*, one of the old breed with thick furred ears and a mustache on his muzzle. If Pronto had ever seen a cow he kept it a dark secret, but between daylight and dark Pronto could put a hundred miles under his hard black hoofs. Lane McLain left the camp in Blocker Gap at seven o'clock. Before midnight he was knocking on Judge Morton's door in Aspinwall.

Morton, in nightshirt and trousers, let Lane in and they talked, low-voiced. Molly came, fully clothed, for she had been sitting up with Agnew. And then Judith appeared, her hair trailing in a braid over her dressing robe. Judith came straight to Lane's arms, and in that moment all Lane's doubts and bitterness were lost, and all his hurt was swept away.

The judge's word of Agnew was reassuring. The arm was bad, but hot foments were reducing the swelling, and the doctor was optimistic. Lane looked in on the sleeping man and then, returning to the living room, sat down on a couch, his arm around Judith. The tension eased out of him. Lane relaxed, and while Morton talked his head bent forward to his chest. "Now I think —" Morton said.

"Shhh!" Judith interrupted and gestured toward Lane.

"Worn out," the judge murmured. "Here. We'll put him on the couch."

Light streaming through the window beside the couch awakened Lane, and he sat up, pushing a cover from his legs. For a moment the unfamiliar surroundings puzzled him, and then as recollection came he glanced out of the window toward the sun low in the east. He rubbed his eyes and his unshaven cheeks and, looking down, saw his dusty boots, his wrinkled trousers, and disordered shirt.

All about the house was quiet. Lane tiptoed down the hall to Agnew's room and, glancing in, saw that Agnew was asleep and that Molly dozed in a chair. He did not awaken her but returned to the living room. More than once Lane had been glad of the convenience a room in town afforded, and now he was doubly glad. There was a suit and change of clothes at Mrs. Tindler's Hotel, and when he saw Judith again he would be presentable. Closing Morton's door carefully behind him, Lane went down the hill.

Aspinwall stirred sluggishly in the early morning. A clerk listlessly swept the sidewalk in front of the Boston Store, and as Lane rounded the hotel corner he saw the swamper opening the Orient Bar. In the hotel lobby Lane took a key from the rack and, climbing the stairs, let himself into his room. The hotel was stirring. There was a rattle from the kitchen as ashes were shaken from the stove, and feet tramped along the corridor outside Lane's door. Grinning, he picked up his pitcher and stepped out. He would beg hot water from the cook.

Lane found Mrs. Tindler in the kitchen. A fire was snapping in the stove, and the woman had set about breakfast preparations. She started with surprise when she saw Lane. "What are you doin' here, Lane McLain?" she demanded.

172

"I came in to change," Lane answered. "Can I have some hot water, Mrs. Tindler?"

The woman opened the stove reservoir and touched the water. "It ain't hot," she said, "but it's warm. What are you doin' in town?"

Lane crossed to the stove and dipped water from the reservoir. "Agnew was hurt," he answered. "I wasn't there, and the boys sent him to town. I came in to find out how he was."

"Oh!" Relief was apparent on Mrs. Tindler's face. "You didn't come on account of Neil, then?"

"Neil?"

"Ain't you heard? No, of course you ain't. The stage was held up yesterday, an' Red Dowd got killed."

Lane closed the reservoir lid. "That's news to me," he drawled. "What's that got to do with Rodgers?"

Mrs. Tindler glanced toward the ceiling and then back to Lane. "There was a man with Dowd," she said. "He was hit, but he got away. They think it was Neil."

For an instant concern showed on Lane's face, and then his eyes grew cold. "That's interesting," he drawled. "Is Buntlin after him?"

Mrs. Tindler made a gesture, a wave of swift impatience. "Of course. He went out soon as they got word. Lane McLain, you're as cold-blooded as a fish. Neil Rodgers was the best friend you ever had, an' when you hear the sheriff's huntin' him you say 'That's interestin'.' I could — I could slap you, I could. Get out of my kitchen! Take your water an' get out!"

Amazed by the tirade, Lane backed away. As he reached the door Mrs. Tindler fired a parting shot.

"You might at least act human, even if you did have a fight with him."

Carrying his water, Lane climbed the stairs. As he reached the top he saw Beth van Brimmer come out of a room at the end of the hall and carefully lock the door behind her. The girl turned and, seeing Lane, grew suddenly white. Lane came toward her, carrying his pitcher and smiling.

"Good morning, Beth," he greeted, his voice low out of consideration for those who might be asleep. "Surprise you to see me?"

"I — Oh yes! You surprised me, Lane."

"I came in last night and stayed at Morton's."

"At Morton's?"

"Mr. Agnew was hurt, and we sent him to town. He's at Morton's, and I came in to see how he was."

"Then you didn't — ? You came to find out about Mr. Agnew?"

"That's right." Lane pushed open his door. "I'll see you before I go, Beth." He smiled again as he stepped into his room, and Beth, waiting until the door closed, hurried on down the hall.

Later, clean, shaven, and in clean clothes, Lane left Mrs. Tindler's Hotel. Neither Beth nor Mrs. Tindler was in evidence, although noises from the kitchen spoke of them at work. On the porch as Lane left the lobby he encountered Pickles. The boy had a bundle under his arm and he stopped short when he saw the boss. Lane frowned. "What are you doing here?" he demanded, forgetting for the moment the reason for the boy's being in town.

Pickles refused to meet Lane's eyes. He stammered, "Them hawses, Mr. McLain. They was plumb beat out —"

"Of course." Lane's frown disappeared. "I'd forgotten for a minute. You're going back to camp today?"

"Right now." Relief was evident in Pickles' reply. "How's Mr. Agnew this mawnin', Mr. McLain?"

"He was asleep when I left," Lane answered. "I'll find out when the doctor comes. You get back to camp, Pickles. Tell Nebraska I'll be out today or tomorrow."

"Yes suh," Pickles agreed and watched Lane as he left the porch. Then with the boss out of sight, Pickles tucked his bundle more firmly under his arm and went into the hotel.

Back at Judge Morton's, Lane found the judge and Judith just sitting down at the breakfast table. The meal was scarcely finished before the doctor came, and they all accompanied him to Agnew's room. Judith and the judge stood at the door while Lane and Molly entered with the physician.

Agnew smiled when he saw Lane. "Awfully good of you to come, McLain," he said. "I made a fool of myself at camp."

"A man can't help being sick when he's hurt," Lane answered.

"But I'm not sick," Agnew protested. "I'm all right. I feel like a fool for lying here."

"Let me see that hand," the doctor directed.

The physician was pleased when he concluded his examination. The swelling was gone down, and the

175

angry red lines had receded. "Last night I wouldn't have given much for your chances of keeping that arm," he told Agnew when he had replaced the bandage. "But today I'm positive that it will be all right. Mrs. Morton, you're to keep him in bed and continue the foments. I'll leave some medicine for him." The doctor continued, speaking to Molly, and Agnew said, "How are things at camp, McLain?"

"Fine," Lane said. "Don't worry about the camp or about receiving those cattle. I'll look after that."

"I knew you would," Agnew said and let his head rest on the pillows.

After the doctor was gone Lane sought Judith in the living room. "I've only a little while," he said, taking Judith's hands. "I have to get back to the gap. You don't know how I've missed you, Judith."

"You're going back today?" Judith asked. "Can't you stay awhile, Lane? Just till tomorrow?"

"I can't." Lane's tone was miserable. "There's trouble at the camp, and I've got to be there."

"Trouble?" Alarm in the girl's voice, and she pulled her hands away.

Lane knew instantly that he should not have spoken. "It's nothing much," he reassured. "But I've got to be there to receive the cattle. I promised Agnew. Let's not waste time talking about the camp, Judith."

"But I want to know," Judith persisted. "Tell me, Lane."

"It's nothing," Lane said, his eyes dark as he thought. "You wouldn't understand it, Judith."

"I understand that it's taking you away again," Judith said. "Must you go? Can't you stay even a day?"

"I'm afraid not." Lane took the girl's hands again. "If I had thought, I could have sent word out by Pickles, but it's too late now. He's gone. No, Judith. I can't stay. Let's not talk about it. Let's use what time we have."

Lane was wrong. He might still have sent word to camp by Pickles, had he but known it. At that moment Pickles stood in Beth van Brimmer's room above the kitchen in Mrs. Tindler's Hotel and looked down at Neil Rodgers sprawled on the bed. Neil's face was sallow from loss of blood; his eyes were closed, and there was a bandage wrapped about his body. Across the bed Mrs. Tindler stood looking at the boy, and Beth van Brimmer knelt beside Neil, her hand holding his protectively.

"I still think you ought to tell the boss," Pickles insisted. "Mr. McLain would fix this all right. He'd fix it so that Neil could have a doctor."

Mrs. Tindler's lips firmed, and Beth said, "No!" breathlessly.

"I'm as good as any doctor," Mrs. Tindler announced. "An' I ain't goin' to tell Lane McLain a thing. Not after the way he acted this mornin'!"

"The boss is all right." Pickles rose in Lane's defense. "He just don't *sabe* things so good right now. He'd take care of Neil all right."

"He's done enough for Neil." Beth's voice was bitter. "Neil wouldn't be here if it weren't for Lane and that Warrend girl!"

Another of Pickles' deities was being trodden, and he scowled at Beth. Mrs. Tindler said, "You done enough, Pickles. You picked Neil up an' brought him in, an' Beth an' me have hid him. You won't tell Lane, will you?"

"No," Pickles agreed reluctantly. "I won't tell him. But I think we'd ought to."

Beth stretched up her free hand to the boy, gripping his own. Pickles freed his hand awkwardly. "I got to get back to camp," he said. "Is there anythin' else you want before I go?"

"No," Mrs. Tindler answered. And then again: "You're a good boy, Pickles. You done enough. You run on now an' don't talk. Beth an' me'll look after Neil."

CHAPTER
THIRTEEN

Lane spent the morning and part of the afternoon at Morton's. He was loath to leave Judith, but with a five-hour ride ahead and certain business still to be transacted in Aspinwall, he finally and reluctantly left the girl. As Lane reached Mrs. Tindler's Guy Pryor appeared from the Orient and crossed the street.

"I heard you were in town," the marshal stated. "I wanted to see you before you left."

"I've got to change clothes and then I want to see Tío Abran Feliz," Lane answered, having shaken Pryor's hand. "Come up."

Pryor agreed and, entering the hotel together, they climbed the stairs to Lane's room. While Lane dressed, shifting from his suit to the work-stained garments he had worn on his ride from the gap, the two men talked. Pryor gave a detailed account of the stage robbery as he had heard it. A pay roll for the Mule Mine had been en route from Junction to Aspinwall, and evidently word of this had leaked.

"Dowd must have known it was coming to the bank," Pryor related, "but he didn't know that Yelland had hired guards to ride the stage. Dowd and this other fellow jumped out of the brush just north of the

179

Handout road and stopped the stage, but the guards cut loose from inside. They killed Dowd the first rattle of the box and hit the other man hard, but he got away. Everybody thinks it was Rodgers, and Buntlin's got a posse out now, looking for him."

"They were both masked, I suppose?" Lane stamped into his boots.

"That's right. But Dowd and Rodgers have been running around together. Buntlin's got a warrant for Rodgers."

"You're not taking any hand?" Lane asked.

"It happened out of town," Pryor answered. "That makes it Buntlin's baby. He's got a couple on his hands now."

"A couple?"

Pryor looked sharply at Lane, who was buckling his belt. "That's right," the marshal agreed. "Buntlin's got a warrant to serve for Harmon and one for Garret. He's had them quite a while, and folks are beginning to ride him pretty hard about not serving them. Didn't you know?"

"No, I didn't." Lane swung his cartridge belt in place and buckled it, his heavy gun settling familiarly against his hip. "I think I could tell Buntlin where he might find Garret and Harmon if he wanted them."

"He don't want them very bad." Pryor's smile was thin and sardonic. "Buntlin plays ball with those two. Where are they, McLain?"

"I think they're someplace south of the gap, over along Rio Bosque. I've got an idea that I ran into them yesterday." Lane had finished dressing, and now he turned to the marshal. "We played a little poker with those two, I think," he continued and went on briefly to outline the meeting below the fence, its cause and outcome.

"But you didn't see them for sure?" Pryor asked.

"Not for sure," Lane agreed, "but I think it was Harmon and Garret and their bunch. I've got to see Abran, Pryor. Come with me?"

"Sure," Pryor agreed.

They left the room and as they stepped into the hall Beth van Brimmer passed them. Lane smiled and nodded to the girl but did not stop. Leaving the hotel, the two men walked south toward the section of Aspinwall known as Chihuahua.

"Are you," Pryor asked, "going to follow up that thing below your fence?"

"Maybe," Lane answered. "I want to get a couple of riders. I'd like to get Pete Feliz and Joe Perez. That's why I want to see Abran."

Pryor nodded. "They're good men," he drawled. "You could use them."

Tío Abran was at home in his long adobe, and the wrinkled patriarch of the Feliz clan listened gravely to Lane's request. Pete, his grandson, and Joe Perez, Tío Abran's nephew, would come to Blocker Gap immediately, he agreed. Lane thanked the old man in dignified Spanish, sure that the men he wanted would appear. As they made ready to go Tío Abran called Pryor back, and Lane waited impatiently outside the door while a murmured conversation took place. Pryor rejoined him finally, and they walked back toward the center of town.

"I feel kind of responsible about Rodgers and you," Pryor said suddenly. "I'm sorry that I put you two together."

"You couldn't help it." Lane's face was hard. "We'd have come together anyhow."

"Maybe," Pryor said thoughtfully. And then: "I wish I hadn't run Rodgers out of town. I should have run Dowd out and split 'em up. Instead I threw them together."

"No more than I did," Lane said curtly. Now that he was away from Judith he had time to think, and Pryor's report of the attempted stage robbery had disturbed him. "Rodgers quit at the ranch after he'd been with me ten years. It made me sore, and I let him go. I should have talked with him. There was something bothering Neil, and I should have found out what it was."

"Do you think Buntlin will get him?" Pryor asked, watching Lane narrowly.

"Not if Neil's all right. Buntlin couldn't catch up with Neil's tracks if the boy didn't want him to and was able to travel. Damn it!" Lane rarely swore, and the oath showed the depth of his feeling. "The kid may have gone haywire, but if he did it's my fault. I'd like to talk to Neil."

Again Pryor's narrowed yellow eyes searched Lane's face. "Even if he *was* with Dowd?"

"Even if he was with Dowd! Mrs. Tindler threw it into me this morning at the hotel. She told me about this business, but I was in a hurry and I turned her off pretty short. She spent a little time to tell me what she thought. She was right about it too."

182

"She can tell a fellow," Pryor drawled, "and most of the time she isn't wrong. It looks like a close race for sheriff this fall, McLain," he changed subject abruptly. "Buntlin and me are running neck and neck."

"You'll beat him," Lane assured. "Well, I've got to get to the gap. So long."

They were at the hotel corner. Pryor took Lane's hand and shook it. "So long," he said. "Good luck." The men parted, Lane striding off toward the Star Wagon Yard. When he was gone Guy Pryor stood awhile, looking thoughtfully up at the hotel, then, his mind made up, walked down the street and entered the doctor's office.

There was no one in the office save the doctor, who appeared from his consultation room and smiled when he saw the officer. "Something on your mind, Marshal?" the physician asked.

"Doc," Pryor drawled, "I've heard that you were backing me for sheriff and that you think I'm a pretty fair kind of man. Is that right?"

"You know where I stand." The small physician was blunt. "I've no use for Buntlin. Of course I'm backing you."

"And I've heard" — Pryor searched the doctor's face — "that you can keep your mouth shut."

"If you mean concerning my patients," the doctor bristled, "I'll tell you that I've never betrayed a professional secret."

Pryor smiled. "No need to get mad," he placated. "Tell you what, Doc. Suppose you put some bandage and stuff in your pocket, whatever you'd need for a gunshot wound, say, and meet me in Mrs. Tindler's Hotel. You could come in through the kitchen and nobody would see you."

"What is this, Pryor?" the doctor challenged. "Are you breaking the law?"

"And me the town marshal? Pshaw, Doc!"

The physician hesitated. Then: "I'll be there in ten minutes," he announced.

"Good man, Doc!" Guy Pryor praised.

When Lane left Pryor on the hotel corner he went to the wagon yard and got Pronto. Striking straight northwest from town, he crossed the Handout road well west of the settlement and, finding a ford in Rio Bosque, kept his line. It was dark, and everyone had gone to bed when Lane reached camp, but his advent aroused the men. When he had unsaddled and let Pronto go to find the remuda Lane was surrounded. Nebraska was there, Ben Israel, the cook, the wrangler, the two vaqueros, and Cuff. Lane eyed Cuff.

"What are you doing here?" he demanded. "Why aren't you at the west end?"

"From now on I stay here," Cuff retorted, unabashed. "I heard what happened. Nebraska told me. The next time I ain't goin' to be left out."

"I was going to send up for you, anyhow," Lane stated. "I've got two men coming out tomorrow, and from now on you and Ben and Nebraska are going to ride the country south."

"We'd already figgered that out," Cuff said. "How's Agnew?"

Lane made his report and asked if Pickles had returned.

"He got in tonight," Nebraska said, "an' Porter an' Harbury an' Raoul were down here awhile ago to see if you'd got back."

"Raoul?"

"He's got a bunch for you to count tomorrow," Nebraska explained.

"I'll see them in the morning," Lane decided. "Seay wasn't with them?"

"Porter said that Seay had gone up to be with his crew." Nebraska's face wore a grin. "I reckon they'd had some hell up there, the way Porter acted."

Lane stretched and yawned. Despite his iron-hard muscles he was tired, weary, and fine-drawn from tension and lack of sleep. "I'm going to bed," he announced. "Good night."

In the morning Lane went up to the camp above the fence. As he rode he heard the bawling of moving cattle, and before he reached the camp he saw the first of the herd. A man cut off from it and rode toward him, and Lane waited until Porter arrived.

"I got in late," he told Porter. "Nebraska said you'd been down with Raoul and Harbury, but I didn't want to wake you last night."

"Jimmer an' Raoul are comin'," Porter announced. "They'll be here in a minute. We want to talk to you, McLain."

Raoul and Jimmer Harbury rode in from the herd, stopping their horses and waiting silently. Lane looked from one to another, waiting for someone to begin. It was Porter who spoke.

"We want to tell you, McLain," he said, "that we didn't have nothin' to do with them wet cows that was bawlin' on the fence. The three of us have lived up to our contract, an' we've brought down every calf we could pick up."

"You didn't need to tell me that, Able," Lane responded.

"But we wanted you to know it." Porter glanced toward Raoul and Harbury, who nodded corroboration. "An' we didn't have nothin' to do with that business south of the fence," the grizzled man continued. "You'd ought to know that. Jimmer had his horse shot an' —"

"I knew it," Lane said.

"Jimmer told us about what happened," Porter continued. "Raoul come in yesterday evenin', an' the three of us talked it over. We're goin' to deliver these cattle, McLain. We're all on that contract an' we're all together, but we ain't responsible for what Seay done."

"Then you think it was Seay?" Lane wanted to pin these men down.

"Who else?" Porter met Lane's eyes squarely. "We had it out with Seay last night. He's gone up to be with his wagons, an' there won't be no more cows go through the gate unless they have their calves. About what happened south of the fence we can't say. But we wasn't none of us mixed up in it."

These men were square. Lane decided to put his hand on the table. "I'm going to have Cuff and Ben and Nebraska riding the country south of the gap," he

186

said. "Agnew won't be back for a while, and I'll have to act for him. If there are any objections —"

"There ain't none from us," Raoul said quickly, and Harbury growled, "It costs money to run a wagon. We can't tie up because Agnew ain't here. You go ahead an' receive for him, Lane."

"Then that's settled," Lane said. "Now —"

"We've been figgerin' things out," Porter interrupted. "We think we're stuck, Lane. We contracted to deliver twenty thousand head. Me an' Raoul an' Jimmer an' Buntlin all signed the contract with Seay. That makes us all responsible. But we don't think we got the cattle." He paused, glanced at the others for reassurance, and then went on: "We think that's what those fellers below the fence were up to. They were headed north with a drive to put it around the fence."

"That's what I think," Lane agreed.

"An' we think they were workin' for Seay," Porter continued doggedly. "What we want to tell you is that we're goin' to put every damned head north of the gap through that gate. The three of us had the cows that we put down, but from what I've seen we won't have enough to fill the contract. Seay just didn't have the cattle he said he had."

"Maybe not."

"Anyhow, that's what we're goin' to do," Porter concluded. "That's what we told Seay. If we have to we'll put our outfits in his country an' round it up, an' if we can't deliver we're stuck."

"How do you mean you're stuck?" Lane asked.

"If we're short we'll have to go out an' buy cattle to fill the contract," Porter stated. "We all signed it an' we're all together. We thought Seay was honest." His voice was bitter.

"Maybe you'll have them," Lane consoled. "You don't know yet."

"But we've got ideas," Harbury growled. "An' if we're right we'll settle with Seay."

"My outfit's at the fence," Raoul stated. "Let's get to countin'."

The four rode toward the gate at a trot.

All the hours he counted cattle filing through the gate Lane considered that meeting. He could see just how those three men thought and reacted. Porter, Raoul, and Harbury were straight, honest as men came. They had had nothing to do with the wet cows being put through the gate, nor with the activity south of the gap. They had made an agreement and they would stand by it grimly, to the bitter end. And the end would be bitter. As Porter said, they had all signed the contract and were all responsible. If the delivery was short, as Lane was sure it would be, these men would be hurt. Perforce they must buy cattle to make up the count and they would have to buy on a rising market. Once their need was known, every man in the country who owned a cow would boost the price. Porter, Raoul, Harbury, and even Buntlin would suffer. But not Seay. Seay owned no cattle. The people in England would be the ones who paid off. Lane was sorry, but it seemed to him that there was no way out of the dilemma. Porter, Raoul, and Harbury had stuck out their necks when they signed that contract with Seay. But perforce Lane admired the men. They were going through with the deal regardless of what it might cost them.

At noon, when they knocked off counting, Lane found his two new men at the wagon. These he dispatched to the camps at either end of the fence with instructions to ride line and fence. Ben, Cuff, and Nebraska had worked that morning, holding cattle after they were counted through. Drawing the three together, Lane gave them orders. "I'll want you to locate what we receive," he instructed them, "and I've already told you that I want you to ride the country south. You know what to do and what to look for."

"Sure," Cuff agreed, "we'll pull out after dinner."

Lane left them, and Cuff, without a word, drew the others aside. "That ain't all we got to do," he said as they stood together. "We got to look after Lane."

Nebraska nodded, and Israel's eyes were narrow. "That's my job," he drawled. "Ah been used to lookin' aftah Mist' Lane."

"Lane don't see it," Cuff said, "but he's in a hole. He thinks he's got everythin' stopped. He puts riders on the fence an' wings an' he has the cows held below the fence to see there ain't none without calves. He puts us to ridin' the country south, but he overlooks his hand. All that wouldn't amount to shucks if they could get him down."

"Porter an' Raoul an' Harbury are square," Nebraska expostulated. "You know what happened. Porter told us."

"An' I know that Seay's still runnin' around loose an' that he's got some pretty salty jiggers workin' for him," Cuff snapped. "We ain't heard where Nosey Harmon an' Clay Garret are. That's why Ben's goin' to ride herd on Lane."

"It'll leave us short," Nebraska said, accepting Cuff's dictum. "We'll have our hands full with just you an' me ridin'."

"An' so we'll count Pickles in," Cuff answered. "There'll be three men at the east end now. We'll all start out together after dinner, an' Ben'll drop back. You an' me'll go on an' see Pickles an' tell him what he's supposed to do."

Nebraska thought that over. "Pickles is just a kid," he objected.

"He's due to grow up, ain't he?" Cuff flared. "Come on; let's eat."

So it was that after dinner, when the three left, Ben accompanied Cuff and Nebraska out of sight, stopped, and, letting down the two wires of the fence, led his horse across. He tacked the wires back in place and, mounting, rode north, coming to a rise above the gate. From this vantage point he could look down and watch the cattle going past the counters at the gate, but Israel wasted very little time in studying that scene. His restless eyes searched the country north and west and east.

That was the first of many such vigils. Ben Israel was assigned the task of guarding Lane and he performed it rigorously. When Lane counted cattle Ben occupied the rise, and when Lane rode south with Cuff and

190

Nebraska, Ben went along. This happened sometimes, for cattle were not counted every day. The flow of stock toward the fence was intermittent, and there were days when no cattle at all were received. The roundup crews north of the fence were working a big scope of country, and as they moved farther from the gap the lengths of their drives increased. On those days when there were no cattle to count Lane rode with his men and found exactly nothing. Pickles, under Cuff's instruction, was also making southward circles and he, too, secretly reporting to Cuff and Nebraska, told of seeing nothing that was suspicious. So for a week the days passed without a change in their even tenor, and then, Porter's crew having brought a herd to the gap, Ben Israel occupied his vantage point again.

It was not a big herd, but counting did not begin until late. The men took time off at noon, and Israel on his knob saw them at the wagon, eating dinner. He could imagine the good food, but he could not partake of it. The work resumed and stock streamed through the gate. Israel eyed the country. The afternoon dragged along and, as it waned, the Negro's sharp eyes spied motion to the north, caught a glimpse of bay hide moving through the brush. He slipped back to his horse and, mounting, rode a circle through the brush until he came to another rise. Dismounting at its base, he took his rifle from the boot and climbed on foot and silently. At the top of the rise he paused. Now he could see the scene below, the last cattle passing through the gap in the wire, the crew that handled them congregated at the gate, the counters meeting. And he saw something else: a mounted man who sat his horse upon the rise and, presently, dismounted.

Israel took two steps and spoke quietly. "Theah're all through fo' the day, Mist' Seay."

Manville Seay wheeled in his tracks. His black eyes were narrow slits, and his lips were drawn into a snarl. He saw Ben Israel, poised and with a rifle in his hands. By accident, it seemed, the rifle pointed at Seay's chest, and Israel's face was calm and composed. Seay did not speak. Gradually the snarl left his lips, and his eyes resumed their normal width. Then without a word he mounted and rode down from the hill toward the north. Israel watched him go and then, returning to his horse, he, also, mounted and rode north. Three miles above the fence Israel reined in. Seay's northward progress was steady. The Negro watched for a time, then as Seay and his horse disappeared turned back toward the gap.

Seay knew that Israel had followed him. He did not look back as he rode, but still he knew. On that rise above the fence Manville Seay had felt death blowing down his neck, and he was still cold with the chill of its breath. Three miles north of the fence he turned east and then, and only then, spurring his horse, he struck a long lope toward the Secate headquarters.

At sundown Seay came slamming in to the ranch. There was no one at the place save a native roustabout and his wife. These were at supper, but, hearing Seay's horse, they came out to see who had arrived. Seay cursed the man bitterly, dismounted, and, throwing the reins to the roustabout, stamped off to the big house.

192

Philosophically the roustabout unsaddled and put up the horse. Returning to his supper, he found his wife preparing a meal for Seay. She took it to the house and brought it back, telling her husband that *el patron* would not eat, would not even answer when she called. Later that evening Seay appeared. Had anyone come? he asked. Had there been any visitors? The roustabout answered in the negative, and Seay disappeared again into the big house. A black mood possessed the man. No one had touched Manville Seay, and yet he was sore as from a physical beating. He had not been handled gently. Porter, Harbury, and Raoul had not spared him, and Seay hated them, but most of all he hated Lane McLain.

On the day that Lane, Harbury, and Ben Israel rode south of the fence Seay counted cattle with Porter. His humor had begun the night before. At the fire, when Lane threw in his face the flat declaration concerning the wet cows, Seay had been tempted but had restrained himself. He wanted to kill McLain then and there, to draw his gun and call the showdown, but he contained his anger. The temptation was great, but there was another, greater temptation and a greater reward. That was the wealth to be gained once Agnew had taken over the Secate and Seay was manager. And so Seay held himself. When Agnew and Lane left he had talked to Harbury and Porter, using all the smooth tact and diplomacy that was his. He found a fairly ready audience, for Lane's brusque bluntness had not pleased the cowmen. But Porter, levelheaded and not entirely trusting, had not been completely won over.

"Sure," Porter agreed, "any man's bound to miss some calves workin' country like we are. An' McLain shot off his head aplenty. But maybe yore foreman did miss more than he should. Jimmer will ride the fence tomorrow an' see how many wet cows he can find. I think McLain's out of line, but we're goin' to know for sure before we go to bat with him."

Perforce Seay had been content with that. He could not win Porter further to his side.

Then the next day, after the cattle had been counted through, Raoul came down. Seay had talked to Raoul, winning agreement from him. Raoul was not so strong-minded as either Harbury or Porter. Raoul was ready to throw in with Seay and refuse further delivery if McLain stayed at the fence, and Seay was pleased. But his elation did not last. Harbury came in on a borrowed horse, with his report of the happenings below the fence, and a stormy session ensued. It was Porter who accused Seay bluntly of hiring men to move cattle back north of the fence.

"I didn't do it," Porter growled. "Jimmer didn't, an' neither did Raoul. That leaves you. You contracted for fifteen thousand head from the Secate. Ain't you got 'em?"

"Sure I've got 'em," Seay snapped. "I've got that many back in the hills."

"Then" — Porter's eyes were thin — "you'd better get to yore wagons an' bring 'em out. Maybe these fellers that shot Jimmer's horse was just stealin' a few, like you say. Maybe they wasn't. We'll give you the benefit of the doubt. But you'd better get yore cattle

194

down an' get 'em counted. If you don't, me an' Jimmer an' Raoul are goin' to throw our outfits into yore country an' round it up for you. An' if you ain't got the cattle, Seay, it's goin' to be kind of tough. We're all on that contract an' we're all responsible. Are you goin' in the mornin'?"

There was nothing more that Seay could do. "I'll go up to the wagons," he agreed surlily, "and get the cattle out. I've got 'em. But this settles it between us, Porter. No man can talk like that to me and get away with it. I'm done with you."

"You hope yo're done with me," Porter answered significantly. "I hope so too. An' I'll tell you, Seay, what I heard Nebraska talkin' about. Nebraska an' them are figurin' to stay in that country south of the fence an' keep it rode. That's just for yore information in case them fellers that Jimmer jumped wasn't rustlin' stock for themselves."

So Manville Seay went north to his nearest crew and spent some time riding between his two wagons and supervising the work. He sent a herd down to the fence to be received and he watched the gathering of another herd. He was trapped, caught by his own cleverness, by his calm assumption that he was smarter than other men, by his contempt for other men. His scheme of pushing wet cows through the gate, cows that would come back to hunt for missing calves, had fallen through. Seay could not buck McLain and Porter and Raoul and Harbury when they were all together. Nosey and Clay Garret with their men had been caught moving cattle, and now the Hatchet warriors rode the country south of the wire, but Seay still had hopes for that plan. He knew that Harmon hated Lane and he believed that somehow Nosey and Clay would circumvent the patrol below the fence and drive the cattle back. But no herds came. In his riding Seay found no stock that had been moved. A country cleaned of cattle stayed clean, and Seay knew that Harmon was not meeting with success. He worried and brooded and came upon an answer. There was one way out of his dilemma, and that was to do away with Lane McLain. When McLain was gone there would be no warriors riding below the fence; no forceful, driving man to battle. McLain was in the road, and the way to get him out was to kill him. Seay rode south to get the job done. He was ready, his nerve wire-edged, his rifle in his hands, when he heard Israel drawl: "Theah're all through fo' the day."

It was pointless to kill McLain and be killed in the act. There was yet something that could be salvaged. In the big house on the Secate, Seay thought and schemed and planned, and as his head cleared he reached an answer. He hadn't killed McLain; he wouldn't kill McLain. There was another man for that job, and so at noon he came from the big house and ordered the roustabout to saddle a horse.

Leaving the Secate, Manville Seay rode west. He cut across the basin above Blocker Gap, noting the sign the cattle had left as they came down to the fence. He entered the Pinnacles and threaded a tortuous way through that labyrinth, and as evening came he reached

Handout and tied his horse to the hitch rack in front of Ryan's Saloon.

Ryan was behind the bar when Seay entered, and through the open door Seay could see Bert Tybert sprawled on a cot in the back room, snoring.

Ryan said, "You ain't been down recently, Seay," and put a bottle and glass on the bar.

Seay took a drink. "When did he get in?" he asked, nodding toward Tybert.

"This afternoon," Ryan stated. "He come in an' asked where Nosey was. We talked awhile, an' then he said he thought that he'd get drunk. He had good luck. Another?" Ryan touched the bottle suggestively.

"Not now. Where is Nosey, Ryan?"

"He left awhile ago. Are you lookin' for Nosey?"

"And Clay."

Ryan bent forward over the bar and lowered his voice, although there was no one present to hear him. "Better leave Nosey alone. He's cussin' you, Seay. Loud an' plenty strong. He says you run him an' Clay into a jackpot."

"You know better than that," Seay demurred. "So do Nosey and Clay."

Ryan shrugged. "Maybe Nosey does," he drawled. "Clay don't know anythin'. Clay's dead."

"Dead? Clay Garret?"

"I ain't talkin' about some other Clay," Ryan stated. "Lissen, Seay, I hear a lot of things an' I keep my mouth shut. I know somethin' about what's goin' on an' I know what you had Nosey an' Clay an' the boys doin'. They were out south of Blocker Gap. Clay an'

Nosey an' three or four more. They ran into Lane McLain an' Israel an' somebody else. Nosey told me this. He says they didn't want to be stopped, an' they took a shot at McLain. An' then there was hell. Clay stopped a slug. He bled to death over by Rio Bosque. Nosey planted him there more'n a week ago."

The bottle in Seay's hand rattled against the small glass as he poured another drink. He threw it down his throat. "Where's Nosey now?" he rasped.

"Nosey said that he was goin' home," Ryan answered. "You don't want to see him. You'd better steer good an' clear of Nosey."

Seay replaced glass and bottle on the bar. "Nobody knows about this?" he asked.

"Nobody but Nosey an' the boys that was along."

"Then don't tell me what I want to do!" Seay snapped and, wheeling from the bar, went out.

CHAPTER
FOURTEEN

A peace officer in Arizona Territory might be forgiven many things, but not lack of courage. When the chips were down he was expected to possess the cold, raw nerve to go up against any kind of proposition. Lacking this quality, Jack Buntlin watched with apprehension the progress of the political campaign. Rumor accused the sheriff of being allied with rustlers, thieves, and card sharps, and Buntlin met these indictments with a laugh and the challenge to prove it. But he did not laugh off the accusation of being yellow. Daily his adherents repeated talk to him, telling him what this man or that man had said, and the pressure mounted.

The roots of the trouble were the two warrants reposing in a pigeonhole of the sheriff's desk. Buntlin eyed the pigeonhole malevolently and more than once drew out the warrants and eyed them uncomfortably. It was time, Buntlin thought, for him to hear from Manville Seay.

Seay's scheme appealed to the sheriff. It was clever; it was tortuous, and it would work. Buntlin waited impatiently for word to go ahead, and when no message reached him Buntlin began to believe that Seay had forgotten and that he would have to act alone. The final straw was a deputation, headed by Yelland and Boss Darby, that came to the courthouse. Buntlin, reading contempt in the eyes of these men, could stand no more.

"You want to know when I'm goin' to serve those warrants, do you?" he snarled as he reached toward the pigeonhole. "I want to know when I've had time to serve 'em. I've been collectin' taxes an' I've been busy huntin' Rodgers."

"We know you ain't found Rodgers," Yelland retorted scornfully, "an' we can find out from the treasurer's office how much taxes you've collected. We think yo're afraid to serve them warrants on Nosey an' Clay. We think yo're stallin' an' we think yo're scared. What we need is another sheriff."

"An' you brought yore candidate along," Buntlin growled, eying Guy Pryor hostilely. "You think I'm yellow, do you? All right, I'll give yore man a chance to show how good *he* is. Come here, Pryor!"

Guy Pryor came to the desk, a tall, broad-shouldered man moving easily. Buntlin slapped the warrants against the palm of his hand. "You want action, do you?" he demanded. "I'll give it to you. You've held a deputy's commission from me a long time, Pryor. You ain't never used it. You want to be a sheriff. All right. Take these an' serve 'em." He thrust the warrants out to Pryor.

"Wait a minute," Yelland commanded, and Boss Darby took a step forward. "Pryor's city marshal. He ain't supposed to work outside of town."

"He's a deputy out of this office," Buntlin declared, his satisfaction plain. "He can serve them warrants or he can back down an' resign."

Pryor accepted the warrants and glanced at them. His eyes were amused. "I'll not resign," he drawled. "You're smarter than I thought you were, Jack. Or did somebody think of this for you?"

Buntlin did not answer the question but glared at the delegation, triumph in his eyes. "Yore candidate's got a chance to show what he can do," he crowed. "Go to it. An' when you fall down on servin' them warrants, bring 'em back an' I'll serve 'em. I'm goin' to have to, anyhow."

"Now wait —" Yelland began. "Pryor's —"

The marshal's even drawl interrupted: "Let's go, Yelland. I've got the warrants and I'll serve them."

There was nothing more to do or say, no argument. Talk still boiling among them, the delegation left the sheriff's office, and Buntlin, having played a good card, tipped back in his chair and grinned.

The grin did not last long, for apprehension began to seep into the sheriff's mind. He had acted without word from Seay, without apprising Nosey and Clay Garret of his intent. Buntlin got out of his chair and, going to the jail door, called the jailer. "You go downtown," he ordered, "an' find Bert Tybert. He's back from Tucson now, an' I want to see him."

Buntlin returned to his chair and teetered nervously. Half an hour passed before the jailer and Bert Tybert entered. Tybert said, "You wanted to see me, Jack? What's on yore mind?"

"Sit down," Buntlin directed, and then to the jailer: "Go on. I want to talk to Bert."

The jailer went out, and Buntlin turned to Tybert. "How's Tucson?" he asked.

"Pretty good. I got back last night. What's been goin' on this last week, Jack? Is somethin' wrong?"

"Yelland an' his bunch have been puttin' pressure on me," Buntlin answered, "about them warrants for Clay an' Nosey. I just handed 'em to Pryor to serve."

"Are you crazy?" Tybert's eyes widened with amazement. "Nosey an' Clay won't stand for that, an' you know it. They'll be in here after you."

"No, they won't," Buntlin assured. "This is Seay's idea." He spoke swiftly, giving Tybert a summary of Seay's scheme. "Nosey an' Clay know all about this," he completed. "They're O.K. or Seay would have told me. I want you to pull out right away to find 'em an' tell 'em Pryor's comin'."

Tybert shoved back his hat and scratched his head. "Do you know where they are?" he asked.

"They're workin' for Seay down south of Blocker Gap someplace. You ask Ryan; he'll know."

Tybert had more questions, but Jack Buntlin forestalled them. "We ain't got time to talk," he stated. "Pryor's got them warrants, an' he'll try to serve 'em. You pull out an' get word to the boys."

Some of the sheriff's unease communicated itself to Bert Tybert. He got up from the chair and settled his hat. "An' I'd better see Seay too," he agreed. "All right, Jack. I'll go to Handout right now."

Tybert left the office, and Buntlin eased his flabby body back in his chair. He had done a good stroke of business.

Striking the Handout road, Tybert made time. He did not underestimate Guy Pryor and he believed that his mission was urgent. He reached Handout shortly after noon and entered the deserted saloon. Ryan was lunching from a sack of crackers and a chunk of cheese on the bar top, washing down the food with an occasional drink. He greeted Tybert cheerfully.

"Have some cheese" — Ryan waved hospitably toward the bar — "an' tell me about your trip. Did you get down to the Blue Ribbon?"

"Yeah." Tybert helped himself to cheese and crackers. "I made it. Is Nosey around, Ryan?"

"He'll be in this afternoon," Ryan said. "He comes in every day. What's new in Tucson, Bert?"

"Not much." Tybert placed a slice of cheese between two crackers. "You know, the last time I was in Tucson, Frank was with me. I kind of missed him this time."

"You an' Birdsall was pretty good friends, wasn't you?" Ryan took a little drink.

"We'd worked together for a long time," Tybert agreed. "I got him up here from Mexico. I thought mebbe he could tie up with Nosey, handlin' them Secate cattle. I never did figure why he tangled with Guy Pryor."

"He wasn't after Pryor," Ryan informed. "He was after McLain. It was just tough luck that Pryor was there."

"But what the hell did he want to jump McLain about?" Tybert demanded. "I'd told Frank that McLain was dangerous."

"Yore friend Birdsall had stole some of McLain's calves," Ryan stated. "I don't guess you knew about it. Remember that time McLain an' Rodgers come in here?"

Tybert nodded.

"Well" — Ryan licked a cracker crumb from his lips — "I guess somebody told Birdsall what McLain said. Mebbe yore friend figgered he'd better get McLain before McLain got him."

"Nosey told Frank!" Bert Tybert said. "That's who done it!"

"Somebody told him, anyhow." Ryan shrugged. "Quit worryin' about Frank Birdsall. He's dead. What'ud you do in Tucson?"

Bert Tybert pulled the whisky bottle toward him. "Frank was a good hand," he said slowly. "He could work in any man's country. Nosey never liked him. He was always afraid that Frank would cut into the pie he was gettin' off the Secate. He knew I'd ruther work with Frank than him. Nosey's too damned stuck on himself."

"Oh hell," Ryan said. "Take a drink an' forget it. What if Nosey didn't like Birdsall? It ain't no skin off yore neck now."

Tybert's fingers closed around the bottle as though he had come to a decision. "I think I'll get drunk, Ryan," he stated. "I meant to get drunk in Tucson, but

I never got around to it. I'll just start with what's in the bottle."

"Not without payin' for it, you won't!" Ryan snapped. "I've had enough trouble collectin' from you after you got drunk."

Tybert threw money on the bar. "Give me another bottle too," he snarled, "an' let me alone. I got some thinkin' to do an' I don't want you buttin' in." Carrying the half-filled bottle and a glass, he retired to the rickety card table at the bar end. Ryan eyed him sardonically.

"Go on an' get drunk, then," he snapped. "I'll tell Nosey you wanted to see him when he comes."

Tybert grunted and took a drink. Ideas, suspicions long held were circulating in his mind. Nosey Harmon had told Frank Birdsall that McLain was looking for him, and Birdsall had gone hunting for McLain. It was plain as the nose on his face. Harmon had steered Birdsall against McLain, and Birdsall had been killed by Guy Pryor. Birdsall had never had a chance against that combination of Pryor and McLain, and it was Harmon's fault, all his fault. Tybert took another drink and then another, in quick succession. All right. Pryor was out after Harmon now. Let Harmon take his chances. Frank Birdsall had!

"Mebbe he was a damned fool, but he was a friend of mine," Tybert muttered.

"What's that, Bert?" Ryan turned from the bar.

"Never mind," Bert Tybert said and took another drink.

★ ★ ★

When they left the courthouse Guy Pryor split off from Yelland, Darby, and their companions. They wanted to talk, to rehash the scene in Buntlin's office. Guy Pryor had no time for talk. He left them on the street and made for the one-room adobe at the edge of town that had been his home since his advent in Aspinwall. As he walked Pryor nodded and spoke to such men as he passed, courteous and pleasant and yet austere. A strange man, Guy Pryor, walking alone down Aspinwall's streets. Always alone.

He unlocked the door of the adobe and, entering, sat down upon the bed. The room was clean and neat, well kept by the native woman Pryor employed. Save for her, no one other than Guy Pryor had entered this place, and now he looked around at the whitewashed walls barren of any adornment, at the gun stand beside the door, at the clothes closeted in the corner, and at the neatly dusted table beside the bed. His inspection finished, Pryor took out the warrants and read them through and, finished with them, he smiled, thin-lipped. " 'To seize the body,' " Pryor murmured, quoting from the warrant, " 'and hold it safe.' "

Returning the papers to his pocket, he began methodical preparations. The heavy short-barreled gun he wore was inspected and checked and returned to the holster. Pryor put on a pair of spurs. As he rose from the bed his elbow brushed the table, upsetting a picture that stood there. He recovered the picture and stood looking at the quiet-eyed woman portrayed. The thin smile left his lips, and he returned the picture to the table. Then, stepping briskly to the door, he took two sets of handcuffs from the gunrack, hesitated, then, selecting a short double-barreled shotgun from the rack, checked its loads and dropped a few extra shells into his pocket. He was ready now, and with a final glance about the room he left, relocking the door from the outside.

The shotgun resting lightly on his arm, Pryor sought the Star Wagon Yard, where he ordered his horse saddled; then, avoiding the center of the town, he walked toward the south. At Abran Feliz' adobe he knocked and was admitted.

No one in Aspinwall knew much of Guy Pryor. He had made his reputation as a peace officer in Carson City and in Trail Town when the railroad was built and drifted into Aspinwall some two years after the silver boom began. The city fathers, having recently lost a night marshal, were looking for a successor for him and were glad enough to give Pryor the job. Rumor whispered that Pryor had killed four men before his advent in Arizona, and perhaps his reputation had simplified to some degree the taming of Aspinwall. He laid down a few simple rules, saw that they were rigidly enforced, and on the side he dealt an honest game of faro in the Orient. When a man broke a rule he was corrected with grave courtesy. If he broke the rule again the marshal was neither grave nor courteous but harsh-voiced and hard-eyed as he ordered the offender out of town. From then on the man was short in Aspinwall and had best not return. Some few had tried it. Five new graves were added to Aspinwall's cemetery after Pryor's advent.

In the course of his duties Pryor made enemies but no friends. He had few confidants. Judge Morton, that humanist, had pierced Pryor's shell, but even the judge did not know the man's history or antecedents. Pryor was a welcome visitor at the house on the hill and frequently, when he was not needed downtown, sat smoking with the judge, drawling comments and showing a keen insight and appreciation. Lane McLain was also Pryor's friend. There was something in common between the two men, a stern uprightness, a fearlessness, and a common code. Lane lived on the Hatchet and Pryor in Aspinwall, and yet they were close. But, like Judge Morton, Lane shared none of the marshal's secrets. The rest of the men in the town and about it offered Pryor a hard respect, knowing that he held himself a cut above them all and that, in deadliness at least, they were not his equals. They spoke to him, gambled over his faro layout, and obeyed his rules.

But there was one group in Aspinwall to whom Pryor was a hero. These were the native people of the place. Speaking Spanish as though born to the tongue, Pryor accorded the natives an even-handed justice and equality, and because of this they believed in him and followed him. So now he was welcomed by Tío Abran. Having stated his errand, Pryor waited while the old man sent a boy running. The boy returned with a man who answered questions. Another came in answer to the patriarch's summons, and still another, until presently Pryor was satisfied.

"*¿Es bastante?*" Tío Abran questioned.

208

"*Es bastante.*" Pryor got up. "*Mil gracias, señor, y adiós.*"

The old man followed Pryor to the door.

In the Orient Bar, Pryor found his deputy marshal and spoke briefly. The deputy had heard the news and nodded understanding to his instructions. At the wagon yard Pryor mounted his horse and spoke a final word to the hostler. "You know why I'm going," Pryor drawled, "but you don't know where I'm going. If anybody asks you, tell them that." And with a faint jingle of spur rowels he rode off.

The gray horse had an easy gait and covered country, following no road. As evening neared so, too, did the Rio Bosque. Pryor crossed the shallows, stopping to let the horse drink. He went on, and presently, from the rise where weeks before Lane McLain and the Hatchet warriors had paused, Guy Pryor viewed the town of Handout. A horse drowsed at the rack in front of the saloon, and that was all. After a long inspection Pryor turned the gray and rode west. Again he crossed the river and worked toward the north, moving slowly and carefully. He startled a little bunch of saddle horses that trotted off a short distance, then stopped and stared at the rider as he passed. Below a low ridge Pryor stopped and scouted forward on foot. On the farther slope were buildings, a rock house, two sheds, a corral which Pryor watched awhile. Returning, he led the gray up the hill into one of the sheds. Tying the horse at an empty manger, Pryor rechecked the loads of the shotgun and sat down, the door of the shed slightly ajar, giving him a view of the corral and house.

Time passed, and the light faded in the corral and shed. Pryor sat motionless. Occasionally the gray shifted his weight or stamped at a fly. Horses watered at the tank below the corral and left again. A fly buzzed, lit, was driven off by a swishing tail. Then through the dusk came a sound, the even beat of a traveling horse, and Guy Pryor stood up. The horse came on, entered the corral, stopped, and leather squeaked as Nosey Harmon swung down. The shed door creaked faintly, and Harmon turned. His eyes grew wide as the color drained from his face, leaving the scar livid. Slowly Harmon's hands crept up toward his shoulders, palms out, fingers spread.

"That's right, Nosey," Guy Pryor commended. "I've got a warrant for you."

Harmon kept his hands at shoulder level. "Warrant?" he demanded. "You got a warrant?"

"Your friend Buntlin gave it to me to serve." Pryor's laugh was mirthless. "One for Garret too. But I hear that Garret's dead. Ease your left hand down, Nosey. Slow. That's right. Now unbuckle your gun belt. Easy. Easy does it."

Harmon's holstered gun thumped to the ground. His face was expressionless. Pryor laughed again. "I know about the hide-out gun," he drawled. "That's next. You can get it out and drop it or you can get it out and use it, whichever way suits you."

Harmon's scarred face seemed to crawl with rage. Pryor waited, speculatively, never taking his eyes from the outlaw's own, never shifting the shotgun. "Well?" he rapped.

Harmon's eyelids lowered. Reaching carefully into his shirt with his left hand, he brought out the smaller gun, holding the butt between thumb and forefinger. This, too, dropped into the dust of the corral.

"That," Pryor approved, "showed sense. I wouldn't have taken a chance on you, Nosey, and there's eighteen buckshot in this gun. One more thing and then I'll read you the warrant. Here." Pryor detached his left hand from the shotgun. A chain jangled; metal flashed in the twilight, and the handcuffs Pryor had tossed dropped close to the corral fence.

"Step over and put them on," he ordered. "Put one on your wrist and clamp the other around a post. I've got another pair we'll use, but I'll feel better when you're tied to the fence. Move, Nosey!"

Reluctantly Harmon took a step, another step, and then he stopped, his eyes widening as he stared past Guy Pryor.

"Don't try that trick!" Pryor snapped. "It's old. Put on those cuffs!" The shotgun lifted menacingly, and Harmon took another step; then from the corner of the shed a gun blared, hammering into the quiet, frightening the horse, and sending him running across the corral. Guy Pryor stood a moment, upright, an odd expression on his face. Then, as a tree falls, he toppled, all his long length straight as he came crashing down. Harmon yelled, a formless, inarticulate screech, and leaped toward the fallen man. Snatching up the shotgun, he pointed it down, and both barrels belched flame, so close to Pryor's body that his coat caught in the blast and began to burn.

"Damn you!" Nosey Harmon screamed. "Damn you!" He threw the empty shotgun at the dead man's head, and from the corner of the shed Manville Seay stepped out, still clutching his Colt with both hands, shaken, terrified, white with his fear and strain.

CHAPTER
FIFTEEN

The livery-stable horse was accustomed to the Junction road and took it without direction. Judith Warrend, leaning back against the seat, watched the aura of light over the western hills while the buggy wheels purred their rhythmic cadence in the soft sand. Wind touched her hair, and her tilted head exposed the long and lovely line of her throat. Crosby Agnew, risking a glance, thought that he had never seen so lovely a picture.

"I feel guilty," Judith said. "We shouldn't have come, Crosby."

The man laughed although he, too, was apprehensive. He had planned this expedition, determined that for once he should have Judith solely to himself. "Why?" he asked. "Surely you would rather ride than listen to the new minister expound."

"But Molly had planned for me to go with her to call on them," Judith said. "I really do feel guilty, Crosby."

"Molly," Agnew observed, "hasn't let you out of her sight. I wanted you for myself, without Molly or the judge chaperoning. Molly acts as though she didn't trust either of us. I'll confess I haven't liked it."

"It has been trying," Judith agreed.

213

"As though," Agnew pursued the idea, "we were two small children that had to be constantly watched. You trust me, don't you, Judith?"

"Of course. But I'm not sure that I should let you drive. After all, you've only one hand. Suppose the horse should run away?"

"This horse?" Agnew laughed. "Don't mention it, Judith. You'll give him delusions of grandeur."

Judith's laugh joined the man's, and the livery horse plodded sedately. "Besides," Agnew continued, "my hand is nearly well. The doctor dressed it today and said that it was healing nicely."

"I was afraid that you would lose your arm." Judith's voice carried a recollection of her concern. "You were very ill."

"That was the whisky Pickles gave me." Agnew laughed again. "How could anything happen with both you and Molly to nurse me? I'm really not very bright, Judith. I should have stayed in bed a month instead of three days."

"I suppose," Judith commented, "that you'll be going back now. When will you go, Crosby?"

"The doctor says that I should stay in town and have my hand dressed every day," Agnew answered. "Really, I'm well enough now to leave. Will you miss me when I go, Judith?"

"Of course. It's been pleasant having you here."

"Just pleasant?"

No answer came from the girl. The livery horse, of its own volition, turned from the road, taking a dimmer way toward the east. Agnew kept his eyes on his companion, drinking in the sweet curve of her lips, her eyes half shuttered with the lashes long upon her cheeks, the wind-touched tendril of her hair that brushed a small ear.

He had known women all his life. As Waite Agnew's son he was accepted everywhere, not for his father's sake alone. Personable and accomplished, Crosby Agnew was welcomed wherever he went, and lovely women were no novelty. Indeed, they had been part of a game he played, a game taken lightly by both players. No one had ever been hurt in those minor flirtations in New York or Boston or Philadelphia. But this was different. An ache welled up in the man, unnamed and unidentified.

" 'Star light, star bright, first star I've seen tonight . . . ' " Judith quoted.

"Tell me what you wish," Agnew commanded.

"You've broken the charm," Judith protested. "Now it won't come true."

"Please tell me."

"I don't know what I would have wished." Judith rested her head on the seat back. "Isn't it lovely tonight? I think I might have wished that I could just ride like this, on and on, forever and forever."

When Agnew first met Judith at Judge Morton's he had admired her beauty and her sparkling wit. They had gravitated together naturally, drawn by their mutual background. Agnew loved music, and it had been a delight to hear Judith play and see her at the piano. But any woman such as Judith would have been a relief in this strange wilderness of the West, and Agnew sensed it then even as he knew it now. Judith had turned to him for similar reasons, seeking a familiar type among the strangers she encountered. That had been at first.

Later, when Judith began her visit at the Mortons', while Lane built the fence across Blocker Gap and Agnew waited for word to come, the girl's companionship had been a release. Neither was serious; simply, they were two of one kind, surrounded by strangers. Their common interests, music, friends in the East, books that both had read, operas heard, and places visited, offered topics for conversation. Each had used the other to stave off nostalgia. But this was different; these last few days had changed the status. Agnew, studying the girl, could remember her concern as she bent above his bed, her relief when first he was allowed to sit up and journey to the living room, her pretty protests added to Molly's when he transferred himself from Morton's to his room at the hotel, and how pleased she had been when, with his arm in a sling and a hostler from the livery driving him, he had come up the hill to visit. Surely he meant more than just a pleasant companion to the girl, a stopgap for her idleness? Desperately he realized how much it meant to him to be important to Judith.

The girl flushed under his scrutiny. "Hadn't we better go back, Crosby?" she suggested tentatively.

"Not yet." Agnew did not realize that his voice was hoarse. "Not for a while. Please, Judith."

He was in love. Agnew knew that he was in love with this girl who leaned back against the seat of the buggy, whose lovely voice had quoted the old nursery jingle,

216

whose clear eyes gazed at the starlit sky. He was in love with her, and she belonged to another man. With a twinge of conscience Agnew recalled Lane, dependable, four-square, honest, engaged now in work that he himself should be doing. He dismissed the thought. It was fair, Agnew told himself almost fiercely; anything was fair when a man loved a woman! If McLain loved the girl he should not leave her unguarded. In McLain's place nothing would have torn Agnew from Judith, not promises or duty — nothing!

"You would?" he asked.

"Would I what, Crosby?"

"Have wished that you could ride like this, on and on, forever and forever?"

"I think so."

"With me, Judith?"

How could Crosby Agnew know that Judith's concern, her tenderness, her freely given companionship had not been for him but for Lane? He had been Lane's deputy. Judith, having punished Lane for leaving her, was contrite. She missed Lane, and when he came, concerned over Agnew, the girl's love welled over. The care she gave Agnew, her thoughtfulness, her companionship were not for him at all but, rather, an overflow of her love and longing for Lane. The tone, the catch in Agnew's voice warned Judith, and she turned to him.

"Please, Crosby," she begged.

The horse, having reached the top of a long ascent, stopped to blow. Below them the country lay spread, twilight still bathing it, the moon tipping the eastern mountains, spreading a soft light across the land. Agnew's voice, hoarse with his emotion, answered: "No! It's too late to stop now. I love you, Judith!"

The declaration was made. It lay bare and bold upon the serenity, like a scar. Judith turned her head away, and Agnew leaned forward, trying to see her face.

"I'm sorry that you said that," Judith murmured.

"I had to say it. It's true. I love you, Judith."

"Please," the girl protested once again. "Take me back now."

"Not yet. Not until I've told you, Judith!"

"But there's Lane," Judith remonstrated. "I'm engaged to Lane. Crosby, you're not being fair."

"Nor you to me!" the man rasped. "Hear me out, Judith! You think that you love Lane. But hear me, Judith! Listen to me! If you love him, why have you been so happy with me? You have been happy!"

"But —" Judith began.

The man's voice overwhelmed her. "You have been happy with me. You can't deny it. You and I don't belong in this Godforsaken country. We're different. You know we are, Judith. Could you live here, with no companionship, no beauty, no one that even speaks the same language? Can you go to the Hatchet and stay for the rest of your life? With mud walls and a dirt roof and no one but a native woman for companionship? Think, Judith. Could you?"

"I'll have Lane," Judith defended.

"You'll have Lane!" Scorn in the hoarse voice. "How much will you have of him? Gone from morning to night while you're alone. Wrapped up in his work, with

218

no time to take you anywhere and nowhere to take you. Would you be satisfied with that? You know better. Can you live without music and friends, without any of the things you know? No, Judith. You can't. It would stifle you."

He could see that the girl was shaken. The appeal had been bold and direct and so savage that it must have had effect. Judith's face showed doubt and hurt, and Agnew exploited the advantage he believed he had gained.

"Think of it. Think of living in this country! You saw a man killed the first night you were here. Apaches attacked you when you went to the ranch. Savagery all about you. No books, no music, nothing! Let me take you away from it. I love you, Judith. Marry me! I'll spend my life making you happy. You'll never regret it."

The moon hung over the hills now, and all the land below was soft with light. Black shadows marked the brush and rocks, and in the stillness Judith could discern blacker moving shadows. Judith straightened as the darker shapes took form. Those were horsemen on the road, two riders leading a third horse that bore a saddle. They paused at the foot of the hill. Agnew, intent on Judith, had not seen their approach.

"Answer me, Judith!" he pressed. "Tell me that you will."

"I — No! Please, Crosby!" Judith's voice was frightened, and Agnew, mistaking the cause, continued his pleading.

"You will! You must!"

The livery horse stood placidly, the lines lax on the dashboard where they had dropped. Below, the riders had disappeared and, heedless of her protest, Agnew swept the girl into his arms, seeking to overcome her resistance. She struggled against him, her hands pushing on his chest, forcing him back. Her voice was muffled. "No, Crosby! Please."

Passion dulled the plea. Agnew's arms were hard, and the girl, stiffening against them, relaxed suddenly. For an instant Agnew was triumphant, believing that he had won. Then he, too, heard the sound, the swift hoofbeats of a moving horse. He released the girl and straightened. There was a rider on the road not ten feet away, a tall man who reined in his horse and stared. Manville Seay's face was etched clearly in the moonlight, a mask of malignant cunning. Gradually the expression smoothed. Seay swept off his hat, and amusement tinged his voice when he spoke.

"Good evening, Crosby. Miss Warrend."

Agnew managed to answer, "Good evening, Manville."

"A beautiful night," Seay drawled. "Beautiful. I trust you are enjoying it?"

"We are just going back," Agnew stated stiffly. "Miss Warrend and I have been riding."

"Riding?" Seay drawled. "Yes, I see. Well, I'll not detain you." He bowed with elaborate courtesy, replaced his hat, and, reining his horse around the buggy, rode on. His laugh came floating back, taunting and sinister.

"I'm sorry, Judith," Agnew apologized when the sound of Seay's travel faded away. "I didn't dream —"

"You had no right!" Judith interrupted indignantly. "Whatever made you act so? You had no right to touch me."

"Perhaps not." Agnew's voice was low. "I lost my head. I love you, Judith; believe me, I do, and, seeing you so lovely and — Forgive me. Please."

The anger drained out of the girl. Agnew was so humble, so contrite, that she could not maintain her wrath. An essential fairness spoke to her. She was equally to blame; she had exposed herself, with this result. If she had not been persuaded to come, none of this would have happened. Swift anger was supplanted by apprehension.

"I was to blame." Judith's voice was contrite. "I shouldn't have come. But it's been so dull in town and — Do you think he'll mention it, Crosby? If Lane found out —" Judith let the sentence stand unfinished.

"Manville won't talk," Agnew said with an assurance he was far from feeling. "Don't worry, my dear. I'll see him and explain. I'm sure that he'll say nothing."

The girl shivered. "Did you see his face?" she asked. "It was — evil. That's the only word I can think of. What he must have thought when he saw us here!"

Agnew resumed the lines and, pulling off the road into a clearing, swung the buggy in a circle. They retraced their way down the hill and reached its foot before the man spoke.

"You should hate me, Judith. I hope you don't."

"No, I don't hate you."

"But you don't love me." Agnew's voice was very soft. "I know that now. I've hurt you, Judith. I'll do anything to make amends."

"I've been wrong too," the girl said frankly. "I think — we'll say it was the moonlight, Crosby. Perhaps we were both a little mad."

"You're being kind," Agnew said. "There is one thing, Judith: if ever you need help, if ever I can be of service, you must promise to call on me. Promise?"

"Of course." Judith placed her hand fleetingly on Agnew's own. "Of course — good friend."

When Manville Seay stepped, gun in hand, from behind the shed corner at Harmon's he was still fearful. He had, before this, killed a man, but never had Seay dealt with one so dangerous as Guy Pryor. It had taken all his nerve, all the courage he could muster to draw his gun and level it at Pryor's back. Indeed, Seay's hand had been so shaken that he was forced to steady it with the other. Pryor was dangerous and deadly as a bull rattlesnake in rutting time. If the shot missed, Pryor would turn; the shotgun would flame, and that would spell finis for Manville Seay. And still Seay had fired, knowing that he must, knowing that if Nosey Harmon were taken into town all his chicanery would be exposed and would lie rawly naked for all to see. He pulled the trigger and saw the man go down, saw Harmon leap and, snatching up the shotgun, discharge it. And then Seay came from behind the shed.

For a moment he did not speak. Harmon, cursing savagely, kicked the dead man, not once but many times, and finally Seay found his voice.

"We've got to get rid of him," he rasped. "Don't do that, Nosey! We've got to get him out of here and get out ourselves. He might not be alone."

Some measure of sanity returned to Harmon's eyes. He backed away from the body and, stooping, picked up the weapons he had discarded. "How'd you get here?" he demanded. "Never mind; you came in pat. Yo're right. We've got to get him out of here."

Seay's mind began to work again. "We've got to fix this so nobody will know!" he rapped. "What did he say before I shot? Why was he after you? He's never worked out of Aspinwall before."

"He said he had a warrant for me," Harmon growled. "He said that Buntlin had give it to him. Damn Buntlin! I'll fix him! Sickin' his dogs on *me!* I'll get Buntlin if it's the last thing I do!"

"Not now!" Seay ordered. "The first thing is to get Pryor away from here. Where's his horse?"

For answer the gray stamped in the shed, and both men jumped, Harmon wheeling toward the door, his gun lifted. The gray stamped again, and slow relief sagged both men's shoulders. "His horse is in the shed," Harmon rasped. "He was waitin' in there for me. Damn him! I thought for a minute somebody was in the shed."

"So did I," Seay agreed.

"What'll we do with him?" Harmon glanced toward Pryor's body. "I tell you they'll be out lookin' for him. It ain't goin' to be easy to hide this."

"We've got to think," Seay answered. He stood staring down at the man he had killed, ideas forming in his mind.

"Take yore time," Harmon drawled. "We got all night."

"We're going to fix this," Seay said. "I think I know how. We'll load him up and pull out north."

"An' deliver him in Junction," Harmon scoffed.

223

"And deliver him in Junction," Seay answered steadily. "His horse, anyhow."

"His horse?"

"If his horse is found in Junction tomorrow morning what will folks think?" Seay demanded.

"They won't think. They'll look around for Pryor."

"And they won't find him. Pryor will be about six feet underground." Seay's mind was working now, his ideas taking shape. "They'll find his horse in Junction and they won't find Pryor. We'll leave the horse tied to a hitch rack. They'll think Pryor left him there."

"And what good will that do us?" Harmon was slow to comprehend.

"This much good: we're going to bury Pryor where nobody will find him. But they will find his horse tied to a rack in Junction. A freight pulls through Junction early in the morning. The talk will be that Pryor was on it, that he pulled out because he was afraid to serve that warrant."

"Buntlin!" Harmon snarled, and Seay saw that he had done wrong in mentioning the warrant. "He give it to Pryor. When I get hold of Buntlin — Where would Buntlin get a warrant for me, anyhow? Who swore it out?"

"I knew about the warrant," Seay said quietly. "Jack told me. He wasn't going to serve it. The Warrend girl swore out complaints against you and Clay."

"The Warrend girl?" Harmon cursed again, a torrent of savagery. "Then McLain's behind it! He didn't have guts enough to brace me an' Clay himself. By God, I knew that he was yellow! Hidin' behind a woman!"

Seay's point was almost won. "Are you going to let him get away with it?" he drawled.

"You know I ain't!" Harmon's eyes were pin points in his working face. "I'll get McLain. Buntlin too. Why, damn him! He —"

"Don't blame Buntlin until you know how it happened!" Seay snapped. "I don't think Jack gave Pryor that warrant. I think that's more of McLain's work. Jack had made Pryor his deputy, you know. The folks in Aspinwall made him do it when Pryor got the marshal's job. Let's go, Nosey. We'd better get at this."

Reluctantly Harmon turned toward the shed. "I don't think it'll work," he complained.

"Then think of something better!" Seay snapped.

Harmon brought the horse and a piece of old canvas from the shed. The canvas covered the saddle, and Pryor's limp body was disposed upon it and lashed in place. They made a quick and thorough survey of the corral and shed, careful to see that no evidence of Pryor's presence was left, and after Harmon had resaddled and Seay reclaimed his horse they rode away. Where an arroyo cut down toward Rio Bosque they stopped and unloaded the body, disposing it against the bank and pinioning it with stones. The overhanging bank was caved so that stones, body, canvas, all were hidden; then, satisfied with a task well done, they went back toward the Handout road, talking as they traveled.

Harmon, more controlled than he had been, gave Seay a brief account of the happenings south of the fence. "They jumped us when we were movin' cattle like you wanted," he stated. "McLain an' the Nigger an'

225

another man. It looked like Harbury, but I ain't sure. Anyhow, we took a shot at 'em to warn 'em off, an' they come down on us. Clay was hit first thing, an' them yellow-liver *paisanos* I had along struck out for the timber. I got Clay into the trees an' he died on me. Right there. Never said a word. I don't know how he made it that far. He was hit hard. I sent one of the Mexicans to the ranch for a shovel, an' we planted Clay. There wasn't no sense to bringin' him in."

Seay nodded agreement. There was indeed no sense in bringing the death of Clay Garret to the attention of the public. "What about it?" he demanded. "Are you going to get some cows around that fence for me? That's what I came to see you about, and it's lucky that I did. Are you going to move some cattle?"

"There ain't a chance," Harmon growled. "I couldn't get a crew into that country. McLain an' them are ridin' it. I can't move cows by myself."

Seay did not press the point. "But you're going to level off with McLain for what he did, aren't you?" he drawled.

"You're damned right I am!" Nosey Harmon snapped.

They were well along the Handout road now, a long rise confronting them, the shadows of the brush upon it black in the moonlight. Seay reined in and Harmon paused, their horses close together. "Here's where we split," Seay announced. "You go on to Junction and put Pryor's horse where it will be found, and I'll get on to Aspinwall."

"What's the idea?" Harmon demanded suspiciously.

"To find out what happened," Seay answered. "I want to know how Pryor got those warrants. And I want to be on hand tomorrow when word comes in about finding Pryor's horse in Junction."

"Go on, then," Harmon growled and started across the road into the brush.

Seay hesitated and then rode after him. "You won't forget about McLain?" he asked.

"Not by a damned sight! And I won't forget that you killed Pryor, neither. You remember that too!"

Seay hesitated and then said, "I'm not likely to forget it. I'll get in touch with you through Ryan. Better stay pretty close until you hear from me."

"I'll look after myself!" Harmon growled, and Seay swung away, back toward the west.

His horse climbed at an angle up the long slope, and Seay, letting the animal have its way, scowled to himself. It might have been better to let Pryor take Nosey. But, no, that would never have done. Harmon would have talked and spilled his guts. This way was best. He needed Nosey for a while, until McLain was out of the way, at least. After that it would be different. Seay crowned the rise, and there in the road was a buggy, its top down. He saw the two on the seat, the woman closely held in the man's arms. For an instant surprise filled Seay, and then fear. His hand swept back to his gun and then dropped away, and the two on the buggy seat drew apart. Agnew and Judith Warrend! What were they doing here? The answer came like a flash, and the fright was gone. Seay swept off his hat with mock courtliness and indulged in a brief colloquy.

The humor of the situation pleased him, and when he rode on he laughed. Momentarily Guy Pryor and the tragedy of the corral were forgotten. Here was a bull whip placed in his hand. He was master of the situation and he would wield the lash!

CHAPTER
SIXTEEN

Porter said, "There ain't a thousand head in the whole country. I don't believe there's five hundred head. I've rode it an' I know." His face was gloomy, and he stared toward the cloudy north.

Lane, looking at Porter and Harbury and Raoul standing about him, felt compassion for the men. They had done their best and they were through. Nothing that Lane could do changed the fact. He tried to console them, although he realized its uselessness.

"Maybe you didn't get all over it," he said. "Maybe there's some more in the hills that you missed. It's been raining, and a man doesn't see too well in a rain."

"Remnants," Porter growled. "Ol' *ladinos* that we could spend a month gettin' out. There ain't enough of 'em to make it worth while. Rain or not, I could see 'em if they was there. We're stuck."

Raoul found a ray of hope and advanced it. "Mebbe Seay —" he began.

"Seay ain't even at his wagons!" Porter snapped. "He ain't been there for some time. His foreman don't know where he's gone or why. We're finished, I tell you. What's the total tally, McLain?"

Lane looked at the tally book. "Fourteen thousand six hundred and three head," he answered. "You'd better make another gather, Porter. If you'll take your crew, and Harbury and Raoul take theirs, you might get the cattle."

"Five thousand head?" Porter looked at Lane. "You know we won't get 'em. It's no use, McLain. They just ain't there. I'm done. Now what I want is to see Seay!"

Harbury nodded, but Raoul scowled at Lane. "If it hadn't been for you," he growled, "Agnew would have taken a book count on these cattle. If you'd kept yore nose out of this business we wouldn't be in a jackpot."

Lane had expected this. He said nothing in answer to Raoul. Harbury's eyes as he looked at Lane held an angry glint. "That's right," he agreed. "You had to butt in, McLain. Do you know what this means? If means that we're short five thousand head of stock. It means about a hundred thousand dollars."

"You went through with it," Lane said. "I'll give you that. You were game."

"An' we got stuck!" Raoul's anger had mounted. "A hundred thousand dollars! That's enough to wipe every one of us out. Damn you, McLain! If you'd kept yore bill out we'd have been all right."

"And what about Agnew?" Lane asked coolly.

"Hell! He's got plenty of money!" Raoul snarled. "What's money to him? It ain't his that he's spendin', anyhow. It's his father's. It's damned funny to me, McLain! We've been yore neighbors for a long time, an' here this Eastern dude comes in an' you take up with him. You went against yore own kind of folks."

"You'd rather," Lane drawled, "have put it over on Agnew than to have had an honest count? Is that it? That's the way you talk. You went into this to cheat Agnew?"

"No, I didn't!" Raoul's anger flashed hot again. "I had the cattle I said I had. If you'd checked the brands you'd know that. But I still say that you sided him against us. I still say that."

"We made our mistake," Porter rumbled, "when we all signed the same contract. That's where we fell down. It's Seay, damn him! He's the one that's short of cattle. Wait till I get ahold of Seay. I'm goin' to make him —"

"You'll have a chance pretty soon." Nebraska, standing beside Lane, drawled the interruption. "There's somebody comin' down the fence, an' I think it's Seay."

The men turned. In the west a horseman rode up from a depression, showed briefly, and then disappeared again. "Seay!" Porter snapped. "Yo're right, Nebraska. We'll quit talkin' till he gets here."

They waited, glimpsing the horseman's yellow slicker as he came at a trot along the wirc, alternately appearing and dropping from sight. Manville Seay rode jauntily, despite his draping slicker and sodden hat, not at all like a man caught in chicanery: assured, confident, and smiling. Reining in, he swung down and advanced toward the group by the wagon. "Howdy," he greeted. "Just get done for today?"

"We've got clear done," Porter growled. "For today an' every other day. We're through an' we ain't got the cattle. Our tally's just over fourteen thousand. Where's the other six thousand, Seay? Where's the cows you claimed you had? We didn't find 'em!"

Seay smiled confidently at Porter. "You didn't know where to look," he answered. "They're back in the hills."

"Then you better hyper out an' get 'em!" Porter's tone and appearance were threatening. "We don't aim to get stuck for a hundred thousand dollars. Not on account of you."

Raoul and Harbury, too, were facing Seay, glaring at him angrily. Seay appeared unconcerned. "I've got a letter for you, McLain," he announced casually. "Here it is." That he was enjoying himself was apparent as he reached under his slicker and brought out an envelope.

Lane opened the letter slowly, watching Seay as his finger ripped the flap. He glanced at the unfolded paper, his eyes widening as he read.

"Agnew sent this?" Lane asked, disbelief in his voice.

"That's his signature," Seay drawled. "Can't you see?"

Slowly Lane's head nodded. "It's his signature," he admitted.

"You could tell the boys what he says," Seay prompted.

"I'll read it." Lane's voice was terse. " 'Dear McLain,' — this is dated yesterday in Aspinwall — 'Dear McLain, By now you will have received the bulk of the cattle bought by me. Mr. Seay assures me that the rest are in the hills and that it will be a costly and lengthy task to round them up and count them. I am sure that this is unnecessary and, therefore, to avoid more delay

232

and expense, we will consider that all the cattle have been received, and I will settle with the sellers accordingly. Your services and that of the crew will be no longer necessary, and I shall settle my bill with you at the earliest opportunity. Thanking you for your help and services, I am, Very truly yours, Crosby Agnew.'"

Lifting his eyes from the letter, Lane stared unbelievingly at Manville Seay. Seay's grin had become a triumphant smirk.

"I expect," he announced, "that you and the Hatchet crew can roll your beds and go home, McLain."

Slowly the purport of the letter sank in. Raoul's face was a map of shifting emotions. At first it mirrored disbelief; then gradually that was dispelled, and, snatching his hat from his head, Raoul threw it into the air and as the hat fell jumped upon it joyfully, his voice ringing out in a shrill whoop of glee: "We're done, by jacks! Done! Agnew's taken our cattle. We ain't short a cow! We're done!" He caught Harbury's shoulders and shook the man joyfully.

Harbury, too, showed the release of pressure. As Raoul shook him, so now the other pounded Raoul's back, and the two indulged in a small impromptu war dance. Seay grinned sardonically at their clumsy antics and turned to Porter. "Satisfied, Able?" he drawled.

"I reckon," Porter growled, "I've got to be. But I sure don't *sabe* this. Agnew was hell-bent to count 'em, an' then he changed his mind. I sure don't sabe it."

"You don't have to understand it," Seay returned. "It ought to be enough for you that Agnew's satisfied and that he's going to pay off."

"Mebbe." Porter pushed back his hat and scratched his head. Harbury and Raoul, their first exuberance over, had stopped their pummeling and rejoined the others.

"How'd you do it, Manville?" Raoul demanded.

"*Everybody* in this country" — Seay's eyes challenged Lane — "doesn't think I'm a crook. That's how I did it. I convinced Agnew that there was no need to go any further with this foolishness. Well, McLain?"

Lane glanced at the refolded letter in his hand and then at Seay. "Well, what?" he drawled.

"What are you going to do?"

"Pull out." Lane's voice was calm. "That's all there is left to do. Agnew's satisfied, and I'm working for Agnew." He tucked the letter into his shirt pocket.

"I'll take that letter, then," Seay announced, holding out his hand.

"It's written to me." Lane's eyebrows lifted quizzically. "I'll keep it."

"But that shows that Agnew's goin' to take the cattle," Raoul expostulated. "That shows we don't have to deliver any more."

"It will be safe with me," Lane drawled.

Seay took an impulsive step and stopped short as Nebraska and Ben Israel moved in concert. "The boss will look after that letter," Nebraska stated. "Don't worry about it."

Seay glanced at Porter, then at Raoul. "Well," he said and jerked his head toward the waiting horses. Plainly he wanted to talk without Lane's presence.

234

Raoul said, "Then take care of it if yo're so set," and, wheeling, walked to his mount. Seay followed swiftly and, more slowly, Porter and Harbury walked away, Porter calling, "Be back in a minute, McLain." The four made a little group, well away from the wagon, each man holding his horse.

"He don't like it." Seay grinned at Raoul and Harbury. "He can't take it. He thought we didn't have the cattle to fill that contract. This is worth a ride in a rainstorm."

"You must have had them cows hid good," Porter rumbled. "We rode all that country north an' couldn't find 'em."

"They're there all right," Seay assured casually. "You just didn't know where to look. Well, what's the program now?"

Harbury glanced toward the west, where a heavy cloud bank hung. The sky was overcast, and an occasional drop of rain spattered sharply, driven by a cold wind. "You sure wanted to get here," he commented. "That's a heavy rain over west, ain't it?"

"Plenty heavy," Seay agreed. "I did want to get here. There was no use in keeping you working after I had that letter. I came right out, rain or no rain."

"I don't like McLain keepin' it," Raoul complained. "It's all we've got to show."

"Agnew won't go back on his word," Seay assured. "You've got nothing to worry about. We'll all go to town and get this settled."

"I'm goin' up to my crew," Porter rumbled. "I'll send 'em back to the ranch. No use of them wastin' any more time tryin' to gather cows, I reckon, an' no use payin' 'em any more. It costs me money to run that wagon."

"That's right," Harbury agreed. "I'll hit for my outfit too. How about you, Francis? Goin' with me?"

"I might as well," Raoul agreed. "No use runnin' up expense. Manville, I was thinkin' pretty hard of you a while ago. I take it all back."

"Me too." Harbury reached out and shook Seay's hand. "I was sure mistaken about you."

"I don't blame you boys," Seay said. "I guess it did look bad. Who I blame is McLain. If he hadn't talked Agnew into it we'd have done this in the first place and we wouldn't have had to spend all this time and money rounding up our stock. When will you get to town, Jimmer?"

"Tomorrow, I reckon," Harbury answered. "I want to get this settled up."

"Me too," Raoul added.

"How about you, Able?"

Porter was frowning thoughtfully. "I'll send my crew back to the ranch," he said slowly. "I'll try to get into Aspinwall tomorrow."

"Aren't you suited?" Seay demanded.

"I don't know whether I am or not." Porter's face told nothing. "I never like to go against somethin' I don't sabe. Well —"

"By joe, McLain don't waste any time," Raoul interrupted. "Look. They're bringin' in the remuda. I reckon he's pullin' out right away."

236

"An' we'd better not waste any time neither," Harbury announced. "It's goin' to rain again."

Indeed, Lane was wasting no time. When Seay, with Harbury, Raoul, and Porter, moved away from the wagon Lane turned to his men. A little outburst of talk followed Seay's departure. Cuff demanding profanely to know what had happened to Agnew, Nebraska growling that the Easterner had lost his nerve. The wrangler, the two vaqueros, and Pancho looked on interestedly.

Lane abruptly checked the outburst. "Cuff, you go and tell Pickles to get his outfit together and bring it here. Nebraska, you'll ride down and tell Emilio the same thing. You'll start home in the morning." He turned and snapped an order to have the remuda brought in, and the wrangler moved.

"Home?" Cuff asked.

"Home! I wish we'd never left it."

"Where are you goin', Lane?"

"To Aspinwall. I want to see Agnew."

Cuff glanced at the sky. "It's goin' to rain again," he predicted, just as Harbury had done. "You'll get wet."

"They're goin' to their camp," Nebraska growled, watching Seay, Raoul, Harbury, and Porter mount. "I thought old man Porter was comin' back."

"No need for them to come back," Lane stated. "They've got what they want."

"So," Cuff drawled. "we work a month an' don't get done an' then we're called off the job. It's damned

237

funny. What's the orders after we get to the Hatchet? Stay there?"

Lane debated a moment. These men had been out a long time, working steadily. "You can go to town," he announced. "I'll be at the hotel, and you can get a check if you want some money. I don't think I'll be in town long."

"Goin' to fly the eagle!" An anticipatory grin spread across Cuff's bearded face. "I can stand some time in town. How about you, Nebraska?"

"You don't want one of us to go in with you?" Nebraska drawled, looking at Lane.

"No." Lane was very positive. "Get the outfit home. Ben, you go with it. There's no need to ride herd on me like you've been doing."

Both Cuff and Nebraska appeared startled, but Israel did not change expression. "How'd you know that?" Cuff demanded.

"I know you three." Lane smiled tightly. "This time Ben goes home. Let's get at it before the rain starts. Here come the horses."

The horses were penned and mounts roped out. As Lane saddled Soldado he gave a few last instructions. Cuff and Nebraska mounted and rode along the fence, one west, one east. Israel nodded his graying head to the last of Lane's orders and spoke a warning. "You be careful, Mist' Lane. It's rained a heap, an' that sand along the Bosque is awful quick."

"I'll be careful," Lane agreed and swung up to his saddle. He lifted his hand to Israel, reined Soldado sharply, and rode southwest, the big bay full of vinegar,

238

showing that he wanted to run. There was activity at the camp north of the fence, and Lane smiled sardonically as he controlled Soldado. Seay wasn't wasting any time, and neither were the others. They had what they wanted and were leaving. Finding that he couldn't run, Soldado struck a steady saddle gait.

Lane's mind was busy as he rode. Something had happened. Just what, he couldn't imagine, but some pressure had been put on Agnew to make him call off the receiving. Seay was behind it, and from pondering the problem of Agnew's change in plans Lane fell to considering Seay.

The man was clever, unscrupulous, and dangerous. Abstractedly Lane considered his own position with regard to Manville Seay. He had never liked Seay; distrusted him; believed that Seay was not entirely straight, and yet until recently he had done nothing about his dislikes and beliefs. Seay and the Secate Ranch had been neighbors for some time, but until now Lane had not turned a hand either way, for or against the man. But now here he was, riding to Aspinwall, thinking about Seay and finding himself stirred and angry. Why?

Lane's mental process hesitated, gathering itself for this introspection. There was first the fact that he simply didn't like Seay. There were some men like that, men whom it was instinctive to dislike and distrust, just as a man was filled with dislike and cold and purposeful destruction when he saw a poisonous snake. Seay affected Lane that way. And then Seay's talk in the Orient had been taunting and irritating, and it was instinctive for Lane to rise and take it out of him. The object of Seay's taunts had been Judith; it all came back to Judith. A small thin smile hovered on Lane's lips. Jud Warrend had warned him that Judith was going to make a lot of difference in his living, and Warrend had surely been right. What he ought to do, Lane told himself, was turn south and head for Casa Alamos, where he belonged. Agnew had made this decision for reasons of his own, and Lane should accept them, but he knew he could not. He was in this deeply, too deeply to back out, and if he could stop it he did not intend to let Seay get away with a thing. Lane had to go to Aspinwall and find out why Agnew had called off the counting.

With the first spatter of rain Lane stopped Soldado, dismounted, and put on the slicker he had tied behind his saddle. He fought Soldado, who pretended fright at the crackling yellow garment, and, mounting again, rode on.

It was dark and still raining when Lane reached Aspinwall and stopped at the hotel. Mrs. Tindler was surprised to see him and eyed the dripping slicker with displeasure. Agnew, Mrs. Tindler said, was not at the hotel. He had gone out.

"You'll likely find him at Judge Morton's," Mrs. Tindler informed. "That's where he spends most of his time." There was a sting in her manner of conveying the information.

"I'll put up my horse and get something to eat," Lane announced. "If Agnew comes in before I get back will you tell him I want to see him?"

"I'll tell him," Mrs. Tindler agreed. "You're goin' to stay here tonight?"

Lane nodded and went out to take Soldado to the Star Wagon Yard. From the Star he walked back through the softly falling rain until he reached the Orient. There were only a few men in the saloon, Boss Darby, Yelland, a few others assembled at the bar. They stopped talking when Lane entered, welcomed him, and made room for him in their midst.

"You've come in about Pryor?" Darby asked, setting out a drink for Lane.

"No." Lane tossed the liquor into his mouth and followed it with a drink of water. "What about Pryor? Has something happened?"

"You ain't heard?"

"I haven't had any news from town."

"Pryor," Darby announced, staring hard, "went out to serve warrants on Nosey Harmon an' Clay Garret. He's been gone right at a week. His horse was found tied to a rack in Junction. an' Buntlin's sayin' that Pryor lost his nerve an' pulled out of the country."

"That doesn't sound like Guy Pryor to me," Lane declared. "I'd be more apt to think something had happened to him. Who swore out warrants for Harmon and Garret?"

"You don't know?" Yelland asked the question.

"I wouldn't ask if I did."

"Judith Warrend swore out complaints against 'em," Yelland said flatly. "We thought you knew about it."

"Judith Warrend?" Lane could not believe the words.

241

"That's who I said. She swore 'em out a long time ago, right after you went out to receive them cattle. You didn't know about it?"

"I said I didn't!" Anger tinged Lane's voice. "Buntlin gave Pryor those warrants to serve? How was that? Pryor was the marshal, not sheriff."

"Pryor was Buntlin's deputy," Yelland stated briefly. He outlined the happenings in the sheriff's office. "An' Pryor took 'em an' went out," Yelland completed. "We know he left town, but we don't know where he went. All we know is that his horse was found in Junction. Buntlin says that Pryor lost his nerve an' hopped a freight. Jack's swelled up like a poisoned pup about it. There's nobody goin' to run against him for sheriff now."

Lane said nothing, and Boss Darby, leaning on the bar, asked, "What are you goin' to do about it, Lane?"

"What am *I* going to do about it?"

"That's what I asked you."

Lane stared at the men around him and they returned that look, steadily and questioningly. "We were goin' to send out for you," Darby said. "It was yore girl that swore out them complaints."

Slowly Lane's eyes traversed the circle, and still he did not speak. "An' Pryor was yore friend," Yelland reminded. "You were backin' him for sheriff. It looks to me —" Yelland broke off.

Without a word Lane stepped away from the bar, and Yelland fell back to give him room to pass. Yelland said, "Them warrants was for Nosey an' Clay; don't forget that. What with Judith Warrend swearin' 'em out

242

an' the trouble you've had with those two, it looks like —" He stopped.

"It looks like what?" Lane snapped, turning.

"Nothin'."

"*Like what?*"

"Never mind, Lane," Darby interposed. "Mebbe Pryor will turn up."

"You started something that you didn't finish!" Lane's hand shot out and caught Yelland's shirt front. "I asked you what it looked like."

Yelland's face showed his discomfort. "None of us here have said it," he announced hastily. "We all know you better, but there's been one or two give up head. They say that you was scared of Nosey an' Clay Garret an' that you got the girl to swear out the complaints an' Pryor to do the dirty work."

Yelland staggered back under Lane's push. Lane's eyes were thin and molten slits as he glared at the men. "You —" he began, and then, without finishing the thing on his mind, wheeled and strode out of the Orient.

CHAPTER
SEVENTEEN

From the orient, Lane crossed to the hotel, finding Mrs. Tindler still in the lobby. "Mr. Agnew ain't come in yet," she began. "He —" The woman stopped, and Lane, wordlessly taking his key from the rack beside the desk, climbed the stairs to his room. Not bothering to light the lamp or to remove his slicker, Lane sat in the chair beside the window, staring out at the street. Light from the Orient and White Palace splashed in the puddles, dappled by the drizzling rain. For a long time he sat staring; then, rising, he mechanically pulled off the slicker and his hat, letting them drop to the floor. He had barely seated himself again when he heard Agnew's voice.

"In his room? Thank you, Mrs. Tindler. I'll see."

Lane went to the door. Agnew had just reached the stair top and came striding down the hall. "Hello, McLain," he greeted uneasily. "Mrs. Tindler said you were looking for me."

"I am. Come in." Lane stepped back from the door, fumbling for a match as he moved. The match spurted flame, and Agnew paused in the opening while Lane lighted the lamp, adjusting the wick carefully as the oil caught. "Come in," he repeated impatiently.

Agnew entered and, closing the door, remained standing in front of it. Water dripped from the coat over his arm, and his hat was wet. "You just came in?" Agnew asked, refusing to meet Lane's eyes.

"This evening. I got the letter you sent by Seay."

"Oh yes. That!" Agnew looked at Lane now and, lifting his hand, removed his hat. The hand was still bandaged. "Seay convinced me that there was no use in any further counting, McLain. I thought I would hold down expenses."

"Seay convinced you?"

"Yes. He convinced me that they really had twenty thousand head of cattle and that we had just been wasting our time."

"Agnew," Lane said slowly, "we put fourteen thousand six hundred head through the gate. That's the tally. I've ridden the country north of the fence, and so have Porter and Raoul and Harbury. There aren't a thousand head in it. You haven't got over sixteen thousand head of stock. Do you believe me?"

"Mr. Seay has cattle back in the hills," Agnew said stiffly, again turning his eyes from Lane's steady stare. "You didn't see them all."

"You're throwing away about eighty thousand dollars, maybe a hundred thousand," Lane warned.

"It's my money." Sudden anger twisted the Easterner's face. "Besides, the cattle are there. Seay tells me that they are."

"Seay convinced you," Lane drawled. "You wouldn't care to tell me *how* he convinced you? I'd like to hear his argument."

"I think," Agnew answered coldly, "that is a matter between myself and Mr. Seay."

"I see." Lane's voice was as cold as Agnew's. It warmed suddenly. "If it's some jackpot you've got into, Agnew, maybe I could help."

For just an instant Agnew hesitated, his expression changing. Then his face hardened again. "I'm in no jackpot, as you call it," he declared. "It's late, McLain, and I know you're tired. I'll not keep you longer." He turned the doorknob.

"I've laid it on the line to you," Lane said wearily. "You know how the deal stands."

Agnew did not answer. "Good night," he said stiffly. "You'll be here tomorrow?"

"I'll be here tomorrow," Lane agreed. "Good night."

Agnew went out, closing the door carefully, and Lane returned to his chair, kicking his slicker aside as he passed. He sat down, rubbed his eyes wearily, and stared out at the street. Whatever Seay's hold on Agnew, it was strong, too strong for Lane to break in so brief a time. He tilted the rocker, resting his head against the antimacassar on its back, and ideas and conjectures revolved endlessly.

Presently he shook his head as though to clear it and, bending, began to tug at a wet boot. He was tired, too tired to think. But tomorrow he would not be tired. Tomorrow he could talk with Crosby Agnew, and tomorrow he would hunt down and stop the gossip about those warrants.

Morning was long in coming. Lane slept fitfully, dreaming when he did doze. When light streaked the east he gave up and, turning on his back, lay staring at the ceiling, thinking. The sky was still gray, forecasting more rain. After a time Lane got up and dressed, struggling into his damp boots. He had made very little sound, and as he pulled open the door and stepped out he bumped into Beth van Brimmer bearing a tray laden with dishes and a small coffeepot.

Recovering from the step he had taken to avoid the girl, Lane caught her arm with a supporting hand to keep her from falling. "I'm sorry, Beth," he said quickly. "I didn't hear you." Then, noting the tray: "Is someone sick?"

Beth's face was pale and her eyes wide. She stammered, "I'm taking — Yes, someone's sick."

"The coffee smells good," Lane commented. "I'm sorry I bumped into you. Excuse me, Beth." He stepped away, smiling. "I think I'll ask Mrs. Tindler to give me some."

Beth said, "She's in the kitchen."

Lane nodded and turned toward the stairs while the girl waited in the hallway. Only when Lane disappeared did she move on.

Mrs. Tindler was in the kitchen when Lane arrived. "I passed Beth upstairs," he said, "and her coffee smelled so good I had to have some."

"Help yourself." Mrs. Tindler opened the oven and inspected the biscuits.

"Who is sick upstairs?" Lane poured coffee into a cup and sipped it.

"Sick?"

"Beth said that she was taking coffee up to a sick man."

"Oh, him!" Mrs. Tindler slid a pan of biscuits out of the oven. "Yes, we've got a sick man upstairs."

"Anybody I know?" Lane sipped hot black coffee.

"Nobody that'ud interest you."

"You've had it in for me lately," Lane drawled. "What have I done to make you mad, Mrs. Tindler?"

The woman shrugged plump shoulders. "I ain't mad," she said. "I'm just disgusted with you."

"Why?"

"I always thought you stuck up for your friends."

"You're talking about Neil," Lane said levelly. "You don't understand about that."

"I understand aplenty. Neil was your friend, an' you went back on him."

"Neil quit the Hatchet." Lane put down his empty cup. "He got out of line here in town, and Pryor asked me to talk to him. I tried to, and Neil made some nasty cracks. I hit him."

"An' then quit him. When he got into trouble you never turned your hand —"

"How could I? I don't know where he is. He's never been found. He —" Lane stopped. His eyes were very keen as he stared at Mrs. Tindler. "Is it Neil upstairs?" he asked quietly.

The panic in the woman's eyes was answer enough. Lane said, "It is. You and Beth have been hiding him."

"What are you goin' to do?" Mrs. Tindler asked hoarsely. "Are you goin' to turn him over to Buntlin?

248

Pickles brought him in, an' we hid him. He — What are you goin' to do, Lane?"

For a long minute Lane did not answer. Then: "I'm not going to do anything. Not now." He looked thoughtfully at the frightened woman beside the stove and then walked deliberately out of the kitchen.

As Lane walked back to his room there were small stirrings as sleepers wakened and dressed to begin the day's business. Lane closed his door and sat down in his chair. He had many things to think about, too many. Agnew's sudden change of heart, Guy Pryor's disappearance, the warrants Judith had sworn out, and now Neil. Lane rolled a cigarette and forgot to light it as he sat staring out of the window, not seeing the street at all. After a time he left the room and went heavily downstairs. He needed the advice and counsel of Judge Morton, but, more than this, he needed to see Judith, needed her with a desperate ache that filled him completely. Leaving the hotel, he walked along its side and began the climb to Morton's house, the wet grass swishing at his trousers legs.

Molly Morton answered Lane's knock. Lane asked, "Is Judith up, Molly?" and Mrs. Morton answered, "I'll see. Wait, Lane." She hurried away, and Lane stood holding his hat, waiting for the girl to appear. A murmur of voices came to him, the judge's bass rumble, and then Judith appeared. She hesitated in the entrance, then crossed the room swiftly, finding haven in Lane's arms, holding him as though she would never let him go, her face upturned for his kiss.

Lane held the girl almost fiercely, pressing her to him as though for reassurance. Then Judith put her hands against the man's chest and pushed him away. "When did you come, Lane?" she demanded. "Are you through? Have you come back to stay?"

"Last night," Lane answered heavily. "I'm done, Judith. Agnew's stopped the work. I'm through for good."

Morton entered at that moment, his voice rumbling a hearty greeting. Lane relinquished Judith to shake the judge's hand and answer his question.

"No, I've not had breakfast. A cup of coffee at Mrs. Tindler's."

"Then you'll eat with us," Morton announced. "What brought you to town, Lane? Are you through at Blocker Gap?"

"I'm through," Lane answered. "Agnew's stopped us. I want to talk to you."

"Sit down," Morton commanded.

Lane sat on a couch. Judith beside him, and Morton took a chair. "Now tell me," the judge ordered, and Lane plunged into his story. During the tale Morton shook his head from time to time, and when Lane finished the man was silent for a moment.

"I don't understand it," he said finally. "I don't know what's got into Crosby. I'll talk to him. It doesn't seem reasonable. You say the cattle aren't there, and yet he seems to be more than willing to take Seay's word. What about Porter and the others?"

"I'd hate to see them hurt," Lane declared. "I'd hoped that Agnew would be willing to settle with them and just pay for the cattle he actually received. I think

250

that Porter and Raoul and Harbury were honest in the number they turned in."

"And you think that Seay wasn't?"

Lane did not answer, and Molly spoke from the door. "Can you come now?"

Breakfast was a silent meal, both men abstract, and the two women not intruding on their thoughts. When it was done Morton said, "I'll talk to Crosby. I'm sure there is some explanation, but I think you'd better stay here and let me see him alone."

When the judge was gone Molly lingered a few moments and then departed, leaving Lane and Judith together. They were in the living room, and Judith patted the couch beside her. "Sit down, Lane," she invited. Lane seated himself, and Judith hesitantly sought an opening. Finally: "I've something I want to tell you," she began. "It's worried me. Crosby and I —"

"Why did you do it, Judith?" Lane interrupted. "Tell me. Why did you?"

"Then you know?" Judith was startled.

"I heard last night. Why did you, Judith?"

Judith looked into Lane's eyes and was frightened. She had never seen them so. "But there was no harm!" she said hastily. "Of course I know that I shouldn't have gone riding with him. Molly has scolded me about it and I've scolded myself. It was foolish of me. I wanted to tell you that I was sorry. I certainly didn't think that Mr. Seay would talk."

"What are you talking about?" Lane's eyes widened. "Riding with Agnew and Seay talking? What do you mean?"

"You said you'd heard," the girl defended. "We slipped away from Molly Friday night and went riding. That was all. And we'd stopped to see the moon rise when Mr. Seay appeared out of nowhere. Of course some gossipmonger might put it in an ugly light, but — really, there was nothing wrong. Mr. Seay told you, of course."

"Seay told me nothing." Lane's voice was tight. "This is the first I've heard."

"I wanted to tell you," Judith said. "I'm glad that no one else did. I don't want any secrets between us, Lane. I'll admit that I was foolish, but nothing was wrong." She paused while she scanned the man's face. Still the eyes alarmed her. "If you hadn't heard, what did you mean?" she demanded. "You asked me why I'd done it. Done what?"

"Sworn out those warrants for Harmon and Garret," Lane said quietly. "That's what I was talking about. Why did you, Judith?"

"Because I was afraid for you!" Judith placed her hand possessively on Lane's arm. "I was afraid of those men. They'd threatened you. I saw that man's gun as plainly as I can see you. And Crosby said that if they were arrested and put under bond they'd have to leave you alone."

"I see." Lane's voice was thin. "Agnew again. You seem to have seen a great deal of him while I was gone." He was skating on a thin edge of anger, holding his temper with an effort. "You made me promise you I'd leave Harmon and Garret alone. Then you swore

252

out complaints against them. Do you know what you've done?"

Judith's anger rose to meet Lane's. "Of course I know. I was protecting you. Let's not quarrel, Lane. Please. You wouldn't understand —"

"I understand," Lane drawled. "I understand a good deal more than you do. You meddled. You swore out those complaints, and warrants were issued. Buntlin gave Pryor the warrants to serve, and Pryor went out. He hasn't come back, and here in town they're saying that I got you to make the complaints and that Pryor went out to do the work I was afraid to do myself. They say I've been hiding behind your skirts!"

"But, Lane! That isn't so!" Judith sprang up to face Lane, who had risen. "Of course it isn't true. You didn't know what I'd done."

In the pause that followed a knock sounded startlingly loud upon the door. Lane wheeled and strode across the room, jerking open the door. Judith heard a man's voice, excited, panting.

"They said you were here, McLain. Pryor's been found. He got washed up from an arroyo. Patrico Maes just brought him in. He's shot to buttons. Somebody got him right in the face with a load of buckshot."

Judith's hands flew to her breast. She saw Lane step back and pick up his hat. The door slammed, its glass rattling, and Judith gasped. Molly, entering the room, saw the girl's white face and staring eyes and hastened to her.

"What is it, Judith?" Molly demanded. "What is it, child?"

"I —" Judith began. "What have I done? Oh, Molly, what have I done?" She broke and, turning to the older woman, sobbed upon her shoulder.

Within an hour Lane came back, Morton with him. They entered quietly and found the women seated together on the couch in the living room. Judith's face was tear-stained, and Molly showed her strain. She sprang up, going straight to the judge, and the big man put his arm around her shoulders.

"Is it true?" Molly asked. "Is Guy Pryor — ?"

"It's true," Morton said heavily.

"But — I can't believe it. He visited us, Henry. He — You liked him. He was your friend."

"And I killed him when I issued those warrants," Morton said heavily.

"No." Lane's voice was almost gentle. "Not you, Judge. Judith, can I talk to you?"

The judge, with Molly still circled by his arm, walked toward the hall. "I'll go back with you, Lane," he said. "Don't cry, Molly. Please don't cry." They disappeared down the hallway, and Lane turned so that he looked down at the girl on the couch.

"When did you and Agnew go riding?" he asked gently. "What day was it?"

Judith looked up. "Are you angry?" she asked, snatching at a straw. "Please, Lane —"

"Tell me the day!"

"On Friday. A week ago. Lane —"

"And Seay saw you? Tell me, Judith. What did you see?" There was desperate intensity in eyes and question. "Think, Judith."

254

"Why, we'd stopped on a hill, I remember. And we were talking. There were two men riding in the moonlight. I saw them down below us, two men, and they had another horse."

"You were on the Handout road? The road we used when you and Jud and I came in?" Still that fierce intentness in Lane McLain.

"That was the road. Why? Why are you asking?"

Lane's shoulders slumped and he seemed to relax. Deliberately he withdrew two pieces of paper from his shirt. They were damp and ink blurred them, but the printing had not faded. Judith, rising, saw the heading.

THE TERRITORY OF ARIZONA
TO THE SHERIFF OF ASPINWALL COUNTY,
Greetings:

"What are those?" she demanded.

"Those," Lane answered very quietly, "are the things that killed Guy Pryor. You said that there were two men and that they led a horse. Then Seay passed you. That was what I wanted to know, Judith."

Judith stared in fascination at the warrants. Lane folded them and returned them to his pocket. The girl stared into his face. Lane's eyes were thin-slitted, their blueness speculative. About nose and mouth the lines were deep, and the stubble of beard he wore accentuated the hard, bold outline of his jaw. "You hate me, don't you?" Judith demanded, reading that face.

"No," Lane answered almost wearily. "You didn't know, that's all. I don't hate you. I love you, Judith.

You're in my blood." He smiled faintly, and the girl, taking courage from words and smile, reached out her arms and clung to him. "Lane!" she breathed. "Oh, Lane, I was so afraid!"

The man bent and almost absently brushed her lips with his own. His hands were strong on her arms as he released himself. "I'll go now," he said. "There are things to do."

Alarm sprang back to Judith's face. "Go?" she demanded. "Where, Lane? What must you do?"

"Those warrants," Lane said. "You had them issued. Pryor was killed serving them. And that makes it a personal matter; don't you see?"

All of Judith's assurance was gone now. She caught Lane's arm. "You're going to find those men," she accused. "I won't let you! You can't go."

"I've got to," Lane said patiently, almost as though he explained to a child.

"I won't let you go!" Judith was wild with her fright. "You don't love me or you'd stay. You wouldn't leave me."

"I've told you that I love you."

Judith freed his arm and stepped back. She was fighting fear, fighting to keep Lane with her, and she used the only weapons at her command. "I won't let you go!" Her fingers tugged and twisted at her ring, freeing it. "If you go now you needn't come back," she challenged. "If you loved me you'd stay."

"You don't understand, do you?" Lane said slowly. "Loving you has nothing to do with it, Judith. I'm

256

sorry. I've got to go." He turned and took two slow steps.

"Lane!"

The man paused, facing toward the girl again. Judith held herself erect, her hand outstretched, the ring in her pink palm.

"You'll be sorry if you go! You needn't come back!"

It seemed to her that she had won. Lane's face twisted for an instant and then settled into heavy bitterness. She thought he would return. Instead he wheeled and, this time, rapidly and without a word, walked to the door.

CHAPTER
EIGHTEEN

Down the hill from Morton's, Lane walked like an old man bent under his years. Judith's last wild words, her last impetuous effort to hold him still sounded in his ears: "You'll be sorry if you go! You needn't come back!" Judith! Spoiled, petted, vain, childish in her demands and yet so sweet, so filled with life, so redundant of promise. She was all a man could ask and all a man could lose. In her a man might sink himself and lose himself until he was no more a man, and in her a man might find delight and manhood. She was, Lane had said, in his blood, and he had spoken truth. Without her life would not be worth living, but there were other values too. Greater values? Yes! In Lane's mind was cold decision, reached not alone through the knowledge he possessed, but through the very fiber of the man. He had no choice to do other than the thing he planned. His whole nature demanded it, and so when he reached the foot of the hill he squared his shoulders and kept on.

Reaching the corner of the hotel, he stopped. Here he had stood talking with Guy Pryor not so many days ago. Lane had seen Pryor's lifeless body, but, standing here, he did not remember the bloated, mangled thing that rested in a courthouse room, but rather Pryor as he had known the man, broad-shouldered, yellow-haired, remote and yet reaching through that remoteness for friendship. Lane walked on, crossing the street, passing the Orient, where men were congregated, their ominous mutter threading through the door. Beyond a small store he went, past a warehouse, another corner, a street, and so at length he reached the edge of town and the small adobe Pryor had occupied.

The door was locked when Lane tried it, and from a house close by a gray-haired woman appeared and hurried across the still-damp, hard-packed dirt. She recognized Lane, calling him by name, and asking if he wished to enter. As did all Aspinwall, she knew of Pryor's death and she exclaimed and muttered a prayer for *el pobre* as she found a key and unlocked the door. Lane went in.

He had never visited the place before and, just within the door, he stopped to survey the room. It was exactly as Pryor had left it: a gunrack beside the door, one place empty of a weapon; the table with a lamp and picture; a letter file. Adornment there was none. The room might have been a monk's cell. Lane examined the picture while the native woman stood silently beside the door. The woman in the picture stared gravely, her steady gaze meeting Lane's eyes. The letter file was open and, drawing out its contents, Lane read the beginning of a letter Pryor had written.

MY DEAR WIFE,

I am sending two hundred dollars by express today. I hope that this sum will be sufficient for the boy to visit his grandmother. You had best go with him.

Pryor had stopped there. Lane did not read the other letters. They were in a woman's handwriting, and Lane returned them to the file and closed it. Looking again around the room, he spoke to the native woman, giving her directions. She was not, he said, to allow anyone to enter this house until Judge Morton came. The woman agreed, and Lane left her. Morton, he thought, would know what to do with those letters and the picture. It was odd that Pryor had never spoken of his wife or son. Yet not odd either. Pryor had never talked to anyone about himself, certainly not to Lane and, Lane doubted, even to Judge Morton. That was Pryor. He had wanted to be a friend, and yet reticence gripped him, and his profession set him apart. Lane returned to town. A man hailed him as he passed the Orient, but he did not pause. When he entered the hotel he met Beth, a pale, distraught Beth, fright apparent in her face.

"Has Agnew come in?" Lane asked, and Beth shook her head.

The lobby was deserted save for the two of them, and Lane nodded toward the chairs under the steps. "Sit down, Beth," he directed. "I want to talk with you."

Beth sat down, Lane beside her. His eyes were kind. "I know that Neil's upstairs," he began. "You were taking him breakfast when I came out this morning."

260

Beth nodded wordlessly.

"Neil's in trouble," Lane continued. "Can he ride, Beth?"

"I — don't — know." The girl spaced her words and then, with a rush: "I think he can. He's much better. The doctor let him get up Monday."

"The doctor?" Lane's tone showed his surprise.

"Mr. Pryor sent him. The doctor's been looking after Neil."

"I see," Lane said, not seeing at all. "You'll have to get Neil out of here, Beth. It's dangerous for him to stay. Neil was with Dowd, wasn't he?"

The girl nodded, and Lane went on evenly: "I was afraid of that. I feel it was partly my fault. Buntlin would arrest Neil if he could find him. Neil will have to go."

"Where?" The girl spoke now. "Where can he go?"

"To the Hatchet. He can get a horse from Tío Abran. Tío Abran won't talk. When Neil gets to the Hatchet, Van can give him what money he needs from my strongbox in the office. He can get horses, too, or anything else he needs. I'll write a note for Neil to give Van. Do you understand, Beth? It's dangerous for Neil to stay. He'd better go tonight if he can travel."

The girl sprang up, her face lighted by amazement. "You — you're helping Neil! I thought you hated him!"

"No" — Lane smiled wryly — "I don't hate him."

"Would you" — the girl hesitated — "would you talk to him? I think it would help."

"No," Lane said. "I expect that Neil blames me for the shape he's in. It wouldn't do to talk to him. You'll have to do it for me. You understand what Neil's to do?"

The girl nodded again, and Lane got up. "I'll write that note," he said.

There was paper on the desk, a pen, and a bottle of muddy ink. Lane scrawled briefly, read what he had written, then, folding the sheet, gave it to the girl. "Talk to Neil before you give him that," Lane directed. "Make sure he understands. You love him, don't you, Beth?"

"I — Yes! I'm going with him."

"Better wait," Lane counseled. "Neil will travel fast when he leaves. Wait till he gets to New Mexico or to Texas and writes to you before you go. Good-by, Beth. Good luck."

"Where are you going, Lane?"

"To find Agnew," Lane answered and walked out.

Men were congregated in small knots on the street, talking. They eyed Lane as he passed, and some spoke, but Lane did not stop. Aspinwall was tense, tight, and excited with the tragedy. Some of these men had been Pryor's enemies; others had been behind him. Lane knew what would happen in Aspinwall. The town would boil and stir and talk. There would be hard words spoken of Guy Pryor, men who would rejoice because Pryor was dead. There would be others who were angry, who would talk of finding Nosey Harmon and lynching him. It would all end in talk. Pryor was not the kind of man whose murder incited mob violence. At the courthouse Lane found a larger group upon the steps, and the men parted to let him pass.

Only Yelland stepped out to meet him, and Lane halted.

"Buntlin's gone," Yelland said, low-voiced. "Do you think he'd have the nerve to go after Harmon?"

"Alone?" Lane asked.

"I think so. Nobody knows where he is. We've been lookin' for him. We want to know what he's goin' to do."

"No!" Lane's voice was hard. "If he went alone he didn't go after Harmon. He'll see Harmon, though."

"You mean — ?" Yelland began but had time for no more. Lane, spying Morton and Agnew in the entry, broke away.

"I've been looking for you," he said when he joined the two. "Judge, will you look after Pryor's things? I went down to his house and looked around. There's some letters and a picture I don't think Guy would like to have made public."

"Certainly," Morton assured. "So that's where you've been? I looked for you."

"That's where I've been," Lane agreed.

"Lane" — Morton touched Lane's arm, drawing him aside — "what happened at the house?" The judge had lowered his voice to a confidential murmur. "Judith was almost hysterical when I came back. What did you say to her? Did you blame her for having those warrants issued? I hope not. That was really my fault, but I thought that they would give us something to use against Buntlin. I didn't dream of this outcome."

"Of course you didn't," Lane assured. "And I didn't blame Judith, Judge. She just didn't know."

Morton's voice was strained. "If I could call them back, I would," he said. "You know that. I'd give anything to undo this damage."

Lane looked compassionately at the judge. Henry Morton had aged in these last few hours. His cheeks sagged, and his eyes were worried. "Nobody can do that," Lane said. "You didn't know what would happen. Nobody knew." A trace of bitterness crept into his voice. "I don't blame you or Judith, either, but — well, I've got to talk to Agnew."

"You aren't planning anything, are you?" Morton's disquiet showed in voice as well as eyes. "You aren't going to do anything rash?"

"I'll do what's got to be done," Lane said firmly. He turned to the waiting Easterner. "Have you got some time, Agnew?"

"Why, yes, I have. Where shall we go, McLain?" Agnew, like Judge Morton, showed his discomfiture.

"To the hotel?" Lane suggested.

"We can talk in my room," Agnew agreed.

The walk from the courthouse had been a silent affair, Lane stepping out briskly and Agnew keeping pace, now and then risking a glance at his silent companion. Now, alone in Agnew's room, Lane faced the Easterner. "I wanted to talk to you about those cattle," he began brusquely.

"Yes?" Agnew said and for some reason showed relief. "What about the cattle? I wrote you —"

"I have the letter here." Lane drew the folded paper from his pocket. "I don't know what Seay did to get this, Agnew. It's not my business; you made that plain last night. Here is the letter and here is the tally book. That shows just how many cattle we received. There aren't over a thousand head left north of the fence. Porter and I are agreed on that."

"Why are you giving me these?" Agnew asked. "I told you in the letter that I was going to take a book count."

"You might change your mind." Lane's face was grim. "I'd like to ask you to do one thing, Agnew. Porter and Raoul and Harbury were honest in the number they guaranteed. If there's a shortage it's with Buntlin and Seay. If you change your mind about a book count I'd like you to compromise with those three, pay for the cattle you've actually received, and not hold them to the contract. Will you do that?"

"Why," Agnew said and hesitated, "yes, I will. But I'm not going to change my mind, McLain. And, besides, I've promised that I'd pay for twenty thousand head. I can't go back on that now."

"You'll find Porter honest." Lane apparently had not heard the last of Agnew's speech. "Harbury and Raoul are honest, but they're not as strong as Porter. I think you'll be able to reach an agreement all right."

"McLain," the Easterner began, "I don't know —"

"I just wanted to get things straight before I left." Lane placed his hand on the doorknob. "You'll have no trouble." He stepped out into the hall, closing the door carefully.

For an instant Lane stood in the hall, looking down its length toward the room above the kitchen. Was Neil there? Lane was tempted to see. He wondered if Beth had given Neil his note, wondered how Neil had received it. Then with a shrug Lane turned and went on to the stairs.

Neil was not in that room. When Lane left Beth van Brimmer in the lobby the girl waited until he was out of sight and then hastily opened the note. Lane had written bluntly to his foreman, directing Van Brimmer to give Neil such money as he might require and to furnish him with horses or any other equipment that he might need. There was no explanation, only the tersely worded order and Lane's signature. Clutching the note, Beth fled to Mrs. Tindler in the kitchen.

Mrs. Tindler heard Beth's story and read the note. "Lane's right," she decided. "Neil's got to go. I haven't drawed an easy breath since Pickles brought him here." The woman brushed straying hair from her forehead and continued, making amends for things she had thought and said. "I was all wrong about Lane McLain. This proves it. He was Neil's friend all the time."

The women went upstairs, and Beth unlocked the door at the end of the hall. Neil Rodgers, his face gaunt and unshaven, rose from a crouch behind the bed as Beth closed the door.

"You'd ought to talk before you come in," he growled, lowering the gun in his hand. "Give me a chance to know who's out there. What's the matter, Beth? Yo're all upset."

"You've got to go, Neil," Beth said breathlessly. "You've got to get away."

"What's the matter?" Apprehension filled Neil's eyes. "Has Buntlin found out I'm here?"

"It's Lane. He —"

266

"He found out!" Neil rapped a curse. "That tears it. He'll tell Buntlin. Damn him! I should have killed him!"

"No. It's not that. Look here, Neil." Beth came to the man, displaying the note she carried. Neil read it, lifting his eyes to stare wonderingly at the girl.

"Lane wrote that?" he demanded. "It's a trap; that's what it is. He wants me to try to get away."

"No, Neil. He meant it."

Neil sat down, the gun dangling between his legs. "Not Lane," he growled. "He's done with me. What's wrong in town? There's been a crowd movin' around. I've heard it. What happened?"

"Guy Pryor was killed," Mrs. Tindler said. "They brought his body in this mornin'."

"Pryor?"

"Yes. You've been too sick to talk to, Neil. You didn't know that Pryor had gone out to arrest Nosey Harmon an' Clay Garret an' that he didn't come back. We didn't want to tell you after all Pryor'd done for you."

"An' Harmon killed him?" Neil rasped.

"Who else could it have been?" Mrs. Tindler spread her hands wide. "Guy Pryor had warrants for them two."

Neil lifted the gun and scratched his temple with its muzzle, never taking his eyes from Mrs. Tindler and Beth. "Who swore out the warrants?" he demanded.

"Judith Warrend."

Neil regarded his weapon speculatively. "An' Lane's in town?" he drawled.

"He gave me this note. I saw him write it. He talked to me, Neil. He said that you blamed him for things and that he wouldn't talk to you but that you were in danger. He said that you were to go to Dad and get what you needed and that you could get a horse from Tío Abran Feliz."

"Hmmm," Neil said, still looking at the gun. "Then where'd he go?"

"I don't know. He said he was going to find Mr. Agnew."

Neil got up, his weakness apparent in the movement. "I'll put on my boots," he said.

"Hadn't you better wait until tonight to go? You can slip out after dark and —"

"I'll go now." The man's voice was very decisive. "I can go out through the kitchen and along the back. Tío Abran will give me a horse all right."

"Are you well enough? Are you sure that you can ride?" All her apprehension was in Beth's voice.

"I'm well enough for what I got to do," Neil answered. "You stay here with Mrs. Tindler, Beth. I'll be all right."

When Lane left Crosby Agnew he was done in Aspinwall. There was no travel on the road he took out of town, and Lane met no one. A mile north of Aspinwall he came to the fork and turned Soldado east on the Handout road.

The sky had been overcast all day, and now the clouds fulfilled their promise. With the first drizzle Lane reached back to touch the empty spot behind his

268

cantle. He had, he recalled, left his slicker in his room at the hotel. Just as well; on this mission he would have no need for a slicker.

Soldado cocked black-tipped ears and turned his head, and Lane, heeding the horse, rested his hand upon his gun butt. South of him sodden brush rasped, and, halting, Lane swung Soldado to face the sound. A rider came through the growth, and Lane's grip tightened on the gun butt. This newcomer was Neil Rodgers, a strange Neil, unshaven, haggard-faced, who bent and swayed in his saddle as he dodged overhanging branches. Reaching the opening of the road, Neil pulled in, and for an instant the two faced each other. Neil was armed, the butt of a gun protruding above the waistband of his trousers.

"Well?" Lane said.

"Yeah." Neil's reins were carried high in his left hand; his right hand rested on his hip.

"Get on with it," Lane said.

"You" — Neil's tone was accusative — "are headed for Handout."

"That's right."

"Because Nosey Harmon's there."

"That's right. Because Nosey Harmon and Seay are there."

"I'm goin' with you."

Lane's eyes sharpened. "Beth showed you that note," he rasped. "You don't owe me a thing. Go on to the ranch like she told you."

"I quit takin' orders a while back," Neil drawled. "Remember? I quit the Hatchet."

"I remember."

"Pryor," Neil said deliberately, "helped me out. I was shot an' down. Pickles picked me up an' slipped me into the hotel after dark. Beth an' Mrs. Tindler looked after me, but I don't think I'd have made it if Pryor hadn't sent Doc."

Soldado moved forward along the road, and Neil's horse kept pace. "Tío Abran told me that Harmon would be in Handout," Neil said. "An' he says that Clay Garret's dead. That old man knows a lot, but I wouldn't bet on all his information."

"I've never found him wrong," Lane said soberly and, his thoughts going back to the encounter below the fence: "Maybe that's why they didn't come back at us. Garret was hit."

"What are you talkin' about?" Neil demanded.

Lane told him of the happenings at Blocker Gap and in the country below, his sentences succinct as a telegram.

"So," Neil drawled when Lane was done, "you might have got Garret then."

"We might have."

"An' Seay was the bug in the molasses all the time. Nosey an' Garret worked for him. Was Seay in on this killin'?" The youngster's voice rasped.

"He was there," Lane answered, "either when Pryor was killed or right afterward. Judith and Agnew saw him and Nosey on this road the night before Pryor's horse was found. Seay passed them on the way to town, and Harmon went on. They had a lead horse. It was Pryor's."

"Is that all you've got to go on?"

"Isn't that enough?"

Neil mulled that over, and Lane, after a pause, added an amendment: "It's enough to make me ask Seay some questions."

"She swore out the warrants, didn't she?" Neil said. "Judith, I mean."

"That's right."

The horses walked through a puddle in the road. "An' that puts it up to you, of course," Neil drawled. "I guess she didn't know what she was doin'."

"She didn't." Lane was very definite.

"I thought I was in love with her," Neil said reflectively. "That's why I quit. She'd been nice to me after I hurt my leg. I was just a fool kid. It made me sore when I found out she was goin' to marry you."

"So that was why? I wondered."

"Yeah. An' Beth left because she was jealous of Judith. It's all kind of mixed up, ain't it?"

"Kind of," Lane agreed.

"I wish I had a smoke," Neil said. "Too wet to smoke though. Let's shake it up. There's no need of stayin' out in the rain any longer than we have to."

"Let's go," Lane agreed and, lifting his reins, stirred Soldado into a long lope.

Away to the west of these two, other riders pointed toward Handout. Cuff Doyle, Pickles, Nebraska, and Ben Israel had obeyed Lane's orders to the letter. By nightfall the camps at either end of the fence had been packed and brought to the wagon. In the morning, during the lull in the rain, the wagon was loaded and camp broken. Riders took the remuda on ahead while Cuff, Ben, Nebraska, and Pickles followed Pancho and the wagon. Three miles south of the fence they came to a draw running water and helped the wagon across, so taking more time. On the far side of the arroyo Cuff drew the others about him.

"I don't know about you fellers," he observed, "but I think that Pancho can get this outfit home by hisself. There ain't no need for us to go to the ranch, the way I see it." He looked around, meeting approving glances from Pickles and Nebraska.

"Me," Cuff continued, "I think goin' to the ranch would be a waste of time. I think we might as well head for town. Lane said we could come in."

"I think so too," Nebraska agreed. "I don't see the use of ridin' to Casa Alamos an' layin' over another night."

"Then," Cuff said, "let's tell Pancho he's the wagon boss an' leave him. You comin', Ben?"

Israel nodded slowly. "I'll go," he said. "I been wantin' to. I don't like Mist' Lane goin' off by himself this-a-way."

"All right," Cuff said briskly, "I'll *hablar* with Pancho."

Pancho offered futile objections, and the four riders swung off from the wagon toward the west. When the rain began Cuff said, "It's goin' to be wet as hell. I'll tell you what I'll do; we'll go by Handout an' I'll buy you all a drink at Ryan's."

"But," Pickles objected, "Ryan's hostile, ain't he? Ain't Handout a bad town for us to hit?"

272

"Pshaw!" Cuff waved aside the boy's comment. "We'll let Handout worry about that. You want to catch cold, kid? Come on. Yo're in good company."

CHAPTER
NINETEEN

On the second straight day of rain Ryan decided that he would have to do something about his roof. It leaked in one corner, and the steady drip was almost as annoying as Bert Tybert. Tybert was drunk, had been drunk for over a week and, from all indications, intended to stay drunk. The man's capacity for liquor seemed to be greater than the roof's capacity for water, and Ryan eyed his customer morosely. He wished that Bert Tybert would get tired of Handout and return to Aspinwall, Tucson, or hell, for all he cared; he wished the rain would stop, and he wished that Nosey Harmon would quit hanging around. There were times, Ryan decided, when keeping saloon in Handout really was not worth while, and this was one of those times. He couldn't really complain about business. Tybert was drinking a little better than a quart a day, and Nosey Harmon had been taking five or six drinks daily, not to mention casual business from the storekeeper, the man who ran the wagon yard, and others. Still, coupled with the rain, the whole thing was becoming monotonous, and Ryan moodily considered closing up and traveling to Tucson to go on a drunk himself. Glass clinked against glass as Tybert unsteadily poured a drink.

274

"Why don't you drink out of a bottle?" Ryan growled. "Yo're spillin' it."

"'S my whishky, ain't it?" Tybert answered. "Whash't to you?"

Ryan scowled and was about to answer when the door opened and Nosey Harmon came in, divesting himself of his dripping slicker after closing the door.

"Damn the rain!" Harmon growled. "Give me a drink, Ryan. Have you seen Seay or had any word from him?"

"You've asked that every day for a week," Ryan snapped, placing bottle and glass on the bar. "No, I ain't had any word from Seay or seen him neither. Why don't you hunt Seay up if you want to see him?"

Nosey abandoned the slicker and poured a drink. "Because Seay went to Aspinwall," he snarled. "I don't stick my nose in that burg, an' you know it."

Ryan said nothing. He had received reports from Aspinwall via various sources, and he knew of the warrants and of Guy Pryor's disappearance. Still, with Nosey half tight and nervous as a bronc under saddle, it was just as well to keep still. Harmon tossed down the drink and poured another."

"How about layin' a little money on the line?" Ryan growled. "You been drinkin' on credit long enough."

The scarred man paid no attention to Ryan's suggestion. "He still here?" he growled, nodding toward Tybert. "Why don't you run him out?"

"He *pays* for his liquor." Ryan eyed Tybert professionally. "He come in here an' said he thought he'd get drunk an', by gosh, he's done it."

Nosey toyed with his glass. "Hear any more about Pryor?" he asked.

"Nothin' today," Ryan equivocated. "There ain't been nobody in from town. Nobody but a fool travels in the rain."

"Then here's a fool," Harmon snapped.

Faint sounds outside the saloon told of a horse's stopping. Harmon faced the door, his eyes alert and his hand on his gun butt. The door opened, and Jack Buntlin stepped in.

The sheriff kept his head bent as he unsnapped his slicker, and water ran from his hat in a stream. "Damn the rain," Buntlin growled. "Has Seay been in here? I want — Nosey! You damned fool, what are you doin' here? Don't you know they've found Pryor?"

Harmon stepped away from the bar, his hand still resting on his weapon. "Found Pryor?" he demanded.

"This mornin'. Patrico Maes found him an' brought him in to town. Said he found him up north of here in the Rio Bosque, layin' on a bank. Looked like the rain had washed him up."

"Yeah?" Harmon drawled thinly, and Ryan bent forward over the bar, his attention riveted on the sheriff.

"Yeah. Pryor got a load of buckshot in the head, an' somebody had spotted him right through the heart with a forty-five. Damn it, Nosey! Everybody knows he'd come out to serve a warrant on you. They know you killed him."

"So they know that, do they?"

"Sure they do."

276

"An' what are you doin' out in the rain?" Harmon drawled. "You wouldn't be lookin' for me, Jack? Mebbe you want to serve the warrant that Pryor had. Stan' still! I know you gave him them warrants!"

Buntlin's ruddy face grew gray. Harmon's voice was light and thin, and he had slipped his gun out of its holster. The sheriff held his hands stiffly out from his sides and stared at the man with the scarred face.

"Sure I gave him the warrants," he said, forcing down his fright and trying to keep his voice from breaking. "Seay told me to. You know about it."

"*I* know about it?"

"Sure. I sent you word by Bert when I handed Pryor them warrants. It was all a part of Seay's scheme."

"You lie!" Harmon's gun had lowered a trifle as Buntlin talked, but now it jerked up.

"Wait a minute!" Ryan growled. "Don't go off half cocked, Nosey. Don't mess up my place. What's all this, Jack?"

"Seay cooked up a scheme," Buntlin answered hurriedly, his voice strained and unnatural. "I had them warrants, an' they was ridin' me about not servin' 'em. Seay said for me to give 'em to Pryor. He figgered that you an' Clay would hide out an' Pryor wouldn't find you. Then I was supposed to take the warrants back an' come out an' bring you in. It was goin' to help me win the election."

"*You* was goin' to bring me in?"

"Yeah. We had it fixed for you to make bond, an' everythin' would have been O.K. I sent you word by Bert when I gave Pryor the warrants."

"I never got it. I don't think you did no such thing!" Harmon's hand tightened on his gun, and Ryan said hastily: "Now wait, Nosey. Bert's right here. We can find out." He came around the end of the bar and advanced to Tybert, shaking the drunken man's shoulder. "Bert! Bert, wake up!"

"Have drink?" Tybert muttered. He was sodden with the liquor and far away, dwelling in some inebriate's world of his own.

"Wake up, Bert!" Ryan snarled. "You've got a message for Nosey. What is it?"

"Ain' goin' tell," Tybert muttered. "Lettum take chanshes. Frank did."

"What is it, Bert?" Ryan rasped, shaking the man again.

"Pryorsh got warrants," Tybert muttered. "Goin' sherve 'em. Let Noshy take 's chanches. Tha's what Frank did." Ryan released the shoulder, and Tybert slumped forward on the table.

"That's it!" the saloonkeeper snarled. "Jack *did* send him out. The drunken pup was sore at you, Nosey. He never said a word about Pryor havin' them warrants."

Harmon's indecision showed in face and lowering gun. "Mebbe you *did* send out word," he admitted, glaring at Buntlin. "Mebbe Tybert did get drunk. But, damn it —"

"It ain't my fault, Nosey," Buntlin hastened to interrupt. "It was Seay's scheme. I thought he'd fixed everythin' up with you an' Clay."

"Clay's dead!" Harmon rasped, "an' Seay didn't fix nothin' with me. I've been waitin' to see him. He said he'd get in touch with me through Ryan." The outlaw lifted his gun again, glanced at it, and then returned it to the holster. Buntlin's sigh of relief filled the saloon.

"You'd ought to pull out of here, Nosey," he said earnestly. "You'd better hit south. Everybody knows that you killed Pryor. McLain's got them warrants. They was on Pryor's body, an' you know McLain ain't goin' to let it drop. An' the whole damned town of Aspinwall is buzzin' like a hornet's nest. Yelland an' Darby an' all of them are talkin' about findin' you. They figure to hang you, Nosey."

"For killin' Guy Pryor, huh?" Under his bushy eyebrows Harmon stared at the sheriff. He laughed suddenly. "Why, damn them! Seay killed Guy Pryor. Right in my corral."

The announcement shocked like cold water thrown on a sleepwalker. Buntlin stiffened, his eyes widening with surprise. By Tybert's table Ryan jerked as though struck by a bullet.

"The hell!" he rasped, and then silence filled the saloon. Ryan walked slowly around the end of the bar, pausing in his accustomed place.

"He —" Harmon began and broke off short.

Again the door swung open, and Manville Seay stepped confidently inside. He pulled off his hat, shook water from it, and, resuming the garment, fell to opening his slicker.

"Hello, boys," Seay greeted casually. "Pretty wet outside."

"Pretty wet," Ryan said slowly.

"What's brought you out from town, Jack?" Seay discarded the slicker and walked forward. "Getting together with Nosey on something?"

"Yeah," Buntlin agreed.

Seay stopped, aware that they were all looking at him and that every eye was hostile. "What's wrong?" he drawled.

"Not much," Harmon growled. "Nothin' that you can't fix. Jack just rode out to tell us that Pryor's body was found this mornin', an' I just said that you killed him."

Again silence, portentous, hard as no spoken word could have been, filled Ryan's Saloon.

Manville Seay had been enjoying himself. When Porter, Raoul, and Harbury left the camp north of the fence in Blocker Gap to go to their wagons and sent their crews home, Seay lingered. He ordered the camp broken and sent men to his two crews sullenly combing country for cattle that weren't there. He watched the activity below the fence where a remuda came in and riders departed on fresh horses. Sure of himself, extremely confident, Seay watched Lane McLain leave toward Aspinwall and laughed as McLain passed out of sight. Then Seay rode on to the Secate. He wanted to see the place, wanted to revel in the knowledge that it was his for as long as he wanted it, that he was in the clear, and that his thievery, his plotting, and scheming could not be exposed.

Seay spent the night at the ranch and in the morning took his time. He was in no hurry. There was something catlike in Manville Seay. He liked to play with his victims. He had promised Porter and Raoul and Harbury that he would meet them in Aspinwall and that together they would finish their business with Agnew. It pleased Seay to keep them waiting, to let Porter and those others squirm and grow concerned, just as Agnew was squirming. Finally he left the place and, still leisurely, riding in the rain, decided that he would stop at Handout. He had walked into this.

"You said I killed Pryor?" Seay rasped, breaking the quiet. "Why did you tell that, Nosey?"

"Because it's so," Harmon growled. "I ain't goin' to take the blame for what you did. You killed Pryor an' I helped you bury him. This damned rain washed him out. Jack says that McLain's got them warrants an' that all Aspinwall's gettin' ready to come after me. Do you think I'm goin' to be the goat? Not much!"

Behind Seay's eyes his thoughts flashed swiftly. He had to do something and do it soon. Buntlin and Harmon were hostile, and Ryan would side with them. He had no friends in this place, none at all. His only friend was his smooth and oily tongue, his quick brain. The door creaked, opening a crack as a gust of wind whipped rain against it. Seay had not caught the latch as he came in. No one heeded the door. Every man in the place save drunken Bert Tybert stared at Manville Seay.

"You know I wouldn't let that happen," Seay declared. "I had no such idea in mind, Nosey. I killed Pryor; that's true enough, but I did it when Pryor had you under his gun. There's been a mix-up, but it's nothing I can't fix. I've got a scheme." He paused.

281

Harmon growled. "Go ahead. I want to hear it."

"I —" Seay began and stopped. Cold wind blew through the open door and, with the wind, came a voice, a slow, even drawl.

"Go ahead, Seay. You killed Guy Pryor and you've got a scheme. We'd like to hear it too."

In Ryan's Saloon men turned slowly, almost woodenly, to face the door. Neil Rodgers stood there, his shirt sodden, water dripping from his hat, his unshaven face fixed in a cruel, hard mask, the butt of a big gun peeping above his belt. On the other side of the doorway, wet shirt clinging to his hard-muscled chest and shoulders, bleak-eyed and thin-lipped, was Lane McLain.

There had been but little talk those last few miles. The horses had alternated trot with lope along the Handout road, and Lane and Neil bent their heads against the rain.

Once Lane thought he heard Neil humming a song, but for the most part he paid little attention, being occupied with other things. Thoughts kept pounding in his brain, monotonous as the steady fall of the rain. Buntlin and Garret. Harmon and Garret, outlaws and killers. Seay, smooth and oily and scheming. Buntlin, weak and grasping and avaricious. Seay had been with Harmon on the night Pryor died. Harmon and Seay, Buntlin and Garret, wet cows at the fence, and a fight below it. Seay's smirk when he handed over Agnew's letter. Guy Pryor's body, the face blown off by buckshot. Judith and Agnew on the Handout road.

Judith! "You'll be sorry if you go! You needn't come back!" Judith!

The horses slowed and walked down into the Rio Bosque's ford. "We can go on if Harmon ain't here," Neil said. "We couldn't get no wetter, anyhow."

"Yes," Lane agreed absently.

It was right and proper that Neil should be along. Neil was always along. Maybe he had been gone awhile, but what of it? This was familiar; this was the way things had always been, with Neil along.

"You'd better get yore mind on yore business!" Neil warned sharply.

The horses splashed out on the eastern side and climbed the bank. In the rainy twilight Lane glanced at his companion. Neil was grinning, and his shoulders carried cocky arrogance. Of all the men Lane knew, only Neil Rodgers could swagger on a horse. It was simple for Neil, very simple. He moved directly, not measuring or balancing thoughts and ideas, but in a straight line to an objective. And suddenly it was simple, too, for Lane McLain. He threw aside his doubts and his shoulders squared.

"It's about time!" Neil rasped. "We're right in town. There's horses at Ryan's rack."

Three horses stood at the hitch rack. A glance at the sodden saddles identified their owners. Buntlin's saddle, Seay's saddle, and the third one must be Nosey Harmon's.

The saloon door creaked and opened a crack as Lane and Neil dismounted. Their horses stood with hanging heads as the two men moved in concert, skirting the

283

hitch rail. A voice came from the saloon: "I killed Pryor; that's true enough, but I did it when Pryor had you under his gun. There's been a mix-up, but it's nothing I can't fix. I've got a scheme."

Neil flashed a grin at Lane and, moving swiftly, was first through the door. Lane followed and as he took position spoke. "Go ahead, Seay. You killed Guy Pryor and you've got a scheme. We'd like to hear it too."

At the bar the men turned slowly to look toward the door. Tybert was slumped across his table. It was a tableau carved from living flesh, and in the quiet Lane spoke again. "Go ahead. Tell us your scheme, Seay. We want to hear it."

"McLain!" Seay rasped.

Here was the finish of a crooked, twisted trail. Nowhere now for him to turn, no loophole that his smooth tongue or agile mind could find. No time now for talk and scheming; this was the finale, and the curtain was coming down. Seay's eyes flashed to Nosey Harmon. Harmon glared malevolently at Lane, small eyes burning with hate. Ryan's hands were on the bar edge, ready to drop to the shotgun concealed beneath the counter. Ryan would buy in. He must declare himself, and on the side of the men he had served. Buntlin's face was pinched and narrow. A rat, Jack Buntlin, but a cornered rat will fight.

"McLain," Manville Seay drawled, "I've let you live too long!" His hand dipped and came up filled with his gun, and a shot crashed in Ryan's Saloon.

The rain betrayed McLain. As Seay moved and spoke, so, too, Lane moved, but the wet leather of his scabbard clung to his Colt. Seay's slug smashed into him, shoving him back against the adobe wall so that he staggered and caught for balance. Neil, too, was caught, wet cloth and leather hindering his draw. Harmon had jumped back so that he was partially behind Tybert's table, where now the cattle buyer, shocked from sodden sleep, was staggering up. Buntlin had pulled and was leveling at Neil. Lane's gun came free.

He snapped a shot at Buntlin and saw the sheriff drop. Then Seay's face was above the barrel of the Colt, a snarling, twisted face that faded out as the gun jumped and thundered in Lane's hand. Seay was down, still trying to shoot, twisting on his side and listing his weapon. Lane fired again, and Seay, propped by his elbow, sagged. The gun fell from Seay's lax fingers; then his head bent; the elbow slipped, and the man lay flat on his face, unmoving. Neil's curse rasped, and Lane hazarded a quick glance. Neil was down, sitting on the floor, his gun braced in both hands. As Lane looked the gun jumped, and into its echoes Neil's voice came triumphantly: "That's for you, Harmon!"

Harmon was under the table. Tybert, one arm waving for balance, staggered toward the door, and, beyond Tybert, Lane caught a glimpse of Ryan leveling a shotgun across the bar top. The gun bellowed, and Tybert pitched headlong at Lane's feet. A gun thundered in Lane's ears even as he leveled off for a shot at Ryan. The saloonman disappeared, and the shotgun teetered on the bar an instant and then dropped, its second barrel undischarged. Men pushed Lane aside, sending him staggering. The room was full of men, it seemed. They were everywhere, familiar, their voices the accustomed voices of the Hatchet crew. Here was Ben Israel leaning over the bar, gun in hand, peering at something that was hidden behind the counter. Here was Cuff jerking Buntlin to his feet and then releasing the man so that he fell again. Here was Nebraska, bent to reach under the table and prod with his gun barrel, and here was Pickles, young and very anxious, staring into Lane's face, his own so close that Lane could feel his breath.

"You hurt, boss?" Pickles demanded. "Are you hurt? Hey! The boss is hurt!"

They left off their seeking, those eager Hatchet warriors, to come to Lane and Neil. Nebraska squatted beside Neil, and Nebraska's question carried to Lane before Cuff and Ben Israel reached him.

"What in hell are you doin' here?" Nebraska rasped, and Neil's answer, accompanied by a twisted grin, came clearly: "What do you think? I come in for a drink, of course."

Then Cuff and Israel were blocking out the view, and Cuff's voice growled: "Lemme look. Damn it, every time you go off without us you get hurt! Hey, Pickles, watch Jack Buntlin! He's tryin' to crawl out!"

CHAPTER
TWENTY

Crosby Agnew finished his cigar and added its stub to the others in the saucer on his dresser. Ashes were scattered on the rug beside his chair; the room was filled with smoke, and rain rattled on the windowpanes. He felt in his pocket for another cigar, failed to find it, and scowled. Not that smoking helped, but it was something to do. Nothing was any good, not smoking or thinking or wishing; nothing changed the shape of things. He glanced toward the bed where his portmanteau lay opened and half packed. As soon as he had done with Seay he would finish packing and leave Arizona. That was all there was left, and he would be glad to go. No need to stay and face Seay's sneering triumph. He could at least avoid that.

A knock sounded on the door and, answering it, Agnew found Judith in the hall, a cloak thrown over her shoulders, rain on her curling hair, and her eyes brilliant with some emotion that he could not determine. She laughed nervously, seeing the man's amazement.

"I had to see you, Crosby. May I come in?"

"Of course." He stepped back, and Judith brushed past, the edge of her wet cape touching his hand as she went to the chair by the window. Agnew closed the door and turned to face his visitor. Judith was examining the place.

"This is the room Dad had when we came," the girl informed. "I remember." She was plainly ill at ease, making talk, her nervousness apparent as she twisted a corner of the cloak in long, slim fingers.

"Yes?" Agnew said. At that moment he hated Judith, just as any man hates a cause of discomfort, however innocent. "You wanted to see me?"

"I — It's difficult to begin." Judith's fingers turned the cloak's corner into a hard, tight strand. "I need help, Crosby."

Agnew sat down beside the portmanteau. "Help?" he asked.

"I want to go away."

"You want me to take you to the Hatchet? Surely, Judith, you don't wish to travel in this storm."

"Not to the Hatchet. Away from here. Out of this whole terrible country." The girl saw the half-packed portmanteau. "You're leaving. Take me with you."

"Oh . . ." Agnew's voice was thoughtful. "I see."

"You asked me . . . Do you remember? You said that if you could ever help me I was to come to you." Judith's plucking fingers stilled, and she met Agnew's eyes squarely.

"I remember." Bitterness tinged the Easterner's voice. "I'm not likely to forget it. And will you tell me why you've made this sudden decision?"

The bitterness was lost to Judith. She leaned forward eagerly. "Because I can't stand it any longer," she flared. "They look at me — Molly and the judge — they stare at me as though I were a murderer. They think it's all my fault."

"Just what are you talking about?" A spark appeared in Agnew's eyes, roused by the girl's beauty and her evident distress. "Tell me, Judith!"

"Lane has gone!" Words tumbled out. "It's on his account. I tried to stop him, but he wouldn't listen to me!" She defended her actions.

"McLain's gone? Where?"

"After those men."

"What men, Judith? You don't mean Harmon and Garret? McLain's gone after *them?*"

"Yes." Judith nodded.

Agnew stared at her thoughtfully. "Because Pryor was killed," he said, explaining to himself. "So McLain's taken that up?"

"I asked him not to. I pleaded with him, and he wouldn't listen to me. I told him that if he went he needn't come back."

"And he went anyhow?" Agnew paused, then continued: "So you're done with him?"

"He doesn't love me. At first I thought he was angry because of us. I told him we'd done nothing wrong, that we'd simply gone riding, and that Mr. Seay saw us. And then —"

"You told him *that?*" Agnew sprang up.

"Why, yes. What's the matter, Crosby?"

The man paced across the room, returned, and, stopping in front of Judith, stared at her. "When?" he demanded.

"This morning. When I first saw him."

Agnew shook his head with disbelief. "But McLain talked to me and said nothing about it." His voice, too, carried disbelief. "He wasn't angry. You told him that Seay saw us on the Handout road?"

"Of course. I always intended to tell him."

"What a fool I was!" Agnew shook his head slowly. "I threw away a hundred thousand dollars!"

"A hundred thousand dollars? What do you mean?"

"I mean" — Agnew's voice was grim — "that Seay came to me and told me that unless I agreed to call off McLain and paid him for twenty thousand head of cattle, he'd see that McLain learned about our ride on the Handout road. Rather than drag you into a scandal, I agreed. And you told McLain!"

"Of course I told him. We'd done nothing wrong. I don't see —"

"No?" Agnew interrupted. "I had you in my arms when Seay discovered us! Maybe we did nothing wrong, but I doubted that McLain would believe it. I sacrificed that money on your account!" Again he made a short turn across the room and back, stopping once more before the girl. "A hundred thousand dollars!" he rasped. His angry eyes softened and grew speculative. "You're worth it, though," he said. "I don't begrudge the money. My offer holds good, Judith. I'll marry you and take you with me."

The words jarred the girl as a slap in the face. Anger, pride, the accusative eyes of Molly and Judge Morton had driven Judith to Crosby Agnew. Crosby loved her, she told herself; Crosby would understand. Crosby

290

valued her, if no one else did, and he would help her escape and forget. And now the man's attitude and words were as stunning and direct as a blow. He had placed a value on her, a monetary value, and behind his voice and eyes was fear, not for her but for himself. Anger flared in the girl.

"You didn't do that for me," she declared. "You were afraid of Lane!"

Agnew could not deny the accusation, for it was true. "Does it matter why?" he demanded. "Isn't it enough that I did it? I'll live up to my word; I'll marry you and take you with me!"

There was quiet scorn in the girl's voice and eyes as she spoke. "That would be a poor bargain. I'm not worth a hundred thousand dollars." She stood up and deliberately moved toward the door.

"But you wanted to get away!" Agnew expostulated. "You've asked me to take you away."

Judith paused by the door, her eyes straying about the room to the sampler on the wall, the faded blue forget-me-nots framing the motto: "HOME IS WHERE THE HEART IS." Finally her gaze came to rest on Crosby Agnew's face. "Because I'm a fool!" she said softly. "A fool! You've nothing to fear from Lane, Crosby. There's nothing little about Lane McLain!"

She was gone. Agnew, confronted by the blank wooden panel of the door, fumbled with the knob and then let his hand drop. He turned, stared at the half-packed grip on the bed, and walked back to his chair, dropping into it. Judith was gone for good. He had read the scorn in voice and eyes and knew that in a measure it was justified. For a full minute he sat still and then, forgetting that he had no more, felt for a cigar. Judith had told McLain of the escapade on the Handout road, and McLain had not been angry. The fact stood out and, with it, other facts. Now there was no need to complete the bargain he had made with Seay, no need to sacrifice a hundred thousand dollars. He could laugh at Seay . . . *Laugh* at him! That was what McLain meant when he spoke of reaching a compromise with Porter and Raoul and Harbury. For the moment Judith was forgotten and, expanding almost visibly, Crosby Agnew tilted back and smiled his satisfaction.

The smile died slowly. It was true that Seay's blackmail was no longer a threat and that he could compromise with Porter and the others. The business could he readily completed, but Agnew's own, personal equation was not so easily solved. Sitting there beside the window, staring out into the rain-filled street, Agnew began to realize that he could not live in Aspinwall or at the Secate. Pride would not allow it. He had made a fool of himself and, remembering Judith and Seay and Lane McLain, the Easterner realized bitterly that he must go. He must talk to Porter and Raoul and Harbury, and because of the talk they would be suspicious. They would know that he had been frightened into an agreement and that now he was backing out. The story would come out, not entirely but in part. No. Agnew shook his head. He could not stay near Aspinwall.

Turning from the window, he looked at his partially packed portmanteau. The trace of a smile touched his lips and made them grim. That packing would not be wasted. As soon as he completed his business, as soon as he could he would go back to the East where he belonged, where the game was played by a different set of rules and where the sight of Judith would not plague him. He must, of course, make arrangements concerning the management of the Secate, but Morton would help with that; McLain too. It all came back to Lane McLain. It always came back to him. Agnew turned from the bed to the window again and watched the rain beat against the glass. Suddenly relief filled him. He would be glad to go, glad to see familiar scenes and faces, glad to hear his father's voice. Impatience filled the man, and he was eager to be done and go back to the place where he belonged!

Judith, having closed the door of Agnew's room, ran blindly toward the stairs. She had sacrificed pride to come to Agnew; he had been an escape, but she could not escape and now she realized it. At the top of the stairs she stopped, her strength departing, her self-sufficiency and arrogance draining away, leaving her weak. She crumpled on the top step, leaned against the newel post, and, hiding her face in her hands, her shoulders shook with the sobs that racked them.

Mrs. Tindler, carrying a pot of tea and two cups, came puffing up the steps. Beth had gone to Abran Feliz' to satisfy herself that Neil had escaped and, returning to the hotel, collapsed. Tío Abran, through the medium of his youngest grandson, assured the girl

293

that Neil had taken a horse and gone, but the grandson added information on his own account.

"Sure," the grandson amplified. "Gran'paw give him a horse an' he got away all right. I asked him where he was goin', an' he said to Handout!"

That was enough. Beth related the news to Mrs. Tindler and added her own interpretation. "Neil's gone to find Nosey Harmon! Guy Pryor helped Neil, and you know what Neil would do!" Tears followed the words, and Mrs. Tindler encircled the girl with ample arms, vainly trying to comfort her. She could not reassure Beth by saying that Neil was on his way to the Hatchet and freedom for, indeed, Mrs. Tindler knew what Neil would do; loyal, impetuous Neil!

"He'll be all right," Mrs. Tindler comforted. "Now don't you worry, dearie, about Neil, dearie. He'll be all right."

In her own mind Mrs. Tindler had grave doubts, but, having partially succeeded in quieting Beth, the good woman padded off to brew a pot of tea, believing more in its efficacy than in any words.

She was delayed. There was excitement in Aspinwall and, going out on her front porch, Mrs. Tindler inquired into the cause. A party of horsemen was moving down the street, Boss Darby and Yelland in the lead, and when a man stepped up on the porch to escape the rain, Mrs. Tindler sought information.

"Where are they goin'?" she demanded.

"To Handout. They're goin' to clean it out. Ain't you heard? Harmon killed Pryor, an' Lane McLain, too, they say. Hey, Joe. Wait a minute!" Mrs. Tindler's

294

informant dived off the porch into the rain. She waited until the riders disappeared and then went back into the kitchen to brew her tea. Now, finding Judith on the top step, Mrs. Tindler was surprised but set down her teapot and cups and bent over the girl.

"What's the matter, dearie?"

Sobs and a muffled "Lane!" were her answer. Mrs. Tindler slipped her hands under Judith's arms. "You come with me," she ordered. "Come along, dearie," and, half carrying, half leading, propelled Judith along the hall to the room where Beth waited.

Judith stiffened at sight of Beth, and Mrs. Tindler unconsciously released her. For an instant the girls faced each other, both with eyes red from weeping, but now there were no tears. Something reached between them, not of conscious thought but of womanhood.

"Beth!"

"Judith!"

They were in each other's arms. Mrs. Tindler sniffed, wiped her eyes with a work-reddened hand, and padded away to retrieve the teapot and cups. When she returned the girls were huddled in each other's arms upon the bed, and they looked up tearfully. Mrs. Tindler set down her tray and faced them.

"There's no use cryin'," she declared. "No use cryin' until there's somethin' real to cry about."

"But Lane —" Judith began.

"Neil —" Beth interrupted.

"They're men!" Mrs. Tindler delivered her dictum. "An' yo're women. Men are always goin' off someplace into trouble, an' women are always waitin' for 'em."

"But — I told Lane not to come back. I tried to stop him and I told him he needn't come back if he went."

"An' you were wrong, dearie," Mrs. Tindler reproved. "Awful wrong. When a woman loves a man she'd ought not to try to change him; she ought to spend her time lovin' him an' thankin' God that he loves her. That's what she'd ought to do. A man's just a man. You wouldn't have one that you could make over."

"But what can I do?" Judith demanded. "What can I do now?"

"Wait," Mrs. Tindler advised, "an' drink a dish of tea."

She might have comforted Judith, assured her that, no matter what had been said, Lane would return. Instead Mrs. Tindler wisely held her tongue. For a while at least she would let Judith study and learn.

No one drank tea. It grew cold in the cups. Time passed, and in Aspinwall's street there were sounds and voices. A call sounded in the hall: "Beth! Are you here, Beth?"

"Dad!" Beth sprang up and fled, and Mrs. Tindler followed. Judith was alone. She heard the voices in the hall, Beth's questioning, Van Brimmer's comforting rumble. The tones diminished and died. Mrs. Tindler looked in through the door, but Judith did not see her. She sat alone, bolt upright on the bed, her whole attention turned inward as she tasted of the bitter brew she had compounded for herself. Mrs. Tindler slipped quietly away.

How long Judith sat and thought she did not know. It was long enough. Long enough to strip away the veneer of living and leave her a woman. Not demanding, aware of her beauty and exacting homage; not imperious and self-assured, but humble, rather, with faults that she could see and find despicable, with traits of character that were not fine at all, but weak and very human.

"Your daddy's downstairs, dearie," Mrs. Tindler said. "Can you come now?"

Judith got up and slowly followed Mrs. Tindler.

Jud Warrend was in the lobby, Molly and the judge with him. They eyed Judith gravely as she approached. Warrend met her at the bottom of the stairs and, having kissed her, assayed heartiness. "Van and I were lonesome," he announced. "We decided to come to town and see our girls."

"I sent Lane away," Judith said, dead-voiced. "I told him not to come back." She buried her face on Warrend's chest, and her shoulders shook with her weeping. The man lifted an awkward hand and stroked her hair.

"Judith," he said. "Baby, don't!"

The sobbing lessened, and Judith straightened. Molly, coming to her, asked, "Hadn't you better come home, Judith? With the judge and me?"

Judith shook her head. "I must wait," she said. "They'll come here first, won't they?"

"They'll come here," Warrend assured. "But you can go with Molly. I'll come to you as soon as —"

"I'll wait here."

Judge Morton walked across the lobby and sat down heavily. Molly joined him. Beth van Brimmer and her father were in chairs below the steps, and Warrend, after a moment, touched Judith's arm. She followed him obediently to a sagging couch. At the desk Mrs. Tindler fiddled nervously with a lamp, sending the flame mounting and then lowering it. For a time no one spoke. Then Morton said, "Judith, you mustn't blame yourself. I — You mustn't blame yourself too much."

"I just didn't know." Judith's voice was dead. "I didn't try to learn."

"Hark!" Warrend exclaimed.

From far away there came a murmur deadened by the rain, a slowly growing babble that swelled and drew nearer until voices echoed in the street. Judith stiffened, and Warrend, starting to rise, sank back again, his fingers gripping the girl's arm until they sank in. Morton was on his feet and Molly, too, was standing, and Mrs. Tindler left the desk, starting to cross the lobby. In the door a man appeared, Boss Darby, wet, with rain glistening on his face.

"Is Doc here?" he demanded. "Rodgers is in my place —"

"Neil!" Beth's voice was a clarion of thanksgiving. She ran to the door, Van Brimmer following her. Darby disappeared to let them pass, then came in sight again, like a jack-in-the-box.

"Say, Judge," Darby rasped, "Buntlin's over there too. He's talkin'. Mebbe you'd better come an' listen to him. Kind of make it official, huh?"

Morton moved eagerly, and Molly, having hesitated an instant, accompanied her husband. The doorway was empty, and only Jud Warrend remained with Judith. He shifted nervously.

"You want to go," Judith said. "Go on. If he's — ? You'll tell me, Dad?"

"I'll tell you," Warrend assured. "I'll come back, Judith."

He too, was gone, and Judith sat alone in the lobby of Mrs. Tindler's Hotel, staring at the door, her eyes wide, her lips parted, waiting . . . waiting. Beyond the door Aspinwall seethed and boiled.

Then Lane came through the door. Lane, bulky with a bandage around his chest where Seay's bullet had plowed, wet with rain, gray-faced and grave-eyed. Drawing off his hat and holding it, he walked toward the girl. Halting, he looked down at her. Judith was very still, a small carved figure on the couch, her face immobile as white marble in the lamplight.

Lane took a breath and held it. Truly she was in his blood. Truly, sitting there, she was all that he wanted, everything that he desired — and she was unattainable. The hat dropped to the floor, and Lane's hands moved, lifting toward the girl, then falling back to his side.

"I had to see you, Judith. Just once more."

He stood drinking in her beauty, graving her loveliness in his mind. Then he turned and walked back slowly to the door, and with each step he took his sodden boots left a wet print upon the lobby floor.

Judith had read Lane's eyes and seen the longing there, the love, the hardly controlled craving. She could not move. Now before her lay those footprints, cleanly outlined, sharp as though imprinted in wet sand. Ben Israel's voice rang in her ears, the Negro's slow drawl as

299

she had heard it long ago: "Them's man tracks, ma'am. If you aim to follow them they'll take you a long ways."

"Lane!"

Lane stopped just within the door, turning slowly, and Judith, rising, fled to him. A woman going to the man she loved, who all her life would follow without question along the path he made and at its end find all she ever wished for in his arms.

ISIS publish a wide range of books in large print, from fiction to biography. Any suggestions for books you would like to see in large print or audio are always welcome. Please send to the Editorial Department at:

ISIS Publishing Limited
7 Centremead
Osney Mead
Oxford OX2 0ES

A full list of titles is available free of charge from:

Ulverscroft Large Print Books Limited

(UK)
The Green
Bradgate Road, Anstey
Leicester LE7 7FU
Tel: (0116) 236 4325

(Australia)
P.O. Box 314
St Leonards
NSW 1590
Tel: (02) 9436 2622

(USA)
P.O. Box 1230
West Seneca
N.Y. 14224-1230
Tel: (716) 674 4270

(Canada)
P.O. Box 80038
Burlington
Ontario L7L 6B1
Tel: (905) 637 8734

(New Zealand)
P.O. Box 456
Feilding
Tel: (06) 323 6828

Details of ISIS complete and unabridged audio books are also available from these offices. Alternatively, contact your local library for details of their collection of ISIS large print and unabridged audio books.